Athena Carstairs is a Romance and F...
desperate need
Fate, is out now
spicy romcom, is

instagram.com/athenacarstairsauthor

THERE'S PUMPKIN ABOUT YOU

ATHENA CARSTAIRS

One More Chapter
a division of HarperCollins*Publishers* Ltd
1 London Bridge Street
London SE1 9GF
www.harpercollins.co.uk
HarperCollins*Publishers*
Macken House, 39/40 Mayor Street Upper,
Dublin 1, D01 C9W8

This paperback edition 2025
25 26 27 28 29 LBC 6 5 4 3 2
First published in Great Britain in ebook format
by HarperCollins*Publishers* 2025
Copyright © Athena Carstairs 2025
Athena Carstairs asserts the moral right to be identified
as the author of this work

A catalogue record of this book is available from the British Library
ISBN: 978-0-00-874533-2

For Soraya, without whom this book would not exist and my opportunities would still be limited.

And for my darling baby, Aria. You made this book a challenge, but when I look at you, I couldn't ask for a sweeter reward.

Playlist

Memory Lane - Zara Larsson 💜
Tummy Hurts - Reneé Rapp 💜
False Confidence - Noah Kahan 💜
A Bar Song (Tipsy) - Shaboozey 💜
Motion Sickness - Phoebe Bridgers 💜
we fell in love in october - girl in red 💜
Lil Boo Thang - Paul Russell 💜
Treacherous - Taylor Swift 💜
Little Things - Ella Mai 💜
Too Sweet - Hozier 💜
I Love You, I'm Sorry - Gracie Abrams 💜
Tornado Warnings - Sabrina Carpenter 💜
Matilda - Harry Styles 💜
Say You Love Me - Fleetwood Mac 💜
West Coast - Lana Del Rey 💜
all my ghosts - Lizzy McAlpine 💜
Sweater Weather - The Neighbourhood 💜
Sweet Nothing - Taylor Swift 💜
Supercut - Lorde 💜
Juna - Clairo 💜
Baby I'm Yours - Arctic Monkeys 💜
Ordinary - Alex Warren 💜
Wildest Dreams - The Native 💜

Author's Note

To you, the reader who has decided that this book sounded worth it: thank you.

Before you read; however, I wanted to bring to your attention a part of this love story that may divide opinions.

The male main character in this story, our beloved August Finch, is autistic. Now, I am fully aware that the Autism spectrum spans far and wide and is dependent on the person, not on the type of autism they have. Writing Gus was the hardest thing I have had to do so far in my writing career, as I know that, unfortunately, he won't be able to portray every form of autism that exists. Therefore, some may find they cannot see themselves being represented within someone like Gus, and I am here to let you know beforehand that that's okay.

Unfortunately, I will never be able to represent the entirety of those with ASD in a single character; therefore, I have decided that in Gus, I will portray people who struggle to be accepted into the ASD community due to their ability to live a completely independent life, free from the 'stereotypical' struggles one might expect.

When it comes to Gus, he represents those who people are 'surprised' to hear they have autism, those who feel they have to mask themselves because, to the world, they seem so ordinary that their autism must be a misdiagnosis. This is for them, and if those kind of people still do not feel appreciated after reading this, then I apologize.

Chapter One

WREN

"So, I've thought of a theme."

My best friend pulls me from my thoughts. "The theme for what?" I ask.

Oakleigh sits across from me in my living room, scrolling through her phone as she aimlessly stuffs popcorn into her mouth. She glances over at me as if I've asked the dumbest of questions.

"Um, the theme for my thirtieth party, duh?"

My eyebrows rise at her playful tone. "Let me guess ... *The Nightmare Before Christmas*?"

"Mm-hm, red wig and everything."

I pause, waiting for her laugh, which never comes. My smile slips and I shift to face her properly. "Wait, you know I'm joking, right?"

All she offers me is a wicked smile and a glint in her chocolate-brown eyes.

"You scare me sometimes," I say, shuddering.

"And yet, you'll miss me when I'm gone."

We'd treated ourselves to a rare (not so rare) night in, loaded with endless snacks, non-alcoholic beer, and hours of ogling Alan Ritchson.

"Hey, how about a fall theme for the party since it's at the end of October?" I ask, just as Reacher takes out six guys on the TV.

I watch her genuinely consider it. A fall theme would allow for Oakleigh to incorporate certain spooky elements from *The Nightmare Before Christmas*, whilst still displaying the class, mystery and beauty that the season has to offer—the warm colors, the slight chill, the pumpkins and the freshly fallen leaves. It's exactly why fall is my favorite time of year.

After a minute, she nods with a smile across her tan face. "A fall theme sounds perfect, actually. It leaves room for open interpretation. We could find some fake leaves and gold silverware."

"Can we even afford gold silverware?" I snicker.

"Hell no, but we can afford gold-sprayed ones from Target."

"Same thing, right?"

"Exactly."

The rest of our evening goes much like that—laughter and drooling over Alan Ritchson until our eyes water uncontrollably from the TV's artificial light.

I've been friends with Oakleigh since high school, back when our chemistry teacher, Mr. Larson, decided it was a good idea to sit us together during our first lesson of sophomore year. For that entire year he suffered through terrible experiments and poorly controlled laughter, and yet he never once separated us. I think he—wrongly—assumed that the laughter was us enjoying the lessons.

Around midnight, Oakleigh decides that it's probably a good idea to go home and give her cat, Ollie, some food and attention, so she packs up half of the snacks and gives me a hug and kiss goodnight.

Just as I'm about to close the door behind her, she pauses in the courtyard. "Oh, my God, I almost forgot!" She doesn't move from the end of the small courtyard as she reaches for her phone and types frantically, brown eyes wide with excitement.

My phone pings in my pocket just as she tucks hers away, swapping it for the keys to her red Fiat 500. I check my phone and see she's sent me a link to a website for this farm two towns away, in Eaglewood.

"What's this?"

"My cousin ordered a bunch of pumpkins from this place last year for that big Halloween party she had, and she had good things to say. Said that the owner was a bit weird, but other than that, the stuff was really good quality."

I lock my phone and shove it back into my pocket. "Amazing. I'll take a look at it tomorrow and see. Maybe even go over there. Gives me a place to start with the planning."

Oakleigh gives me a sympathetic smile. "I seriously appreciate you doing this for me, Wrennie. I hope you know that. Please don't think I asked you for any reason other than you're a kick-ass planner. The fact that you're also my best friend and that you know me better than I know myself is just a bonus."

We exchange the kind of smile that only comes with years of friendship before I blow her a kiss and head back inside. I watch out the window until I see her car pass by, content that she's safely on her way home.

Now that I'm alone, I let the smile fade and the worries flood to the surface. I let it mar the smooth brown skin of my forehead and show the wrinkles that are probably already setting in at the ripe old age of twenty-seven.

I knew that leaving my old job at the dentist was a risk. Yet things with my party planning business, Second Nature Events, were picking up and it was almost impossible to juggle two full-time jobs. So, I quit. I took a chance and dived into the unknown that is being a self-employed business owner full-time. But business has been slow the past couple of months.

I know deep down that it's the location. I've run the town of Beckford dry, and now there is nothing left for me here, personally or professionally. Beckford isn't the smallest of the five towns that surround Lake Carlow, but it's small enough that there really isn't much need for a party planner when you can easily hire out city hall any time. When I started, the hype of having someone to help host the "best party the town had ever seen" was what helped me get my name out there, but now people realize that they still have to pay me at the end of it. And yet, this is where I remain, glued to this house by the memories I've made in it.

My engagement ending hasn't helped since everyone in town knows Adam and me, but it has been a temporary—albeit confidence-slashing—hindrance.

It's okay, though. A dry spell is never forever. At least that's what my dad always tells me. It's going to take a lot more than a diminishing business and a failed relationship to make Wren Southwick give up! Things will get better, especially with this chance that Oakleigh is giving me. Instead of wallowing in self-pity, I plan to use Oakleigh's party as a rebranding opportunity, a chance to both put a smile on my best friend's face and get my name out there again.

Since sleep seems to want to evade me, I take a seat at my breakfast bar and crack open my laptop. I'm fueled by determination and a refreshed outlook—and, possibly, all the sugar from the snacks—so nothing is making me tired for at least another hour.

Oakleigh is the definition of extroverted, so her guest list is going to be long. I'll need a large space for the event and that means that city hall isn't going to cut it. I need somewhere new, somewhere with potential.

I pull up the link that Oakleigh had sent me.

It's a quaint farm with a surprisingly large amount of land attached. Even though the pictures have been taken in what looks to be the summer sun, the land is still overrun with a fall-like hue—gold-colored leaves, hay bales scattered in the distance, and, at the heart of it all, a rustic red and blue barn that needs some love.

A photo of three men catches my attention. Three outrageously attractive men, all of whom are smiling as if they don't have a single care in the world. I see why Oakleigh's cousin had chosen this place. All three guys look completely different, and yet you can tell they are related. Their smiles carry the same hint of mischief, their eyes lit up with the same lighthearted glint.

Except for the guy on the end. There's something about him

that I can't quite put my finger on. Something about the small dip on the side of his lip that tells me he's not as genuine as his relatives'. Something to do with the way his free hand is clenched at his side as if something about the situation has him wanting it to end just as quickly as it began.

He's the most handsome of the three, that's for sure, with sandy brown hair that looks caramel in the sun, brown eyes that hold a softer glint than his companions, and a strain to his plaid shirt that tells me there's more underneath it than you'd originally imagine. The man is huge, big enough to lift his biggest pumpkin right over his head without breaking a sweat. Wide, imposing shoulders fill out the fabric with ease, giving him a formidable presence that I can feel even through the screen.

I shake all thoughts from my mind, reminding myself sternly that after leaving my cheating ex less than six months ago, the last thing I need is another man.

I click through the menu to: *About Our Farm.*

Goldleaf Farm was established by the original Finch brothers back in 1941. Their vision began with nothing more than an acre of land, and a handful of pumpkin seeds—an active attempt to help their fellow soldiers during the war effort. Now, thanks to the efforts of three generations worth of Finches, including Edward Finch's three great-grandsons—Samuel, Sebastian and August—Goldleaf Farm is now the proud owner of three acres of prime land, mainly focused on the production of pumpkins, corn and the maintenance of their collection of rescued animals.

Goldleaf Farm are happy to provide all of your pumpkin needs, whether that be for some Halloween carvin', or some good old-

fashioned pumpkin pie, there's something for everyone down here on the farm.

"He looks like an August," I think aloud as I catch sight of another photo of the three brothers, this time surrounding a man who looks to be in his late seventies or eighties. The first two from earlier are hunched down so they are level with the seated older man, but the last one—whom I assume is August—remains standing, no longer bothering to hide his displeasure as he barely smiles at all this time.

I look up the opening times for the farm and see they will be open tomorrow from 8am until 5pm, which is perfect. I shoot Oakleigh a message to say that I'm going to visit the place tomorrow and she replies not five minutes later to tell me she wishes she could come too.

After some quick research into potential event spaces in the neighboring towns, I snap my laptop shut with a yawn and head upstairs to bed. The thick winter duvet soon swallows me and I immediately feel myself drifting off, the thrill of finally getting back into planning fluttering in my chest.

Chapter Two

WREN

This morning, before heading over to Eaglewood, I take a minute to mentally prepare myself for today. I consider calling the farm just to make sure that they're open, knowing that sometimes smaller businesses have to occasionally swap and change hours due to low staff.

In the end, I follow my gut, which tells me going there might make a better impression. If placing an order goes well with them this time, maybe I can make them a supplier for future events. The best way to do that is to show them that Second Nature Events is a company that can be taken seriously.

Usually, it's times like this that I would call my parents and ask them for advice. They're the most loving parents a girl could ask for, and they've always done everything they can to make me feel loved and wanted. I think they wanted to show the love they worried Finn and I missed out on when we became orphans at the ages of three and five. But now, after two decades of having to clean up my messes, I want to give them a break, for once, especially after the whole Adam incident.

When we all found out about his other girlfriend in another town, my parents insisted I come back to live with them whilst Adam packed up his stuff and moved out. Since he decided to take his sweet time doing so, I ended up living at home for two whole months. Should I have pushed him to get his ass out sooner? Of course, but my parents enjoyed being needed, and if I'm being honest, after that breakup, it was nice to feel wanted.

Currently, they're on a cruise around the Caribbean for their anniversary and I'm determined to only ever call them with good news. So, until this party is guaranteed to be a success, I'm avoiding calling them.

Not long after I hop into my SUV and start the drive to Eaglewood, my phone starts to ring on the car's Bluetooth system.

"Hey, biatch," I greet my best friend.

"Hey hey" she replies, sounding very chirpy for someone who is hours into a thirteen-hour shift at the hospital. "Are you there yet? I spoke to my cousin about it this morning and she said that this farm is seriously a hidden gem."

"I can see why she said that." I chuckle. "Have you seen the photos on the website?"

"Is the place cute?"

"The men in it definitely are."

"Oh, really?" I hear her fumble around on her phone, the background noise of the hospital, complete with heart monitors and PA announcements, coming through the hospital speakers. "Oh, sweet mother of God."

I can imagine her staring at the photo. Brown eyes wide like a child at Christmas.

"Bitch, this is your idea of cute? This is not cute, Wren! This is every woman's favorite porno come to life! God, the things I could do with these three." She mumbles the last part and I'm glad I'm stopped at a red light, given my eyes are pinched closed with uncontrollable laughter.

"What are the chances that they're all single?" she asks dreamily.

"Very, very low, sweetie. The world doesn't offer one gift like that very often, let alone three."

"One is all I need, sugar." After a moment of laughter, I hear her pause and then sigh. "A patient needs me, boo."

"No problem. I'll let you know how it goes."

"Take a photo of the hot farmers for me, please. Preferably one without their shirts on if they're okay with that."

I chuckle as I indicate my right-hand turn. "If any of them are single, did you want me to kidnap them and bring them to you?"

The sound of my best friend pretending to cry fills my car. "I love you so much, do you know that?"

We say our goodbyes and I bring my full attention back to the road as I drive out of Beckford and start on the windy backroads that lead to Eaglewood. Despite only living two towns away, I've never actually taken the time to visit. Compared to Beckford's town center, with a Target and a McDonald's, Eaglewood lives in the dark ages. It isn't surprising that you often see a lot of people from there popping over to use our amenities, since the most they have is a general store and some chic cafés on their main road.

Even the roads leading to the town are almost devoid of technology, with nothing but spotty signal along the whole road. But one thing that's for certain is that even these roads seem to have more character than my town. Mine is uniform, minimalistic and with a distinct lack of color. The houses all need to look the same, the signs on the fronts of the stores need to be in the same font; it's all very monotone.

And yet, as I drive closer to Eaglewood, I can see the houses start to change. There are only a few, every mile or so along the road, but each one is completely different. Some are time capsules showcasing the house's history in every layer of cement and brick. Others are the kind you see in movies: white picket fence, wraparound porch, a dog perched on the steps basking in the autumn sun.

I wish I lived somewhere with more character like this, but at the time, Adam had insisted on staying in Beckford. Being the naive, love-struck woman I was at the time, I thought that giving up my choices was the same as compromising. Whilst I still hold some anger within my chest, my house still holds the good memories Adam and I made, and that makes it hard to think about selling and starting over somewhere new. But recently there has been a sense of longing brewing within me, a need for somewhere more than where I am. Last I heard, Adam had moved somewhere near New Jersey, but I have no plans to move so far. My family is spread out between these five towns, and it's comforting knowing that there is only one lake separating us. I wouldn't want to move any further from my parents and brother than was completely necessary.

As I enter Eaglewood, and signal becomes a thing again—almost—I pull up the website for the directions.

"Drive to the end of the main road and turn left. Then continue down for about a mile until you see a willow tree on your right," I recite to myself as I put my phone away. "Sounds easy enough."

As I drive down the main road, I fall in love. The friendly smiles that are exchanged between locals as they pass one another, the fairytale atmosphere as I drive in between trees that separate the sidewalk and the road. As I drive over russet leaves and fallen berries, I crack open the window and the smell of coffee and cinnamon welcomes me. I indicate left at the end of the road, take a deep breath and excitedly drive towards Goldleaf Farm.

———

The farm is just as charming in real life, but it definitely needs some TLC.

The barn is even more bruised and battered than it was in the photo, dead grass and discarded tools surrounding its exterior. Corn husks are lined up in neat rows behind it, the grains not yet ripe enough to harvest.

To my right is the farm's main building, which could be better described as a shack. Peeling blue paint covers the outside and a crumbling white door stands wide open at the front.

Between the barn and the shack, you can just about catch a glimpse of one of the pumpkin patches, with a gorgeous variety of amber, burnt orange and cream pumpkins dotted with green. Some are the size of one of my tires, while others look no bigger than a newborn baby. Curling vines wrap themselves around each one, as if they are protecting them from the elements and raising them as their own.

The satisfied bleating of a goat reaches my ears, and yet, only the scent of pumpkins and fresh air fills my nose. A kind of contentment overcomes me as I stare out at the open space.

I smile to myself as I hop out of the car and wander around. I imagine myself harvesting pumpkins with my future children, their smiling faces and lighthearted laughter making me feel complete as they work as a team to lift up one of the larger pumpkins. Children that were ripped away from me by a man who wanted all without giving anything.

Up close, the barn doesn't look to be in any better condition than it did at first glance. The blue and red paint had peeled off long ago, leaving a wet, old brown color in its wake, and though one of the windows on the side is broken, no one has bothered to even attempt a patch job. Curious, I peek around the open door, wanting to see inside.

The barn looks as if it was once used to house farming equipment, big enough to hold at least two good-sized tractors. Even with the autumn sun flowing through the broken window, the space remains in eerie darkness, a haunted look clinging to every crevice. Farm tools sit discarded on the cracked wooden floor, and hay bales are piled up in each corner, hiding from the elements. Cracked wooden boards form a makeshift balcony overhead, some boards missing from the worn railing at the edge. My heart races as I let my eyes float over to the edge of the barn, where shadows seem to live and breed.

"Okay, Wren," I whisper to myself, "pull yourself together because there is no way that something is going to jump out and attack you."

The creaking of the floorboards rushes each beat in my chest and cracks the silence. Whilst the barn's potential shines, that doesn't stop me from seeing it for what it currently is … creepy as hell. No amount of science is persuading me that the noises I'm hearing aren't the echoing of a ghost's footsteps, or that the straw that glides across my feet isn't the stuffing from an evil scarecrow lurking in the corner.

"Soooo time to go," I mumble.

Just as I'm stepping back to leave, pain flashes through my body and I scream until my throat becomes hoarse. On instinct, I close my eyes and flail my arms around me, hoping to spare myself from another attack from the evil spirit.

It's only when a deep voice booms, "What the fuck?" that I dare myself to open my eyes. My screams continue when my eyes meet two slanted, rectangular ones and a loud bleating echoes around the haunted space.

With every one of my screams, the goat in front of me bleats just as loudly, as if I'm the one that bit it.

One of my frantic steps away ends with me getting one foot caught behind the other, sending me flying towards the ground. Something loud falls to the ground, and just as I brace for impact, a strong arm wraps itself confidently around my waist, halting my tumble in its tracks, and a final shriek escapes me as my hands connect with a rock-hard chest and a muscular arm wrapped in a sling and a bright orange cast.

The entire space falls back into its eerie silence, and even the dreaded goat doesn't dare to make another sound.

My world seems to stop as I stare at a strong chest covered by a cotton t-shirt. Trying to recenter myself, everything, from that damn goat to the stranger's chest, all feels as if it has been crammed into the same second, a blend of time that leaves me feeling nothing and everything.

"You okay?" the deep voice asks, not sounding at all as if he actually cares.

"Yeah," I whisper, my breath coming out as a puff of air against his chest.

"Then you can stop touching me."

It's now that I realize his arm has vanished from my waist, and the only thing keeping us in such close proximity is my hand clutching the t-shirt he's wearing underneath a recognizable plaid shirt.

I jump backward and try to discreetly wipe the tingling sensation away from my waist, and he rubs at his chest.

When I look up at my savior, I find myself eye to eye with what appears to be a very pissed off Finch brother with his arm in a sling.

"Now you can tell me what the fuck you're doing in my barn."

Chapter Three

GUS

Her touch doesn't bug me, and that bugs me.

There is something about the way she's grabbing my shirt like a lifeline, something that makes me want to hold her there until she is fine. Which is why I'm so grateful when she leaps back, putting some much-needed distance between us. I roll my shoulder carefully to help ease the twinge of pain that has come from helping her, and push my glasses back up my nose.

She shakes her head, brown curls flying, and she steels her features, a look of annoyance taking over what would otherwise be a pleasant face to look at. "The real question should be why the hell did your goat bite my ass?" she snaps as she glares at Emilio.

"Emilio doesn't bite people," I answer blankly.

"Well, I have the bite mark on my ass to prove that that's a bunch of crap."

She has a beauty spot above her lip that my eyes keep flicking to. There's about a one-in-four-hundred chance of someone having a beauty spot in that exact position. Less than a one per cent probability.

I spout facts when I'm uncomfortable. And I'm suddenly very uncomfortable.

"What are you doing in my barn?" I ask again as I look around me for the axe that I'd dropped while rushing to stop her fall.

She frowns, dark eyebrows dip down towards honey-brown eyes that glisten like jewels in the sunlight, even in the shade of the old barn.

"The door was open," she replies snippily.

"So you thought you'd just let yourself in even though the place doesn't belong to you?"

"The door was open," she repeats impatiently.

"And that makes a difference how?"

She presses her lips together and I watch the action with a fixation I've only ever had for facts. "It doesn't."

"Exactly." I move to the side and motion towards the doors. "So why are you still in it?"

Her honey eyes flash again, and a single eyebrow rises, and immediately Sam's words from five years ago come into my mind.

Sometimes, Auggie, it's not what you say, but how you say it.

"Are you always this impossible to talk to?" she demands.

"I'm autistic, I'm told it's in my nature."

"Being autistic doesn't mean you're automatically impossible to talk to."

"Well, then I suppose it's just my charming personality." I flick my hand towards the door. "After you."

She steps forwards but falters as soon as Emilio bleats at her. She surveys the goat warily. When Emilio bleats again, she holds a pointed finger at him, glaring through squinted eyes. "Don't you dare bleat at me like I'm the one that just groped you. I'm accepting nothing other than an apology, mister. Until then, I don't want to hear it."

"Why did you even let him near enough to bite you?"

Her head whips towards me. "You think I let him bite me? He came into the barn when my back was turned!"

"Leading me to wonder once more why you were in the barn in the first place."

"I—" She stops herself and huffs like a child before pushing past me and storming out of the barn.

My eyebrows scrunch together, and I look down at Emilio, who looks up at me with his big eyes. "I seriously can't have misinterpreted that, can I?"

Emilio bleats once, a sound I take to mean: "Women, am I right?"

With a sigh and a shake of my head, I pick up my axe and reluctantly follow her.

She has marched herself over to the black SUV that had caught my attention when I came back from the field.

Bash chooses that moment to exit my office, immediately smiling at the stranger in a way that makes me walk towards her faster.

"Well, hi." He smiles and holds out a hand for her to shake. "I'm Sebastian, one of the owners of Goldleaf Farm, but please call me Bash. Everyone does. It's a pleasure."

The woman's frown instantly vanishes and is replaced by the kind of smile that makes my chest squeeze. I marvel at how quickly she switches from angry at me for no reason, to being nice to my brother who she has seen for all of two seconds.

"Nice to meet you, Bash. My name is Wren. I'm a party planner over in Beckford."

"Oh, him you're nice to," I mutter.

She turns to glare at me. "He is not the one being rude after his goat bit my ass."

"A goat bit your ass?" Bash questions.

"A goat bit my ass," she confirms.

"It hasn't been proven that Emilio bit her ass," I interject.

"Emilio bit her ass? I thought you said Emilio had cut it with the biting," Bash says, sighing.

"He has cut it out, which is why I said it hadn't been proven that he bit her."

"Why would I lie about him biting me?"

"Because you got caught somewhere where you didn't belong?" I offer.

"Where were you?" Bash asks.

"I was looking at your barn," she explains, her tone soft and polite when she speaks to my brother. "Like I said, I'm a party planner. I have a fall-themed event coming up and when I saw the barn, I thought it had a ton of potential to be an event space."

"We don't do events," I say.

She sends another glare in my direction as she leans against her car. "That's why I said potential."

I'm tempted to poke my brother with the butt of my axe for the way he's failing to hide his laugh.

"My main reason for coming, however, was your pumpkins. A relative of a friend of mine ordered a bunch of pumpkins from you last year. She said you guys were really good and so I wanted to order a bunch for said event." She smiles at Bash before adding, "If that's okay with you, of course."

Bash's mouth opens to respond, but I cut him off. "No, we can't help you. On both counts."

I twist the axe in my hand, ignoring both my brother and my annoyance's shocked expressions.

"What do you mean you *can't*?"

"Yeah, what do you mean we can't?" Seb whispers.

I allow myself a moment to take her in—the wild brown curls, the almost golden eyes, the way her jawline effortlessly slopes towards her neck. There are no sharp lines to her, just soft edges and round features. And yet, with me, she speaks with a sharp edge. She flits between polite and angry like she isn't used to being anything other than annoyingly nice.

I twist the axe once more and start towards my office. "I meant what I said."

"Auggie!" Bash whispers desperately as he rushes behind me. "What are you talking about, man? We need the orders."

"We don't have the manpower, Bash. We have you, half of me and sometimes Sam. That's not enough to even get the orders we have done on time."

21

"Well? Do I get to know why you can't?" Wren asks as she follows us into my office.

I sit at my desk and the chair groans under my weight. It isn't the best-looking office in the world, but it's what I'm able to afford—a ratty-looking armchair in one corner, a tired plastic chair opposite, and a worn-out desk that is barely holding up the ancient computer and stacks of unfinished paperwork that has piled up since I broke my arm. Paperwork that is going to take me even longer to finish since my writing hand is now broken in two places.

"We're working with only one and a half men harvesting at the moment. We're going to be behind on our orders as it is. I can't afford to take on any more."

"But you don't even know when I would need them for."

"You came here from two towns over instead of just calling on the phone like a normal person. That means you're on a time limit and not just perusing for your own amusement."

"Or," she scoffs as she steps further into the office and leans on the edge of my already struggling desk, "it just means that I wanted to see the place for myself, out of excitement for doing what I love."

"That's a less likely option." I swat at her hands with my good one. "Stop leaning on the desk, it's struggling enough as it is."

Her mouth falls open. "Are you trying to say that I'm fat?"

"Well, statistically you would be too heavy for this desk, so if it's in reference to that, then yes, but if you're asking if I think you're fat in general, then, no."

She stares at me in disbelief, full and distracting lips stuck in a confused grimace. It's difficult not to notice things about her, things that would have been completely obsolete on anybody else. It's hard to pretend that the symmetry of her face isn't appealing, or that the way she raises her eyebrows every time I speak isn't a little bit cute.

"Look, even if I could get the pumpkins harvested in time, as you can see, the admin required for it would figuratively kill us. I'm two weeks behind on it as it is. So, again, sorry, but I can't help you."

She lets her body fall into the free seat, defeated, and yet her face seems contemplative. I try to ignore her and the secret looks Bash is sending my way so I can get to work.

As expected, she can't even let me do that. "Okay, well, what if I made a deal with you?"

My hand freezes halfway to the on button on my computer. "What if you what?"

"What if I made you a deal? I'm the owner of a business just like you. So how about we help each other out? That way, you can get on with your sourpuss ways, grumpily sat behind your desk, grumbling to yourself about paperwork that you can't do with the hand you don't write with, and I get a chance to line up more work in town for after we're done."

Neither Bash nor I reply straightaway, and she takes that as a sign to keep going.

"I need a venue for this party. What if I helped you guys fix up your barn and I used it as the venue? I have some people who could help me out and that way, when I order pumpkins from you, you guys are saved the delivery costs and time because you only need to bring them over to the barn. And then, by the end, you guys will have a newly renovated barn that you can use to hold events during the summer and the fall

23

—and as storage the other six months of the year—and I get my name out in Eaglewood."

My eyes find Bash's green ones, both of ours wide.

Logically, it works out for the better, but my pride doesn't want me to admit that to her. It would help us out greatly—bring us business from Beckford whilst also leaving us with a new barn. Events would be a good way to utilize the space, especially during times that hold significance, like Christmas and Halloween. Plus, like she said, I won't have to worry about delivery when I only have to let Mori pull the pumpkins from the field to the barn.

The only problem is…

"You seriously think I have money to fork out to pay for a new barn? Last time I checked, two employees on a farm didn't exactly equal thriving."

"I have tons of old paint from when I repainted my house. Plus, my brother, Finn, is a contractor. That means a major discount on flooring and wood, and I can ask if he and his team can help with the construction work."

What I say next isn't brought on by any agreement in logic, or by some sliver of excitement at the thought of a new barn. No, it's her—that look of hope that sits on her face so clearly that even I can see it. Facial expressions and social cues are my biggest downfall, and yet I can read her so easily, like a book written in my language. I see the way she leans forward slightly with every sentence, how her voice rises in both pitch and volume. I see the excitement in her eyes, and the ability to give any other response slips away.

"Give me some time to think about it."

It's the first time since I met her twenty minutes ago that

one of her smiles has been directed at me and I swear at myself for letting it happen. It's a secret weapon of hers; it must be. That's the only reason it can possibly be so disarming.

She jumps up from her seat with a new sense of purpose. "Really? Oh, my God, thank you so much!"

She pulls a sticky note and a pen from my table, excitedly scribbling on it.

"Here's my number and my email. Whenever you make a decision just call me."

She squeals and jumps and she leaves the room, hugging a confused Bash on the way out and I find it suits her more, this kind of excited chaos. It's something I find equal parts annoying and endearing, and that alone makes me want to say no. But I need to think about the company...

So then why is she already wriggling her way into my mind?

Chapter Four

GUS

Two Weeks Earlier

"You'll need to keep your arm in the cast for eight weeks to start off with. If your shoulder is healing slowly then we might need to keep it in a sling for another couple of weeks after that."

Doctor Shakari speaks as she finishes up with the disgustingly orange cast on my arm, but her words go in one ear and straight out the other.

"I'll book for you to come in in four weeks' time so we can change it."

I see her lean forward, hoping to catch my eye, but my gaze is fixed on the blue curtain that separates me from the rest of the emergency room. Focusing on something else sometimes helps me to block out the overwhelming stimulations of the

27

world. It doesn't help that I can see her in my peripheral, distracting me from the wall of sterile blue cotton. It doesn't help that her brown eyes are looking at me with an embarrassing amount of pity, mahogany softening to a warm chocolate due to an idiotic sense of compassion since she knows the truth. She of all people knows why the pale blue in my eyeline is, in this moment, so important.

She offers a sad smile and my stomach twists. "I made it orange because I thought it would blend in with your work a little. You won't have to think about it as much."

The good doctor often makes the mistake of associating autistic with childish.

After several moments of silence, I see her nod slowly, thankfully accepting that I am not planning on talking unless she asks a question that requires an answer.

"Is there anyone who can help pick up the slack on the farm whilst you're out of commission?" she asks softly.

I offer a stiff shake of my head. Apart from my brothers and I, there isn't a single person left in this town to help out with the farm. No one in our small, closed-minded town is going to be bothered enough. They'd be much more content with being fucked off that their orders were not delivered on time.

She sighs whilst she cleans up and I take that as my sign she's done. I only need to pull myself up from the hospital bed she sat me on, my legs long enough that my only option is to let them spread out in front of me. I pick up my plaid shirt from the bed and start towards the curtain.

"August," Doctor Shakari calls. My hand pauses in front of the curtain and I tighten my grip on my shirt. I turn my head so she knows I'm listening.

"I'm sure if you asked around there would be people in the town willing to—"

"Thanks for the patchwork, Doc." And I leave her pointless words behind.

Present Day

"How long are you out for again?"

"Six more weeks … minimum."

Sebastian blows out a breath as he leans back in the seat opposite. He runs a hand through his brown hair. "That's not great, but it's also not the end of the world. I'm going to come in earlier and stay later to help you with the paperwork."

I shake my head. "You need to focus on the harvest. I'll be working half as fast as I was before and asking Sam for help is about as useful as the crap on the bottom of my shoe. There's no benefit to losing one more person to admin." I can feel his desperate stare on the top of my head. "There's even less benefit to opening an events space when we can't spare anyone to manage it and we definitely can't afford it."

A small smirk graces my brother's face. "You sure you're not just saying that because of a certain hottie you argued with earlier today?"

"No," I snap. "I'm saying that because there is no way you can harvest three fields of pumpkins by the end of the month and help 'Scream McGee' out with the barn as well."

Bash's eyes roll. "You underestimate me, clearly."

"No, I don't. One field contains fifty-two rows of

pumpkins. One pumpkin takes roughly three minutes to harvest, if you include the time between checking it hasn't rot and actually removing it from the vine. Therefore, if you were to do it yourself, assuming that there is roughly one hundred and … twelve pumpkins per row, that would mean you would be spending three hundred and thirty-six minutes per row, or just over five and half hours. That equals seventeen thousand, four hundred and seventy-two minutes—just over two hundred and ninety hours—to harvest one field alone. Now take into account the following factors…" I list them off as I hold up a finger for every item. "… Sam can't help you every day throughout the harvesting period because he's fucking useless; time needs to be added for how long it takes to attach Mori to the sled, stack the crates onto the sled, and move Mori from one location to another as you work your way down the row; and finally, whilst you can carry a bit, your stamina is naturally very low and you roughly require a break of at least ten minutes after every seven pumpkins harvested."

The room is silent as Bash stares at me. We look similar enough that you are able to see some kind of relation, but no one ever guesses brothers if they meet us for the first time. Whilst I am all sharp features and deep frowns, Sebastian is soft smiles and booming laughs. His dark brown hair, and green eyes create a large contrast to my lighter strands and brown gaze.

Sebastian always looks at me with confusion, but never judgment. At least that's what he told me. Facial expressions are an enigma at the best of times.

"You scare me sometimes."

I shrug and lean back in my desk chair. "It's basic math."

"So is Wren's proposal, Auggie. In the long term this is the perfect way to make some extra money and get the farm looking more appealing to our customers."

"It's too unbalanced. She is gaining less than we are in this situation, so I don't trust it."

Bash tilts his head. "Dude," he says blankly. "She's making a name for herself in Eaglewood. You know what they're like here. They're all vultures. Anything new and they're all clawing at it like the last scrap of food in winter."

He's not wrong. The people in this town are so used to cutting themselves off from the world that when something new comes along, they lunge at it. They treat every change in the town like it's either the plague coming to Eaglewood, or a blessing in disguise. As someone who relies on routine and is the biggest enemy of change, you'd think that this mindset would be some kind of twisted turn-on for me, and yet it's exactly what I hate most about this town.

Judging by the way Wren spoke to Bash earlier today—all charming smiles and polite nature—I wouldn't be surprised if they all come to the farm to kiss her taut ass. Huh, maybe Emilio did bite it.

"Just think about it and give her a call, okay? Maybe even ask her out on a date."

I cringe as he stands up and starts towards the door. "Why the hell would I do that?"

Bash turns to smile at me. "You may be shit at reading other people, Auggie, but whether you like it or not you're an open book. And I could tell for a fact that you like the shit out of that woman."

Chapter Five

WREN

The Sweet Cinnamon Café encompasses everything a small town should—cozy atmosphere, quiet yet judgmental gossip and the juxtapositional stares of business owners who can't decide if they want to welcome the extra customers or tell the newbies to go away.

A guy with closely cropped red hair and a cautious smile greets me as I walk up to the counter.

"Welcome to the Sweet Cinnamon Café," he drawls. He looks me up and down. "You're new."

"That obvious, huh?" I chuckle.

"No, just that it's a small town. I'd remember a face like yours. It's too symmetrical and young not to."

I touch one cheek and then the other with a shy smile. "Well, thanks. I'm liking you already."

"Hard not to." He winks. "Now what can I get for ya?"

"Do you by any chance know what the two guys up at Goldleaf Farm drink?"

He scoffs. "Ah, you're one of those ones."

"Those ones?"

"The ones who want to try and score with the Finch brothers."

"What?" I squeak.

"I don't blame you." He smiles. "I've tried a few times myself."

"Oh, no no no, it's not like that, I promise," I nervously chuckle. "I'm possibly going into business with them and so I wanted to start off on the right foot."

Green eyes widen and I swear that the entire café quietens. The barista watches me as I nervously switch my weight from one foot to the other. When I look over my shoulder, sure enough I have about half of the café's eyes on me.

I turn back towards the barista. "I said something wrong, didn't I?"

He shakes away his shock, but his eyebrows remain cocked. "No, not wrong, just weird. I've never heard of anyone going into business with the Finch brothers before."

"Why not?"

"Well, people never usually have a problem with Sebastian, he's like a big fluffy unicorn, but others have been known to … clash, let's say, with Sam and August."

My head tilts. "Okay, August I understand. I didn't have the best time with him yesterday, but I haven't met Sam yet."

"Sam is … complicated. Known to be a bit on the angry side. He always did have a short temper, even in high school."

His eyes flick downward, accompanied by a frown that I don't think he knows is there.

"You went to school with him?"

He shakes his head. "I was in the same grade as August, but my older sister was with Sam. She always came home with some complaint or another when it came to him and whilst I wasn't in their grade, I was ... you know"—he awkwardly clears his throat—"I was in the same school. You hear a lot when no one cares if you're listening. And Sam never cared."

"Huh," I breathe, more to myself than to him.

"But, hey, if they want to go into business with you then you've gotta be stronger than all of us put together."

"They can't be all bad."

"We'll see." He smiles. "You wanted both the boys' orders?"

"Yes, please. Plus a cinnamon latte with oat milk, if you don't mind."

As I pull out my purse, he stops me. "I always allow the first one on the house for newbies that I like."

Even though I know he's not hitting on me, I still feel heat blossom in my cheeks.

"Thank you so much." I stuff my purse back into my bag and move towards the collection counter. "My name's Wren, by the way."

"James, but you can call me Jamie. Everyone does."

Jamie and I continue to chat as he quickly and expertly whips up my order. He asks me where I'm from and I supply the information, still aware that the other customers have only half gone back to their previous conversations. Beckford has its own rumor mill and its fair share of gossip, but they are at least more discreet about listening in. As soon as I mentioned possibly going into business with August and his brothers, I literally heard chairs move closer.

Jamie fills me in on the rough ins and outs of the town—who to avoid (Sandra, the library clerk) and who to keep my mouth shut around (Connor from the hardware store). I don't know whether or not he's genuinely joking when he throws his name into the mix on that last one. His laugh isn't particularly convincing.

When he's finished all three drinks, he grabs a pen and writes "August" on one, "Bash" on another, and "Newbie" on the last one. I thank him and promise to return tomorrow morning. I rush out the café and away from prying eyes. I feel like I can breathe deeper when I step back into the crisp, autumn air as the wind gently swipes my brown curls from my face.

I realize that Jamie never made a coffee for the final Finch brother. There sure seemed to be some underlying tension between them judging by the way Jamie spoke. Either way, I know it's better to be prepared for a man with whom I'm never going to get along with no matter how hard I try.

———

The clouds threaten a heavy spout of rain by the time I get to Goldleaf Farm, their dark gray tint hovering over the barn I ache to see both one more time and never again.

"Well, look who it is!" a cheery, low voice calls. Bash walks towards me with a mischievous smile and a glint in his bright green eyes. "I was hoping you'd come back."

"Oh?" I ask, my eyebrow raising. "And why is that?"

"Because my brother Sam didn't believe me when I told him about the woman who stood up to the infamously grumpy August Finch. I needed you to come back so that when it happens again, I can record it."

I let out a genuine laugh, one that ricochets off of the main building and back to us.

"Well, I'm sorry to disappoint but today I intend on going back to nice, kind, patient Wren. I do have a potential deal on the line here after all."

"Is nice, kind, patient Wren just as interesting as sassy, witty Wren?"

I shrug and turn to grab his coffee. "I'm not sure, but she does come with coffee."

His lips twitch when he sees his name written on the top of the cup. "A woman after my own heart. If it didn't already belong to someone else, it would be yours by now."

We both stand in a comfortable silence, him admiring the roasted, slightly caramel taste of his black coffee with vanilla syrup, me taking in the tummy-twisting feel of nature and simplicity that surrounds me. I've always known I'd have been perfectly content living a life like this—a life filled with a complex simplicity. It's quiet here, comforting and frugal all on its own. I love it. I admire it.

"Oh, before you go and see him," Bash begins, pulling me from my thoughts. I turn to him expectantly, my hands tightening on my own cup of coffee. "I know he can be difficult. Auggie is blunt and self-assertive and, most of the time, just way too honest." He lets out a breathy laugh.

"But he's a good guy. It's not easy for him to live in a town that isn't the most open-minded."

I offer Bash a small smile.

"All I'm trying to say is that the spectrum is different for everyone on it. The things which usually just have one meaning to us can have several to him, and vice versa. He's not always aware of how he says things because to him it's a predictable response, so pull him up on it. You'll find he becomes a lot easier to talk to after that."

It makes me smile to see a brother's love so abundant in Bash. It's clear that he cares for August, so much so that he wants to give his brother the chance to be understood before being judged.

I put a comforting hand on his shoulder as I pass by him towards the office. I've only known the man for not even half a day and I can already see that Jamie's description of him is bang on. The man really is a unicorn.

As I let myself into August's office, his coffee in my free hand, I make a promise to myself to be more patient with him just as Bash has asked me to.

He's at his desk, one hand stuck gripping his brown locks to the point that it looks painful, the other still bound in a nauseatingly orange cast and black sling. His head is down and I can tell by the sharp cut of his jaw and the tense set of his shoulders that he's not having a good time. I tilt my head as I take in the sight of him—plaid shirtsleeves rolled up to the elbows showing the slightly tanned skin that covers toned muscle and undeniable strength.

"If you've come back in here to badger me about the girl from yesterday, Bash, then allow me to tell you to fuck off now and save you the time it would take to tell me how you think I like her and want to marry her or whatever the hell it is you think," he says without looking up, his hand releasing its hold on his hair and moving to cup his forehead instead.

I almost laugh.

"Oh, man, that's a shame, I was planning on sending out wedding invites today. Whatever will I tell the family?"

He jolts, head zipping up as he pins me in place with wide brown eyes that are dull with lack of sleep. Purple bags are beginning to form under his eyes which are almost blocked by his mop of blonde chocolate waves atop his head. Good thing I've brought coffee.

"What are you doing here?" he asks with that tone that tells me he doesn't actually care about the answer.

I step further into the office and place the coffee on the only clear part of his desk. "I come bearing gifts."

He stares at the paper cup as if he can smell poison. His eyes skim over his name written in black marker on the top and his face scrunches up.

"You don't even know what coffee I like."

I hold back an eyeroll. "That's the beauty of a small town, the people who work in the coffee shop do."

He picks up the cup and sniffs the steam that escapes through the hole in the lid. A single eyebrow shoots up.

"What can I say, I'm amazing."

He takes a tentative sip and when it has his approval, he

sits back in his seat, his unbuttoned shirt sliding off him to reveal the plain black tee that stretches itself across a broad chest and wide shoulders. I avert my gaze.

"Is this your attempt at buttering me up so I'll say yes to working with you?"

"What? Nooo!" I laugh awkwardly as I drag out the "no" until it is embarrassingly obvious that I mean "yes".

His head tilts, waves falling into his eyes and kissing the end of his nose. "Why the hell are you talking like that?"

I take a seat in front of his desk.

"Never mind. Anyway ... since we're on the subject ... any news on whether or not you want to do up the barn?"

He fixes me with this look and there's something about it that unsettles me. Previously, he's never really looked at me ... he watches me, like an impossible math equation and it concerns me that this one look has the capacity to capture all of my attention in an instant. He analyzes every one of my movements—every flick of my eyebrow, each time I allow my mouth to lift in a smirk meant to rile, and he seems to pay particular attention to my lips any time that I lift my cup to my mouth to taste the sweet and bitter blend of my coffee.

It's one of those stares which you aren't quite sure if it's done out of interest or out of disgust.

He sips his coffee once more, eyes glued to mine. "I'm still undecided."

"What's holding you back?"

"You."

"Me?"

"I don't trust you." When he is met with no response, he rolls the shoulder of his injured arm and continues.

"When looking for a business partner, one should typically look for more than a pretty face and a confusing personality. So far you've done nothing to prove you're anything more than that."

He speaks as if the knowledge of my apparent beauty is something he came to terms with long ago, but that can be anxiously dissected by my own brain later.

I clear my throat. "I am a lot more than that," I say uncertainly, mainly because I'm not sure that I am. My breakup with Adam mixed in with the painfully quiet period for the business has really taken its toll on my confidence. I know I'm all over the place sometimes—shy one minute, outspoken the next—and that is down to my forever fluctuating belief in myself and my ability to be the confident woman I once was. It's the reason why I'm so afraid of committing to anyone else. Why my head and my heart have both been on strike, allowing me to easily sit in my dark pit of self-pity and occasional pessimism.

Then again … I stayed with a man like Adam for so long so how confident can I truly have been?

"Prove it," Gus leers, the tiniest hint of a smirk tugging at the corners of his pink lips.

"What would you like me to do, Gus, show you I'm not going to jump off the bridge just because my friends did it?"

He stands from his chair and the room shrinks as broad shoulders and a tall figure take over the small office space. He stalks towards me; his movements composed but tense. My breath shallows and for a brief, pathetic moment, I believe myself to be the object of the desires of a man I've just met and not the reason for his frustration.

It looks natural on him—this level of confidence that others have to spend decades begging for. Every speck of dust, every atom in the air follows him and so does my gaze.

When there is nothing more than a single step between us, I jump up from the chair. My stance seems pathetic in comparison given that I reach no higher than his chest. I'm small, even with my knee-high heeled boots, and I want to shrink at the intensity of his towering form.

The chair behind me blocks me from creating some distance between us as he swallows it up. He takes that final step until one breath in is enough to have my breasts flush against him.

His hard gaze narrows at something on my face. Whatever it is, he looks both intrigued and annoyed by it.

"Less than one percent," he mumbles gruffly.

"What?" I whisper, so enchanted by the atmosphere that I don't want to interrupt it.

Thick, dark eyebrows dip. "There's a less than one percent chance of you having this beauty spot in this specific place. Did you know that?"

I open my mouth to respond, but suddenly he reaches out to gently trace a finger across it, cutting off both my words and my air supply. I snap my mouth shut as he runs his finger along the spot that holds all of his attention.

"Hey, guys, I'm making a run to the bakery, do you want any—" Bash's words are cut off mid-sentence by the sight of Gus's hand stuck in the air and me scrambling away from him, grateful that there is now something that separates Gus's intensity from my shy temperament. "Am I interrupting something?"

"No!" I all but yell, my voice breaking. I clear my throat

and try again. "No, no. Nothing at all. I was just going. Gus needs more time and I really should be going anyway so I can sort out some stuff at home since I'll be coming and going from here for a while."

"You're staying in town?" Gus asks in a low voice, arm still stuck in the air.

I avoid eye contact as I answer. "No, I just make the drive down each morning."

Any evidence of a thick and electric atmosphere has dissipated, and in its place is a stuffy awkwardness.

"I should go." I repeat.

With one last sparing look towards Gus, I pick up my now cold coffee and leg it out of the office.

Chapter Six

GUS

S ince Bash is the most annoying idiot in my life right now, I've somehow ended up on Main Street, heading towards the bakery for some fucking tarts. Wren, thankfully, has headed home to—according to her—continue researching food and drink options for the party.

God, she infuriates me. She gives me the same look the rest of the town does, with her fancy clothes and perfectly manicured nails, she looks as if every conversation with me is an inconvenience. Which is why I can't figure out for the life of me why she ends up using those nails to crawl her way into my thoughts every hour. I need her gone and I need her gone fast.

The main street leads out of town one way, and towards the lake at the other end. After finding somewhere to park, I start pacing down the street, very aware that I still have an unending pile of paperwork to sort out back at the farm.

Several people send curious looks in my direction, curious as to what Gus Finch could possibly be doing so far from the farm with his bad attitude and blunt conversation.

The most heavenly smell reaches my nose, letting me know that I'm finally outside of "Doughnut Miss This", a brand-new bakery that some new girl opened about a month ago. The sweetness of sugar and the faintest hint of lemon mix together and even if I wasn't here for Bash, I'm pretty sure I wouldn't be able to resist.

I've dealt with Wren Southwick for the second time this week, I deserve a treat, don't I?

I open the door and step in, a bell above me ringing as I enter. A woman stands behind the counter, restocking the lemon tarts in the display. She seems to be around Wren's age, large round glasses surrounding shy eyes. I push my own further up my nose as she offers the only other person in the store a kind smile.

"Did you want anything else other than the strawberry tart, Cally?"

Cally Ranson smiles back before shaking her head. "No, thanks, Lori. My husband would kill me if he saw me buying even one." When Lori pauses at her words, Cally adds, "We're supposed to be doing a workout program together which includes no sugar for two months."

Lori visibly relaxes, and I find myself wondering what I've just missed within Cally's words to support such a reaction. "No worries, I promise I won't tell."

"You're the best."

Lori spots me and gives a shy wave. "Hiya. I'm Lori. Welcome to Doughnut Miss This."

"Hi," is all I say in return.

When Cally hears my voice, she spins around, shock quickly turning to distaste.

"August Finch," she says.

"Gus," I correct her.

She looks me up and down before snapping herself out of whatever trance her shock put her in. "I'm surprised to see you here."

"I live here."

"Gus Finch," Lori buts in. "You own the farm down the road, right?"

"Yeah."

She nods in confirmation. "Yeah, I've heard … of … you."

I grunt, but don't ask anything else. I already know the type of shit she's going to have heard. Cally huffs out a humorless laugh, but when she sees me watching her, she stares at me for a few seconds before blinking nervously and taking a step back.

Everyone falls into an awkward silence as Lori and Cally both watch the ground with an uncomfortable level of interest. I don't know what I can do in this moment to explain to Lori that whatever shit people spread about me isn't anywhere near the truth, but at the same time I don't really care enough to do so. Is there a tightness in my chest as someone who has never met me before looks almost scared to look me in the eye? Sure, but that's not my problem. I want to yell "Next time, do what Wren did and find out for yourself instead of listening to futile gossip." Yes, Wren still hates me anyway, but at least she took the time to see for herself. There I go thinking of Wren Southwick again.

"Did you want to order something?" Lori asks from behind the counter, eyes flicking from me to Cally like she's watching a tennis match.

Grateful for the segue, I reply, "Yeah. Two strawberry tarts for my brother."

She gets to work and I maneuver myself around Cally to get closer to the counter.

"What is that smell?" I ask her.

"Do you need to ask so rudely?" Cally asks.

I turn towards her, pushing my glasses up. "All I did was ask her what that smell was?"

"So you can tell her it smells bad, I'm assuming."

Why the hell is that what she assumes?

"No, so I can know what the smell is. I like lemon."

Lori blushes. "Oh, that's a new addition actually. It's a lemon and elderflower tart."

I like elderflower, too.

I go to say that I'll take two, but then I take a second and reassess. After clearing my throat, I ask, "Is the base the same as the strawberry ones?"

Lori nods.

I stole one from Bash last week and the texture didn't make me want to throw up.

"I'll take two," I tell her.

She smiles awkwardly and gets to work.

"Right, yes," Cally mumbles behind me. "Well, it was nice to see you, Lori, I'll see you later."

"Bye, Cally."

The bell above the door rings as she leaves.

"I'm sorry about that," Lori apologizes, surprising me. "She's never normally like that."

I turn to look at the door Cally just left through. "She is with me. I'm used to it."

I decide not to dwell on it any further, not wanting to let anything ruin my day more than it already has been. I really hate coming into town.

"How much do I owe you?" I ask.

I pay what I owe and seem to surprise Lori when I say thank you before heading out. I take a bite out of one of the tarts and groan to myself—a perfect balance of sharp and sweet, the pastry just the right texture for my sensitive mouth.

Immediately after finishing the first one, I turn around and head straight into the bakery. When I enter the store for the second time, Lori looks shocked to see me.

"Hi."

Her expression turns to mild concern. "Was everything okay with the tarts?"

"Yeah, they're great."

She pushes her glasses further up her nose and I mimic the gesture. She still looks confused bordering on concerned. I move further into the store, my broad shoulders taking up most of the space. I look down and realize that there are a few crumbs from the tart I scoffed down lingering on my plaid shirt and I quickly brush them away, an embarrassed blush creeping up my neck. The awkward atmosphere makes my skin itch.

I'm frustrated with myself. Why the fuck do people feel it okay to share their assumptions about me with others? And why do I let it happen? I am straightforward and blunt, yes,

49

but not rude to people I've never met. I say things how it is. Having a conversation with others has never been my strong suit, but I at least used to try my best before this town decided to write me off as a rude, egotistical asshole.

Not only has this town put a massive dent in my self-esteem along with my ability to believe in myself, but so did I. I put a massive dent in my self-esteem because I let them do it. People like my father made me believe in a future, in being who I am without apology, and then took it all away from me. Stripped it from me and took away any belief I had in deserving either of those things. My career counts as my future and it's the only thing I have left that cannot be taken from me. Well, not until I'm broke anyway.

But now there's Wren, this woman that's come out of nowhere and completely upended everything, demanding we rebuild the barn for her benefit. The bad part is that I'm completely aware that I'm most likely going to say yes eventually. What's worse is that I'm going to say yes because of her and I know it. Bash teases me for me and I deny it, but he's right. I don't like her but I want her and that makes me hate her.

I need Wren Southwick gone.

Clearing my throat, I finally speak to Lori. "You able to do a bulk order for a party at the end of the month?"

Surprise swims behind her glasses. "You want me to provide food for a party?"

"Yeah, on the farm."

Even more surprise. "You're having a party on your farm?"

"The party planner is … persuasive." Even though it's not set in stone yet. And despite her sexy glares and bitchy personality being an equally persuasive reason as to not do it, I find myself asking, "So do you think it would be a possibility?"

"I've never done it before, but you've given me enough notice. I'd be more than happy to try. How much would you be needing?"

Internally, I breathe a sigh of relief. One step closer to saying goodbye to Wren Southwick once and for all.

───────────

Since things seem to be working in my favor today, I decide to see what else I can do to ensure that Wren's time at the farm is cut down to its absolute minimum.

I remember that Jamie knows the ins and outs of this town so he'll probably be the best person to ask for some advice.

"Gus," he says as I step into the Sweet Cinnamon Café. "I thought Wren picked up your coffee this morning."

"I'm not here for coffee."

"Well, I would ask if you're here for me, but I know I'm not that lucky."

"Don't you think one Finch brother is enough?"

"Good point. You are all a lot of work." Jamie leans onto the counter so that we are in our own little soundproof bubble. Not that there is any such thing in this town. "What can I do you for?"

"I need some advice. I have a difficult party planner who won't leave me alone."

"You're coming to me for advice on women? Bit of a gay stereotype, don't you think?"

"That's not why I'm here," I say, agitated. "I need the names of people who have done this kind of thing before."

He's suspicious, but he asks, "Specifically in Eaglewood?"

"Yeah." I watch my foot as it scuffs the checkered tiles.

Jamie watches me with uncertainty, and I don't blame him. The chances of finding me in town on a manhunt for people I can talk to? Well, you'd have a bigger chance of the sun shining out of my ass. It's so obvious that this is out of the ordinary for me and even though I've been considered to be quite a monotone speaker, my lying skills aren't exactly pristine.

Jamie hums lowly as he watches me with a raised eyebrow. "People drinking at this party that you're magically allowing on your farm?"

"I don't fucking know."

"Alright, alright." He begins making a coffee the moment he sees Tommy from the hardware store walk in. I would wonder how he manages to remember all these orders, but I know the orders of every local that orders from me as well. "Then you'll want to talk to Colin, he can supply the booze."

Noted. "Anyone else?"

He thinks on it as he hands Tommy his coffee. "The only other one I can think of is Mickey at the Thompson. If you need to cater this thing, he's your man."

My chest lightens as I make progress with ridding myself of the most annoying of women. I can't really remember the last time I was this excited since Dad left last year. I feel the rush under my skin from the new sense of determination and inspiration. I've kind of missed this feeling. It's exactly how I used to feel during harvesting season or when it came time to sow the new seeds. The excitement of seeing the progress as

52

the seeds turn to sprouts, knowing that eventually you'll have made something that can be eaten, decorated or planted all over again. When I sold the first pumpkin that I planted myself, I was on cloud nine and nothing was going to dampen the swell of pride in my chest when I did.

Now, I spend half of my time wondering if that swell of pride was nothing more than a bloom of happiness for the first time because I was needed by something.

"Thanks."

He shrugs like he's used to dishing out information. "You feel like telling me why you're suddenly in the mood to be helpful?"

"It's not being helpful, it's making sure Wren needs to visit Eaglewood as little as possible."

He looks amused. "The whole of Eaglewood?"

"Yep," I say before turning and heading out. "Staying away from my farm is not far enough."

Chapter Seven

WREN

My house is a small cottage ten minutes out from the edge of Beckford. Even though they aren't particularly up to date with the world in this town, it seems they are at least open to the idea of the younger generation moving here. The lady Adam and I bought the house from finally managed to book herself her dream holiday to Egypt and then decided to sell once her vacation was coming to an end, so she could stay out there for a year. She was only too happy when we asked to buy the place.

By the time I've driven back home, packed a bag for tomorrow, worked on Oakleigh's party some more and gotten ready for bed, it's late, and despite not doing much with my day, the excitement that I was feeling earlier has now drained away, leaving only exhaustion in its wake. I don't take in much of anything. I make sure I'm aware enough to find my way to the living room and that is the end of Wren Southwick for the night.

This morning, I'm feeling refreshed. But worry still wraps around my head like a ribbon tied too tight. I ran out of Gus's office like a thief in the night. No man has ever looked at me with the hunger I saw in Gus's eyes and it has shaken me. It was either that he didn't want to hide the heat in his eyes, or he didn't know how. It's the part of August Finch that holds the biggest mystery so far—how is one man able to show everything and nothing at the same time?

But then again, maybe that was his intention. Maybe he wanted to throw me off knowing that I'd back down and he'd have more time to think of a reason to say no to our deal.

As I wrap myself up in my light blue dressing gown and wander down into the white and oak kitchen, I make blind guesses as to what it would be like to work with Gus, what it would be like to see him every day until we finish the barn. There is an arrogance which leads me to think that we'd end up fighting it out with the farm's discarded tools by the end of the first week. And yet there is a small part of me that wants to see just how deep the well that is Gus Finch runs; see if my immediate opinion (other than that he's extremely good-looking) is merely misinterpretation.

I grab the milk I bought yesterday, pour it into my cereal and think to myself that everything is probably not all that it seems.

It's not until midday, after a phone call with Oakleigh to offer an update and discuss decorations for the party, that I make it out of the house and over to Eaglewood's Sweet Cinnamon Café.

I'm not surprised by the stares and whispers as I enter. The sweet smell of chocolate and the bitter scent of coffee are the perfect start to my afternoon and so a few curious locals aren't going to deter me.

Jamie offers me an aloof smile from behind the counter, his red hair covered by a baseball cap. You could spot his pink jumper from a mile away, especially when he's paired it with some green corduroy pants.

"Hey, newbie," he greets. "Survived day one I see."

"Afternoon, Jamie." I pull my card from my purse. "I didn't stay for too long. I live over in Beckford. You'd be surprised how easy it is to avoid being the newbie when you're two towns away."

"You're living my dream, babe." He taps a few buttons on the till. "Want the same as last time?"

I nod. "The guys' coffees too, please."

He smiles slyly. "So your attempt to woo the Finch brothers was successful then?"

"I'm not wooing anyone!" I turn to face the locals who don't even bother to conceal their efforts to eavesdrop. "I wasn't wooing anyone, I promise."

"Good!" says an older woman sitting against the window. "Those Finch brothers are nothing but trouble."

"What makes you say that?" I ask, my curiosity getting the better of me.

She turns in her seat and the café quietens further. "All that youngest one does is stay on the farm and ignore everyone. Then, when he does talk to someone, he has the gall to be rude and obnoxious. He called the other day to tell me that my order for the library would be late and I told him that was unacceptable. Just because he's broken his arm? If he hadn't gotten rid of all his staff, then his arm wouldn't be causing any issues."

A warning look from Jamie tells me it's probably best not to mention the slightly selfish outlook on that one. I do find it interesting that Gus apparently let all of his staff go, however.

"He's always been a strange kid, Sandra," says a balding middle-aged man sitting a few tables away. "I remember back when I used to teach him, he always used to come into school with ear plugs. I had to constantly tell him that they weren't allowed but he wouldn't listen. He almost lived in detention because of it."

Okay, not too sure about that one either.

"Let's not forget about what happened when Erica came to town. Now that was a rough month," a woman chips in from across the café.

"I think the situation with Melina was worse than Erica, wouldn't you say, Millie?"

"True," she agrees as I realize that I've now been weaseled out of this conversation. "Then again, even his own father always used to talk about how strange he is. He's always been rude. He even had the audacity to tell me that my shoes were horrible."

Jamie whispers into my ear. "He told her that they weren't a good idea for winter. She was wearing stilettos in the snow. Tripped over four times."

Interesting.

By the time I leave the café for the second time, I am once again the object of people's stares and conversations. Jamie tries to tell all of them to get back to their "old people chats" about bingo and the next town hall meeting, but the smell of fresh meat is too tempting for their small-town noses to bear.

Just like the day before, I grab the three cups of coffee and start the drive to Goldleaf Farm, my head filled with even more questions about August Finch.

GUS

She came at 8:40 in the morning the day before, so when 8:45 came and went, I realized that she wasn't showing up, and after mentally chastising myself for being disappointed by that, I got back to the shit I had to do.

At nine o'clock, it was time to check the vines.

Eleven a.m. meant a late breakfast and now, at midday, it's time for—

"Knock, knock."

That light, slightly raspy feminine voice I've already memorized floats towards me from the door. She's leaning against the door frame, everything about her posture screaming that she is entirely at ease in this moment. How, I'm not sure, especially when the mere sound of her voice has my muscles locking up.

She has on skinny jeans and knee-high boots which could give even old man Smith a heart attack. Pair them with the turtleneck that stretches itself across her breasts like a second skin and I'm a man on the edge. I found it distracting enough the first time I met her—hair a wild bush of mahogany curls atop her head and those almost hazel eyes wild and frantic. Now, they spark with fire and her curls sit along her back as the dim light of my office reflects off of each strand.

"So, when you handed me your number and said 'call me when you've made a decision' … that was just bullshit, wasn't it?" I mumble as I lean back in my chair. Her eyes flick down to my chest and back up, not quite quick enough to escape my notice.

She shrugs after pushing herself off of the door frame.

"Why aren't you staying in Eaglewood?"

It throws her off, but she hides it well. I let my smirk show as she lowers her head, and it's gone by the time she lets her gaze meet mine once more.

"It's just easier," she eventually grumbles.

"Easier for who?"

"For my bank account," she snaps. "Like you said to me, I don't have money to fork out on renting an apartment here *and* paying a mortgage."

"Then why keep coming here?"

"What can I say? I'm an eager beaver."

"What exactly is it about beavers that makes them eager?"

Her shoulders lift in a silent laugh. "It's just a phrase. I'm pretty sure it's just because the words rhyme."

That's stupid. "Right."

She places a coffee in front of me and sits down. Once again it has my name written on the top.

"You brought this at eight forty yesterday."

I see the pause of her hand as she brings her own drink to her lips. She tries to take a sip normally, and I refrain from asking the purpose for such a reaction.

"Did I? I didn't even check the time before I brought it over."

"So, for all you know, it could have been five in the morning?"

"That's an exaggeration and you know it."

"It isn't actually. It's an accurate interpretation of the information you just gave me."

She looks annoyed and a chuckle sits on my chest. Has no one ever stopped to think that maybe I'm just saying things as they are? That I'm merely forming a sentence and associating it with the proper tone that implies whether or not it's an opinion or fact.

I look away and roll my shoulder. With my free hand, I reach for the coffee and take a sip. That familiar combination of coffee and pumpkin floats over my tongue and I all but groan. It's a taste I love, but it's currently being dampened by the knowledge that I'm drinking it at the wrong time. When I woke up this morning, I had expected her to bring a coffee again, because if there is one thing I can deduct about Wren Southwick, it's that she's stubborn enough to bring coffee every day until I say yes. It's partly what makes me want to say no.

Now that she's brought me exactly what I expected to have almost four hours ago, I'm bombarded by the usual feeling that comes with the slightest change. The closest analogy I can offer is that it's as if I have a million and one ants crawling under my skin. Not that it's scientifically possible to have a million ants crawling under your skin because both you and the ants would die, but the sensation is imaginable all the same.

I close my eyes and twist my head from side to side in a pathetic attempt to control my reaction. Getting overstimulated isn't something that I need her seeing. I don't need a woman like Wren knowing that I struggle with something as simple as drinking coffee at a time that wasn't self-appointed.

"I still haven't decided, by the way." I put my coffee back on my desk and clench my fist under the table. "Despite my brother trying to make the decision for me."

We sit in silence, and I welcome it even though it's awkward. When I find the confidence to slide my gaze back up to Wren, I find her watching me through slitted lids.

She's analyzing me and I'm surprised that's something I'm noticing so easily. Slitted eyelids usually equal anger, exactly like it did when she glared at me the first day I met her. But it's all there in the cute little tilt to her head and the way her lips tease me with a hint of a smile.

"What about a trial period?" she asks.

"How the hell do you conduct a trial period to rebuild a barn?"

"It's not a trial period for the barn; it's a trial for us. To see if we can work together. The barn gets fixed regardless because let's face it, it seriously needs a touch-up either way. We can fix the things that desperately need it to start off with, such as the upper level, the broken windows and the flooring. If you find that it's too difficult and I'm too untrustworthy because of my—how did you put it? Pretty face?—then we part ways, I find a new venue, but you still have the help from my brother and his team to finish the work. Oh, but I still get my pumpkin order either way, I'll just be nice and say that if we part ways, I'll lessen the quantity to make it easier on you guys."

I run my hand through my hair and adjust my glasses. "How long would it take you to find a new venue?"

She scoffs. "What do you think this is, my first day? I'll find a backup so that it's ready to go in case I need it."

My eyes float around my desk to the incomplete invoices, the tax returns and the unprocessed orders. I lift my wrist to look at my watch which now sits on the wrong side thanks to the disgustingly orange cast that decorates my right wrist. I'm twelve minutes late.

I readjust myself in my seat and clear my throat. "Next time you come by, make sure it's either before nine, between eleven and twelve, or after two. If you're bringing coffee, then don't bring it after nine."

There's the anger. There's a big difference between the two emotions when I see it on her. It's no longer a puzzle I have to work out, maybe because I can't help but analyze her every expression. Or, maybe because the fire in her eyes cannot possibly be anything else. She doesn't bother to hide anything in that brown and green gaze.

"If you're going to talk to me, make sure you're not doing it like a butthead."

"Butthead?" I question.

She offers a single nod.

I don't want to tell her that I don't understand. Most people mistake misunderstanding for stupidity these days.

"Right," is all I can find to say.

"By that I mean that you can't talk to me so rudely all the time."

I scratch my beard, completely perplexed. Thankfully, Bash chooses this moment to walk into the office. He looks cautious as he walks in, green eyes nervously flitting between Wren and me as if sensing the energy in the room before opening his mouth.

"Everything okay in here?"

"Everything is fine," Wren says at the exact same time that I say, "I think she was just telling me that I'm an asshole."

Bash smiles. "Glad to know she's telling it to you like it is."

I glare at him fiercely. Bash is used to my "sour personality" as Wren puts it, mostly because he knows it isn't sour at all. I'm just sick of being nice to people first and then being treated like an idiot just because I'm different. They hear the word "disorder" and take that to mean the same thing as "incompetent".

Wren turns towards Bash, her lips breaking out into a smile that threatens to cloud my judgment.

"Gus was just agreeing to a trial period to see how working together pans out."

Bash looks impressed. "Really?" he beams. "Well, isn't that good news. I was just telling him yesterday how good it would be if we took you up on your unbelievably kind offer."

She pretends to be shocked at the news even though I told her just minutes before that he wants to work with her. There is just no need to be so fucking dramatic. Both of them.

"Can we move on? I'm currently ... seventeen minutes behind schedule here."

They both roll their eyes at me.

"Okay, so when can you get your brother down here to help out?" Bash asks Wren.

"I can ask him to stop by tomorrow afternoon. He lives in Renford so not far to travel."

Renford is the town next to Beckford. It's the biggest of the five towns that surround the lake we all share. It's more of a commercial town, complete with everything from factories to four-story shopping malls. I've never been able to imagine living in such chaos.

"And how much does he plan to ask for?"

"That's the best part," Wren smiles. "He owes me a million and one favors, all of which just so happens to equal the rebuild of a brand-new barn."

"What did you do for him? Give him a kidney?"

"I'm joking, Gus. I'm going to split the money I make on this party with him," she says with a playful eyeroll. She stands and holds a small, delicate hand out towards me. "So, what do you say, Finch?"

I glare at her hand despite the way my fingers itch to reach for it. "Fine," I grumble, my eyes flicking to two light brown gems that sparkle with mischief. I take a deep breath and finalize the deal with six words that I'm sure I will regret further down the line. "Let's see what you got, Southwick."

Chapter Eight

WREN

Even though August's attitude infuriates me in a way that no one ever has before, I still find myself purchasing his coffee from Jamie this morning—making sure I've got plenty of time to deliver it before the hour that he deems as "late". When I collect the goods from my new favorite barista, he sends me a knowing smile and a wink, along with a whispered, "You seem to be spending a lot of time over there."

I smile politely, but my cheeks still blossom with heat as I tuck my chin into my scarf. Scurrying away from the Sweet Cinnamon Café seems to be my permanent exit strategy now. It's funny how, to a small town like this one, every change is analyzed, especially when that change is an outsider.

As I drive over to the farm, one of the guests for the party on speaker phone, Gus pops into my head for what feels like the millionth time since I met him. The more I think about it, the more I understand that yes, August Finch annoys me, but I think it's because he challenges me. He pushes me, makes me look at myself and wonder where the line is between kind and naive. He makes me see what I want and fight for it instead of just lying down and letting others trample all over me, and I don't even think that he's doing it on purpose. I think he's just naturally an ass who seems to bring out the fighter in me.

As I step out of the car, the autumn wind nips at my curls, sending them flying across my face and into the open air behind me. The clouds above are tinted gray, but not enough to threaten any rain. Over the four days I've come here, it's become even colder, the somewhat warm chill has become a brisk cold that tells of the oncoming storm mentioned in the weather report this morning.

My attention shifts to the barn when I hear the laughter that floats from the open door. It's a low, almost melodic laugh that warms my chest and fights off the autumn chill. I've heard Bash's laugh before and it's not his. Sebastian laughs as if it's the last time he will ever do so—it's loud and booming and infectious. This laugh is almost shy, reserved, as if the owner feels he shouldn't be allowed to be so happy.

I stop to listen, reveling in the knowledge that as far as I'm aware there is only one other person who the calming sound could belong to.

When I reach the barn and silently slip in through the door, lo and behold, there he is—August Finch with a heart-stopping smile and a body-warming chuckle that lifts his chest as it leaves him. He runs a hand through thick brown waves as he stares at the floor. I can still see the smile on his face—lopsided and innocent. It softens the harsh cut of his jawline and adds some color to his cheeks. He looks just as shy as his laugh sounds.

I move to see who is making him laugh so easily, only to find my brother—of all people—jabbering away whilst he watches Gus, whose dark brown eyes are glowing.

Finn Southwick is many things, but funny has never really been one of them. He's a very reserved, very anti-social being, hence why he chose to work in construction. It means that he only needs to communicate with others in a professional capacity, leaving him to spend time with his own thoughts as he hammers nails and levels concrete. That's not to say that Finn isn't a very kind, very lovable person. He's always been the big brother I need exactly when I need him, he's just never been one for conversations that require laughter and jokes.

I clear my throat quietly, hoping to not interrupt this lighthearted moment, but alas it's enough for the sound to travel around the vacant space, bouncing off of the loose floorboards and broken beams.

Gus's laughter halts in its tracks as he spins to watch me with wide eyes. Any hint of his smile disappears, any trace of contentment washes away with the sound of his laughter, leaving only the sour-faced, closed-off Gus that I've been meeting the past few days.

Finn looks up in surprise, but Gus's expression reflects what I assume is annoyance at the mere presence of me. I try my best not to be offended, but it's hard not to feel the sting against my skin. It's difficult to pretend that the warmth I felt due to the sound of his laughter hasn't just dissipated and left behind the September chill.

With a subtle shake of my head, I try my best to ignore the

tension in my chest and skate over to them, floorboards creaking under me. I hold Gus's coffee out to him and try to smile casually. "Good morning."

He skeptically eyes the cup before slowly taking it from me, his finger softly brushing against mine, sending a soft buzz up my arm.

"Morning," he replies, suspicious.

I turn to my brother. "Morning, bro."

Finn's eyes flick between Gus and me. "Morning, Wrennie. No coffee for me I take it?"

"Sorry, I didn't know you would end up coming over this early, but here, have mine."

He shakes his head with its soft brown curls that have grown long enough that they move with the action. "No, no. It's yours. I'll grab one a bit later."

I shove the cup towards him. "Take it. I can grab one when I stop by the flower shop."

"Why do you need flowers?" Gus asks.

"I don't *need* flowers. I just thought it would be a nice way to brighten up my kitchen." When the awkwardness begins to settle into the ever-shrinking space, I add, "So how is it going in here so far?"

"It's going well," my brother replies after a sip of cinnamon-flavored goodness. "I'm just looking around at the structure and everything to get a feel for it, but I've been talking to Gus at the same time. He's a nice guy."

I can't control the way my puzzled expression moves from my brother to Gus. He frowns down at me which is no surprise. I turn back to my brother. "Really?"

Finn's head tilts. "Why are you so surprised?"

"Your sister and I aren't exactly best friends. You'll find that she—ironically—finds me rather uptight."

"Ironically? What the hell is that supposed to mean?"

"Irony is when something happens in contrast to the situation's expectations. You will usually find that it concludes itself with a hint of amusement for those observing its occurrence."

"I know what irony means, you ass."

"Then why did you—"

"I was asking you, what you mean when you say it's ironic that I find you uptight?"

He watches me blankly, but you can see genuine confusion swimming in his eyes. "You say you know what it means and yet to answer your question I would yet again have to explain the meaning."

I open my mouth to respond, but shut it again at the last minute, instead closing my eyes and taking a deep breath. When I turn to my brother who is crouched down looking amused, I can feel the way my smile strains. "Do you think I'm uptight, Finn?"

"No comment," he mumbles.

———

An hour later, Finn finishes up with his inspection. I sit myself on a hay bale, laptop on my lap as I look through backup venues as well as possible ways to cater the party, especially now that Oakleigh has sent me a first draft of the guest list along with who on that list has special dietary requirements.

"Well, I have good news and bad news," Finn says as he packs up his tools.

"Start with the good news," I reply just as Gus says, "Start with the bad news."

Finn, for what feels like the fifteenth time since I got here, flicks between the two of us with evident uncertainty. After a moment of silence, Gus sighs and mumbles, "Start with the good news."

"Okay," Finn says hesitantly. "Well, the good news is that there is a lot of potential with the barn. I don't see any mold and the wood that has been eaten away needs to be removed anyway, so all in all it's possible to get it done without tearing the whole thing down."

"And the bad news?" I ask.

I hate that his sympathetic gaze is directed at me. "I'm sorry, Wrennie, but the bad news is that I don't see everything getting done by the date you need it. Especially since my team is only halfway through another project. It would literally just be you and me at the beginning."

"You, me and Oakleigh."

"I somehow rest my case even more than I did before you said that." He cringes bitterly.

Can you tell Oakleigh and Finn have never really seen eye to eye?

"Well, how far out would we be?"

He avoids my gaze. "Maybe a month?"

A month? Surely it can't need two whole months to sort out a few wooden beams and some paint?

"You're sure?"

He nods once even though there's no point. Finn Southwick

never lies. He softens the truth, sure, but he never tells a lie. I know for a fact he's just given me the least amount of time to soften the blow.

"And to get it done by when I'd need?"

He looks around the open space. "I don't see it happening, Wrennie."

My lip finds its way between my teeth as Adam's words from our breakup float back into my head: *Maybe events just isn't your calling, Wren. Have you ever thought of that?*

The tears threaten to spill. I was on the right track. Things were going so well. I was finally getting my chance to improve on the business and now it turns out that Adam might have been right this entire time. He told me when I quit my job that it wasn't worth the risk, that I was putting his future in jeopardy not just mine, and I didn't listen. At the time I was just so annoyed that he didn't believe in me that I felt more determined than ever to pursue it.

What a naive woman I've turned out to be.

I can feel eyes on me and my shame shines darker. I turn away from both men, my face hot and my chest tight. There's no thinking clearly, no logic that can calm my anxiety. There is only this feeling of unending doom, as if every decision was riding on this, and now that it's out of the window everything else is too.

"Wren?"

I hate it. I hate that he softens his voice even though he never has for me before now. I hate that there is sympathy in his tone. I hate that there is an unexplained reason as to why he says my name—just my name—and my chest does lighten fractionally. I hate that we dislike one another immensely and yet he still affects me in a way I have never experienced before.

A hand places itself on my shoulder and its warmth spreads to my skin even through my jacket, jumper and t-shirt.

"You good?" Gus asks and it's too much.

"I need some air," I say in a rushed voice as I move towards the door, thankful for the fact that he lets me.

GUS

I stood frozen when she left, staring after her, unsure of what to do next. I'm not sure if I was waiting for her to come back or simply trying to wrap my mind around what had happened, but it had kept me rooted to the spot.

Finn had to explain to me that Wren was overwhelmed and had walked out because she needed the space to calm down and think things through. When he spoke about her, every word had been laced with a mixture of protectiveness and pride. Bash spoke the same way whenever he was defending me and so it was easy to interpret it for what it was.

It was strange knowing that what Wren had experienced was her feeling such an understated emotion. When she feels, it always looks so complex, you would never think it could be something so ordinary, because she isn't ordinary.

Now, here I am, sitting in my office chair, eyes focused on nothing at all, thinking about how her feelings in that moment are something I feel more than I care to admit, and yet seeing it on someone else is somehow such an alien experience. I can't see any similarities between us that would show her experience to mirror mine and yet there she'd been, right in front of me, feeling exactly that.

Maybe it's that knowledge that made me do what I did next. Maybe it's the way that up until now, I still can't seem to get the image of her on the verge of tears out of my head, or how I watched her run off into the morning cold. Either way, whatever the hell it was has made me feverish with a need to right the wrongs even though I'm not sure any wrongs have been committed.

Chapter Nine

WREN

"Morning, newbie," Jamie greets as I step into the café with a scarf covering half of my face.

I shimmy it down until it's around my neck. "Will there ever be a morning where I'm no longer 'newbie'?"

Jamie shrugs, his flashy yellow glasses falling further down his nose. "I usually change it to their name after the first week, but I'm not sure if I'll stop with you. It suits you too much."

I laugh as I pull out my purse. Jamie really is on track to be the first friend I've made here. I've spent so much time having Oakleigh as my only friend, forever depending on her to fill in the empty time slots that surround my life, especially before and after Adam. It's wrong, I know, and it's a terrible thing to want, but I love her so much and she, along with my brother and my parents have been the only constants I've ever known.

It feels nice to now have at the very least the possibility of one more person filling in the gaps surrounding my life.

Even though my latest setback with Oakleigh's party has me feeling like a failure already, I still decided to come back to Eaglewood, hoping that a change of scenery and a long walk along the lake will aid me in finding a new venue. I never expected to see so much potential when I saw the barn, so who knows? Maybe I will get lucky a second time?

"Oh, I wanted to call you to ask something, but I obviously didn't know your number."

"Oh, my gosh!" I hastily scribble my number onto a napkin and hand it over to him.

"First time a girl's given me her number like this … interesting."

"I'm guessing it's the first time a girl has given you her number, period."

He looks impressed. "Oh, okay then. She's a feisty newbie this morning."

"Sometimes she bites," I joke. "Now what is it that you wanted to ask me?"

He starts on my coffee order, heating up my oat milk at the same time as putting a double shot into a cup. As he works, he talks.

"I wanted to see if you would be interested in coming with us to the town hall meeting tonight?"

"You guys have those here?"

"Nowadays, it's only really when Sandra demands one. But they're entertaining as fuck."

"Should I really expose myself to potential ridicule so early?"

Jamie shrugs as he adds cinnamon syrup to my coffee. "It'll show you're just as brave as I thought you were."

The Eaglewood town hall is ten times smaller than the one in Beckford, and also a hundred times older. It's all old wood floors and grubby bathroom tiles.

Several members of the town flood inside and take a seat in the main hall which holds a bunch of foldable chairs. A few of them send me quizzical looks and I shrink into myself knowing that I really don't have any justifiable reason to be here.

"Just ignore them," Jamie whispers.

Moving further into the room, Jamie and I take a seat at the back, not on the last row, but a couple of rows before it. I look around and take in the sight of everyone conversing with one another. They all look serious as they discuss what I'm assuming are possible reasons for the meeting being called into action. It was nice spending the day in the café. Instead of heading back to Beckford just to come back again, I rooted myself to one of the comfy armchairs and cracked open my laptop. Thanks to Jamie's endless supply of coffee and my noise-canceling headphones, I managed to send out invites (with a TBC on the location), confirm some of the decorations with Oakleigh, and order them to my house.

One of the women who discussed Gus in the café—Sandra, I believe—stands at the front—past middle age, she leans on her cane as she watches everyone chat and take a seat. She casts a critical eye over us all, silently—but not subtly—judging everyone around her.

Another older man stands next to her, conspicuously whispering into her ear.

"That's Mayor Johnson," Jamie explains. "He's nice enough, but useless if Sandra is in the room."

I see Nigel across the room and give him a small wave. Nigel is a kind old man who owns the florist on Main Street. As I walked to get a coffee this morning, he was nice enough to stop me and introduce himself and his wife. He waves back and when his wife sees me, she waves as well.

"Good evening, all," Mayor Johnson greets. "Welcome to today's meeting. Now none of us are new to how this goes, so who would like to start us off."

Much to no one's surprise, Sandra speaks up first. "I will." She steps to the middle where everyone can see her. She tosses her graying blonde bob to the side. "It's come to my attention that we may have a problem with people getting their pumpkin orders this week."

Oh, boy.

"I felt it crucial that this town be updated and notified on the current delay on their orders, otherwise it would be considered unprofessional and uncouth on August's part."

The room breaks out into mumbles and the scraping of chairs as people turn around in their seats. I duck down.

"I am also aware that a certain deal has been struck between Goldleaf Farm and one"—Sandra checks a piece of paper in her hand—"Second Nature Events? Bit of an odd name if you ask me."

Okay, well that was just uncalled for.

"August, can you please confirm both of these?"

Gus is here? I look around, but I'm unable to locate him. It's only when a recognizable deep voice behind me says, "Thank you, Sandra, for once again airing out my business unnecessarily."

I spin in my seat and see a mop of brown hair—a man that is instantly recognizable to me despite having his head down. Maybe it's the way his hand grips his hair like it's a lifeline, or the orange cast that peeks out through the plaid shirt and the two rows of people separating him from me.

Sandra, with her bloodhound-like ears, scoffs from across the room. "The town deserves to know."

"In his defense, Sandra," Nigel's wife, Simone, speaks up. "I'm certain that August or Sebastian would have called those who placed an order with them to let them know. Wouldn't you, Gus?"

"That's what businesses typically do to avoid losing customers, Simone, yes," he retorts.

I send a glare in Gus's direction when I hear his tone, even though he hasn't seen me yet. Simone is only trying to help.

"And yet he hasn't done it," Sandra argues.

"How would you know? You didn't order anything," Bash pipes up.

Yet again, Sandra scoffs. "I have my ways of knowing things. It's my job to know what goes on in this town."

"I thought that was the mayor's job?" a middle-aged man says from the middle of the room.

Sandra sputters as she tries to find a comeback to what is a rather obvious argument. How she thought she would win that one I have no idea.

"August," Mayor Johnson steps in, looking around awkwardly. "If you need the help, we can figure out a way.

This is the first harvest since you let everyone go and now considering your most recent proble—"

"I don't need any help," Gus says calmly, but I can hear the warning in his tone.

"You'd rather send out all of the orders late?" a woman near Sandra asks.

"I'd rather everyone stayed out of my business unless I ask them to do differently."

I hear someone nearby whisper, "Just because you want to be rude to everyone in town, doesn't mean you need to purposely inconvenience us."

What are these people on about?

I lean over to Jamie. "Why are they being so harsh?"

Jamie, who is currently glaring at whoever just whispered that comment, sighs. "No one knows why Sandra is the way that she is. I put it to her being bitter and alone, but mine isn't the only theory. As for the rest of the town … well, let's just say that not everyone's mindset made it into the twenty-first century."

I spin around again. Gus still has his head in his hands and for once I find myself with the urge to go over there and comfort him somehow. Place a hand on his back and tell him not to listen to them whilst gently tugging his hand out of his hair before he gets a bald spot. Something tells me that Gus isn't exactly one for a friendly shoulder, easily deciding to instead mistake it for pity.

To be honest I don't blame him.

If he sees me watching him, or feels my gaze, he doesn't acknowledge it, but Bash offers me a small smile which I return before turning around.

"How late is late, August?"

I can hear Gus release a breath before he says, "It's Gus, and the people who ordered from me will know how late when they receive my phone call, if they haven't already."

"Well, how do you plan to conduct the harvest of not just the pumpkins, but the corn as well?" Sandra asks snootily.

"I plan to harvest the corn when it's ready, which it currently isn't."

Sandra huffs like a child before looking to the mayor and slamming her cane onto the floor. The mayor simply shrugs.

"You're sure you don't need help, Gus?" he asks.

There's a pause before his response follows. "I don't need anyone."

Chapter Ten

WREN

I've been reluctant to return to the farm since my overreaction yesterday. The weight of embarrassment still sits on my chest despite Finn calling me to tell me that there is no need to feel embarrassed, that we all get overwhelmed sometimes.

What he doesn't say, but what sits in the middle of our phone line like a lump in the throat is that I don't. I don't do overwhelmed, not when I try my hardest to focus on the positives even if it kills me. I start my mornings with affirmations, I make myself find positives alternatives when it feels like there's no other way.

Or, at least I did before Adam and I went our separate ways and I found my positivity being held up in front of me like it's the most inconvenient quality.

God, maybe I'm not doing as well as I thought.

A dry spell is never forever.

You're right, Dad. I shouldn't be wasting my time feeling bad for myself when things could be so much worse. And even if they were worse, they wouldn't be permanent.

Deciding that I need to brighten my day, I get ready to go and do the one thing I meant to yesterday but never did, instead choosing to listen in to the town hall meeting.

It's not the first time I've stepped into Flora and Flowers since coming to Eaglewood. The day that Nigel and Simone introduced themselves, I made sure to stop by for some flowers to make my new, exciting, albeit not confirmed, career venture with Gus begin on a bright note. A chance to wake up in the morning and feel like the storm is finally passing me by. Now, as I step into the store once more, it feels more comforting than most stores in Beckford ever have.

"Morning, Nigel."

The florist pauses his arrangement and sends me a kind smile.

"Good morning, Wren," he beams. "I assumed you would stop by at some point today when you didn't show up yesterday."

"I know, I'm sorry. I thought I would stop by for something to brighten my week before heading over to the farm."

"Those boys aren't giving you any trouble now, are they?" he asks, fatherly concern wrapping itself around every word.

"Nothing I can't handle, Nigel." I laugh lightly. "Now how is my new favorite florist doing?"

"Oh, well aren't you a sweetheart?" A blush coats his slightly wrinkled cheeks. "No wonder people here are starting to like you."

"They are?" I turn to him, perplexed. "I've never really had a chance to talk to anyone else."

He wraps a ribbon around his finished bouquet. "The fact that you bring the boys a coffee every day and treat the locals with kindness has already told us all we need to know about you. You're a good one, Wren. Besides, Sebastian told me that a smile is never far away when you're around."

My cheeks are starting to match the pink hydrangeas that he's just finished wrapping. Whether it's summer or winter, I suspect that you can always find a touch of brightness in this store if Nigel's personality is anything to go by. Red roses, blue narcissus and white peace lilies sit in old vases that have been nailed into the wall, so that each flower stands stark against the sea of green behind. Various leaves and different variations of baby's breath add depth and dimension to all of the pre-made arrangements on display. Eucalyptus and delphinium hang from the ceiling, making you feel as if you are walking into a fairytale land filled with magic and fairies.

"I'll be with you as soon as I can, Wren. I'm just finishing up this order for Lori who owns the bakery down the street."

"Take your time!" I check my watch. I still have half an hour before Gus begins to moan about the time I bring him his coffee.

I marvel at the profound collection of nature all around me and I laugh to myself quietly as I find myself comparing this to what I see at Goldleaf Farm. In Nigel's store, there is vibrance and light. Even though it's fall, it speaks of endless summers. And yet, Gus's farm brings warmth and tenderness. It makes you feel as if you're at peace, with its acres of land and silver fir trees.

"Now then," says Nigel as he steps out from behind the counter. He's a similar height to me, his shoulders slightly brought down by the weight of time. His thinning hair atop his head mostly gray with the occasional brown streak peeking through. Blue eyes glitter with years of kindness, proof of it clear in the crow's nests on either side. "How about this one? I did look at it when I put it together earlier and think that it was something that might suit you."

He picks up a medium-sized arrangement that is filled with yellow roses, eucalyptus, white lilies and yarrow. It's unsurprisingly stunning. I have yet to see an unattractive bouquet put together by Nigel.

"It's gorgeous," I breathe. "I absolutely love it!"

"I thought you would," Nigel smiles. "Bright and lovely, just like you."

"If you keep this up, Nigel, I'm going to have to steal you from your wife." I jest, of course. Simone is just as lovely as Nigel and they belong together.

"Oh, well that wouldn't be hard," Nigel chuckles as he makes his way back behind the counter. "Just poke her in the hip and you'll be fine. She's had a bad one since the particularly naughty summer of two thousand and seven."

A few more laughs and a promise that I would never dream of separating him from his beloved and I race back to the car, my new bouquet resting on the back seat. I'll put them in water at the farm. The bouquet that I found at the supermarket are pretty much dead only two days later, sitting in the living room in the window that provides the most sunlight.

I head straight for the Sweet Cinnamon Café. When I enter the café, thankfully fewer whispers than normal make their way around the cozy space. I'm surprised when I see someone other than Jamie behind the counter.

"Hello," I greet her politely. "I'm Wren. It's nice to meet you."

"Oh, you're the newbie!" the girl almost yells, hand slapping down onto the counter. She holds a hand out towards me. "I'm Lola. I'm Jamie's cousin."

"A pleasure," I smile. "Is Jamie okay?"

"Oh, yeah, he's fine!" she says loudly. "He just had a really long night, so he asked to switch shifts with me. No biggie."

Lola is a very loud individual. I love it. She reminds me of Oakleigh—a little chaotic but with such good intentions.

"Did you want your usual? Jamie already filled me in on what it is."

"If that's okay. Plus an extra cinnamon latte with oat milk for my brother."

"You got it," she beams. She starts towards the large red and white vintage-looking coffee machine, but she turns back abruptly. "Oh, I heard that Sam is on the farm today if you want me to add his order, too."

Do I trust myself to carry five coffees? No.

Do I want to make a good impression on the last and final brother? Yes. I've heard a lot about him, but I want the chance to get to know him myself before listening to town gossip.

I offer Lola a weak nod. "That would be great."

Whilst she's not as fast as Jamie, she still makes the coffees quicker than I ever could. Just like her cousin, when she finishes a coffee, she uses a black marker to write down the name of its owner on the lid, calling me "newbie" again.

I pay, say a goodbye to Lola, and walk out of the café slowly for the first time since I arrived in Eaglewood.

I was grateful there wasn't anyone behind me as I was driving over to Goldleaf Farms because I was driving well under the speed limit. It was very difficult not to, what with five coffees on the floor in front of the passenger seat. The bumps along the road leading to the farm were an added challenge and whilst it would usually take me three minutes to get from the end of the road to the farm, today it's taken a good solid seven and a half. Add in the fact that I spent the entire time on the phone (over Bluetooth, of course) to a DJ I know in Redford, and it's a miracle my entire passenger side is not covered in coffee and sugar.

I breathe a sigh of relief when I put my SUV into park and look over to find the floor around the coffees still bone dry.

I force my eyes to stay on the task at hand and not move their gaze over to the barn. Everything I felt yesterday will come flooding back if I look over and I need to go into this day in a positive light.

I jump out the car with my head down and rush over to the passenger side and grab the coffees, holding mine in one hand and everyone else's in a drinks holder. Like the world's worst gymnast, I try and balance my way from the car to the main building.

Just as I'm halfway there and starting to actually believe I can make it, a shout comes from the barn and I jump, leading to a couple of drops of Finn's coffee to leap out of the cup.

I mutter a curse, try my best to wipe my hand onto my brown knee-length jacket, and reluctantly look up towards the source of the noise.

When my eyes raise, my coffee slips out of my hand as a surprised breath leaves my chest.

Chapter Eleven

WREN

There's no sound of paper meeting grass that follows once my coffee leaves my grip. There is no warmth that spreads through my thin knee-high boots as coffee seeps through the fibers.

Instead, there's a low, somewhat sexy grunt as someone manages to catch the cup less than a second after it slips from my hand. I tear my eyes away from what used to be the barn ahead of me and turn towards the man who just saved my precious libation.

"Thank you so mu—" The last word becomes trapped, stuck to my tongue by the shock of seeing none other than August Finch in front of me, my coffee in his free hand, some drops of the sweet nectar dripping from his fingers.

He looks frustratingly attractive, as always—brown hair messy from his fingers raking through it over and over; a plaid shirt tied around his waist, this time of the yellow and blue variety; somewhat overly distressed dark blue jeans and a typical pair of brown work boots. He's groomed his beard since last night, what I imagine used to be rough strands now cut down into more of a thick stubble.

He has me pinned with an annoyingly adorable stare, head tilted, nose scrunched and dark brown pools glinting with curiosity. Seriously, why does someone so infuriating have to be so handsome?

Of course, just like always, he has to ruin the view by opening his mouth and letting words escape. "Are you really that petty that you stop saying thank you just because it's me?"

I can't resist the thrill that runs down my spine and the deliciously dirty fantasies that enter my mind when he lifts two wet fingers to his lips to suck off the coffee. He grimaces at the taste.

"Too sweet."

I let out an exasperated sigh as I roll my eyes, grateful that his attitude has the pool between my thighs drying up. "I wasn't stopping because it's you I have to say thank you to. I was stopping because I was shocked that you helped at all."

His thick, dark eyebrows flinch. "You think so lowly of me? Well, I can't say that I'm surprised, what with you being uptight and all. You would think that everyone else is somehow less, wouldn't you?"

"It's not even nine in the morning, do you seriously have to be this much of an ass so early in the day?"

"Do you seriously have to be so difficult so early in the day? I haven't even had my coffee yet."

He hands me back my coffee and takes his instead.

I spare him the snide remark that I have sitting on the tip of my tongue, and turn back to the barn.

"What's all this?" I ask.

I don't miss the fact that he pauses before he answers me, nor the almost nervous sound of him shifting his weight beside me.

"Finn and I found a way to make it work."

"You found a way to make what work?" I reply.

"Getting the barn done by the end of the month."

I feel a drop of coffee flick itself from my cup onto my neck as I turn abruptly. He looks skittish, avoiding eye contact with me and finding more interest in the way the dying grass gently sways in the wind.

"How?" I ask on a whisper.

"It was a puzzle," he mumbles. "I'm good with puzzles. It was no big deal."

My world pauses for a second. "Wait a minute ... it was your idea to try and get it done on time?"

"I don't see the big deal, Wren. You needed it done, I found a way to get it done."

Hearing my name on his lips is a surprisingly enlightening experience. There's a hint of possessiveness within it that sends a tingle down my spine. He tries to cover it with a thin layer of annoyance, and yet it's there clear as day. It lowers his already bass-filled voice until it's low and smoother than silk. If he keeps saying my name like this in the future, then I can already see myself losing almost every argument we have.

"You found a way how?" I attempt to rid my voice of its awkward high pitch.

He chooses not to answer me and instead starts towards

the barn. Obviously, thanks to his long, toned legs and my inability to walk with four coffees in my hand, he is halfway there by the time I've taken all of three steps. He either notices that he's left me behind, or he hears my overdramatic sigh (really couldn't tell which one), because he lifts his head up towards the sky as if searching the heavens for some patience. He spins around, skulks back over to me, plucks the coffee holder out of my hand and proceeds to once again speed off leaving me to struggle to keep up with my little legs.

When we get closer, I see that there are quite a few people. Bash carries a bunch of rubbish towards a skip whilst Finn and Jamie are lifting up a beam and fixing it into place. The last guy I don't know, but I would recognize him anywhere. It's the other brother from the photo—Sam.

For someone who is apparently supposed to be the grumpiest of them all, I can tell that his slightly softer features look a lot less frustrated than Gus's. His brown hair is up in a man bun at the back of his head, and I can see the ice-cold blue of his eyes from twenty yards away. His muscles flex without any restriction thanks to his sleeveless undershirt. He's a big guy, but I know that he would be lost if Gus were to stand in front of him, his shoulders dwarfing Sam's by a mile.

Why am I comparing?

I'm not entirely sure. But what I am sure of is that if Oakleigh were to find out I was currently in muscle heaven, she would murder me for not letting her know.

Finn and Jamie spot me first, so I walk over to them and Gus surprisingly follows on behind me. He hands Finn his coffee who says a polite thank you to both of us.

"How did this happen?" I ask in awe as I turn in a circle to grasp everything that's happened so far.

The walls of the barn have disappeared, the discarded tools placed somewhere else and the hay bales hidden from view under tarpaulin. The dodgy balcony has been taken down and now all that remains is a shell. Brand-new wooden beams that will make up the foundation for the walls and the roof.

Finn shrugs. "Gus was adamant he wanted it done by the party. When I reminded him that we needed more people he went and asked Jamie—well, demanded, really—to help with the work throughout the night. I also managed to move some things around with my team and scramble together three of the guys to come over tomorrow."

My mind replays Finn's words over and over in my mind like a track on repeat. My heart jumps and pleads with me to calm down, but I can't.

"I didn't demand that he help," Gus mumbles under his breath.

"You stormed into the coffee shop and all but dragged my ass from the behind the counter," Jamie states playfully. He shoots me a wink when our eyes meet.

When the dark, almost jet-black of Gus's eyes meet the hazel of mine, I can see for the first time a man whose face and eyes seem to be at odds with one another. I see a depth to August that I've only seen once before, when he looked at the beauty spot above my lip like it was the thread that would make him snap.

In the space of a single moment, everything else begins to fade away, leaving just the two of us wrapped in our own bubble. The sounds of work, drills and shouting around us dim and in its place there is a silence that feels strangely intimate.

I step closer and I see his leg twitches as if he wants to maintain the distance between us.

"You worked through the night to get this done?" I ask him slowly.

He clears his throat and rolls his shoulder. "Yes."

"Why?"

He shrugs those broad shoulders but doesn't respond. And for the first time since meeting Gus, I wonder if maybe I have him all wrong.

Chapter Twelve

GUS

"I just need the one," Nigel says as he pretends he isn't surveying the closest pumpkin patch. "I'm going to surprise Simone with a pumpkin pie."

I take my time filling out the order form because the last one that I rushed, I ended up messing up the numbers, meaning someone who ordered two pumpkins ended up with seven ... somehow.

"Harvesting season is coming up soon, isn't it?" Nigel asks.

I grunt in confirmation.

"Are you going to be able to handle it with your injury?"

I shrug with my free shoulder and finish filling out the form. It takes me a lot longer than usual since I'm attempting to write with my left hand.

Nigel chuckles. "I forget how chatty you can be."

"Your order is done. I'll get it to you tomorrow."

"Thank you," he grins. He returns to his not-so-subtle

observation of one of the pumpkin patches, arms crossed over his button-down and windbreaker. His graying hair moves with the wind that seems to be increasing in both strength and frequency. Just as I'm about to leave him to it, he adds, "He'd be proud of what you've accomplished here, August."

If I wasn't already having a shitty day, that comment would have soured it completely.

I mumble an "Mhmm," and hope that he doesn't continue. I clearly overestimate my luck.

"I'm being serious. He would think this is amazing."

"Well, then it's a shame he ran off, isn't it?"

Nigel spins to me, a small smile tugging at his lips. "I wouldn't say he ran off."

"Oh, you wouldn't? What else would you call flying to Vegas to get married and never coming back?"

He takes a deep breath. "I would call it being lost."

I scoff in disbelief. "If you want to be lost, then be lost, but don't drag others into your shit just so you can find yourself. I'll see you tomorrow, Nigel."

I make it to the steps leading to my office.

"Make sure you listen to that advice when you begin working with Miss Southwick." His tone is kind, but his words are firm, a warning.

"If only someone had told him that before he met *her*." I storm into my office without waiting to hear one more word.

Nigel and my dad were friends once upon a time. They grew up together in town, but when my dad met Marina, all of his other personal relationships kind of went to shit. They ran away to Vegas for a shotgun wedding and we never saw him again. All we were left with was a shitty group text to say that

Marina didn't like the small-town life and so they'd be settling down in California.

Some people pretended to be shocked, even went as far as judging me for not bothering to hide my lack of surprise. I was and still am the one person not affected by it and for that, there has to be something wrong with me. Or, maybe it is affecting me and I just refuse to acknowledge that. Never mind that the relationship between me and my father was a shitshow before he met her. Never mind that I lived a life where Bash felt like more of a father figure than he did.

I drop myself into my desk chair and lower my head, careful not to fold my shoulder awkwardly. Most would call it a stupid reason; why I ended up breaking my arm, but I wouldn't change a thing.

Well, maybe I would try and accomplish the task in a way that doesn't land my arm in a cast during harvesting season, but I wouldn't change the fact that I tried.

As I let the darkness quell my pending overstimulation, my mind continues to drift to thoughts of a stubborn woman with brown curls and a testing attitude—without my permission, might I add. I don't want to think about her. I don't want to acknowledge her unmatched beauty, or her chest-tightening smile. It's an inconvenience.

She's annoying, she's a smartass, and for some reason everyone seems to like her even though she's a demon in disguise.

I try and remind myself that having the barn redone will be good for business. It's a chance to pull in more money which, if I'm being honest, I'm down-playing how much more we need.

It's partly my fault, I've accepted that. My inability to say no to an animal in need of rehoming is pitiful and my attitude towards the customers that are based in Eaglewood could maybe do with some work. I'm not stubborn enough to fool myself into thinking that I run this place perfectly. My Autism gets in the way at times, preventing me from making changes that need to happen until it's too late and making it so that everything needs its sometimes unexplainable reason.

But I try my best. I try because so far no one else is showing that they want to. My father may be a piece of shit, but my grandfather deserves to have the one thing he dedicated his life to be treated with respect.

"I'm trying to think of something witty to say."

I groan loudly when I hear her. Of all the things I don't need right now, her particular brand of shit makes the top of the list.

"What do you want?"

"I want to talk to you about the barn. You never gave me a reason."

"I never gave you a reason for what?" I know exactly what.

She leans on one leg and folds her arms, a thick but perfectly shaped eyebrow rising in defiance. "For why you worked so hard to make sure we could meet the deadline."

I groan once more and give my hair a rough tug. "Why are you so keen to know?"

"Because it's unusually nice of you, so I'm suspicious."

"If there's one thing I can promise you, it's that I wasn't trying to be nice when I did it."

She scoffs. "That I can believe."

She steps closer to the desk and my stomach tightens at the

lack of distance between us. She leans on the desk and bends over until she's level with me. "So tell me why."

God, the things I would do to her, bent over like this.

"What did I tell you about my desk?"

"Has nobody ever told you that it's rude to comment on a woman's weight?"

"Has anyone ever told you that you're a pain in the ass?"

Wren sighs and lifts herself making the desk groan slightly. Her glare still remains fixed on mine, and for the next few minutes we stay trapped in our awkward silence, locked in a battle of wills. Once I realize that she's not going to back down, I surrender with an eyeroll and exit the office into the open space of the farm.

I take a deep breath and push up the free sleeve on my plaid shirt. I hold my shoulder and slowly lift my arm, keeping my elbow bent. A twinge of pain flares up from my elbow to my shoulder and I wince, the stiffness from lack of movement making my muscles and bones resist the action. I can feel the muscles slowly withering and losing the mass that I've tried really hard to build over the years.

"How did you do that to your arm?" Wren asks behind me.

I shrug and move towards the field, already knowing that she's going to end up following me.

"There was a puppy."

"A puppy?" I can hear her struggling to keep up, and, as if of their own accord, my legs slow their steps.

"A puppy," I repeat. "It's an animal. A name for a baby dog?"

I can all but hear her roll her eyes as she follows me. "Thank you for that," she says sarcastically. "What do you mean that there was a puppy? Are you trying to tell me that a baby dog somehow managed to break bones that are sat underneath your million and one layers of muscle?"

I pause walking, shoot her a puzzled look, and continue on. "No, idiot. There was a puppy stuck on the cliff at the edge of our land. I fell onto the next ledge trying to reach it."

Chapter Thirteen

GUS

My feet cease their steps when I hear her stop.

When I face her, I'm faced with a confusing expression. She doesn't look mad per se, more disbelieving mixed with frustration. Her eyebrows dip down just as her nose scrunches up and those full, brown lips of hers are ajar. She's stuck in place, but I can't quite grasp by what. Her black boots don't even do that toe shuffle that she does.

"What?" I ask uncertainly.

"You risked your life to save a puppy?" Her voice is but a whisper she lets the wind carry over to me.

I look away and look back, my neck suddenly hot and itchy. "I'm starting to get a little insulted by how often you're surprised by the good things I do."

And I mean it. I understand that I'm difficult to talk to and that I'm stubborn even on my best days, but the one thing I know for sure is that I'm not a bad person. When I was younger, I started off wanting to always be there for others until I realized that the world was mostly going to see me as unreasonable and incapable. So, I hid that part of me and have continued to do so ever since.

So, yes, maybe her surprise at my good deeds is slightly warranted, but I didn't think it would be impossible to imagine me doing something good for the hell of it. I'm not the fucking Antichrist.

Her eyes widen as she takes in my serious expression. "I didn't mean to offend, it's just…"

"Just what?" I ask, taking a step towards her. "It's just that Gus Finch is so much of an asshole that he must surely kill baby animals for fun, or start fires for the hell of it, right? Surely, because he can be difficult to talk to at times, he must be some kind of sociopath in the making."

She leans back and it's only now that I realize I took a few more steps towards her and am now chest to chest with her, so close that I could count every freckle that cuts across the bridge of her nose even without my glasses. I'm so close that I can see the distress that flashes so brightly in those hazel eyes.

What the hell is she doing to me?

Just as I'm about to move away, she grabs the open part of my plaid shirt, making both my body and my breath halt.

No one moves. It feels like neither of us is even daring to breathe, so unsure by this moment that the only thing left to do is to do nothing at all. Her curls move as the wind picks up, just like my own hair that falls into my eyes. The breeze ruffles my shirt, but her hand holds it in place. She stares at her hand, just as confused by the action as I am. My glasses begin to fall down my nose, but I make no move to push them back.

Eventually, after what feels like an eternity, she slowly moves her thumb, feeling the worn-out cotton as it glides across her skin. There is no skin-to-skin contact, and yet I feel the heat from my neck travel down to my chest until it's in line with her hand. She feels it, I think. Or, maybe that's just the cold settling into her bones.

I move back. "I spoke to some people about your party."

"Oh?" Surprise lights up her face.

"I spoke to Lori who has agreed to do some cakes and shit. And Mickey has said he'll do the food for you if you want. Colin from The Locke and Key will also handle your drinks. I gave them your email address so you can discuss prices and options with them."

It takes a second for her to reply. "You did that for me?"

Yes, my mind lies, whilst I say out loud, "No."

"Okay?"

"I did it to speed things up. The more stuff that gets sorted now, the less you need to come here."

She flinches, but any reply stays locked away, making me wonder I've spoken harshly.

"If you're cold, you should go inside," I mumble, my voice lower than usual.

Even with the wind blowing around us, I can hear the way she shakily exhales before she shakes her head.

Disappointment washes over me when the unavoidable clearing of my throat breaks the tension clean in two, leaving us to once again return to the Wren and Gus we were before. Our energies are no longer entwined and I let out a sigh of relief because I'm not sure what staying in that moment would have made me do.

I pull my glasses out of my pocket and put them on, pushing them to the bridge of my nose when there is once again some space between us. Wren looks flushed, the deep red of a blush visible underneath her light brown complexion. Her chest rises and falls with each subtle sway of her body and I have to stop myself from reaching out to steady her.

"I need to go and check the pumpkins. Harvest season starts tomorrow and it's going to be a long one this year."

Her gaze finds mine—mine a brown that sits in the shade, hers in the sun—and for the first time, there is no annoyance, no anger, just … nothing.

"Could I maybe come and help?" She asks.

"You want to help?"

She nods. "If I'm going to work with you on the farm, it would be helpful if I actually knew the farm. Besides, it's something new to learn, and you might need some help carrying something."

"I'm pretty sure that whatever you could carry with two hands, I can still carry with just one," I scoff.

Her eyes narrow to a playful glare. "I'll have you know, August, that I am a regular at my local gym where I spend a lot of time doing deadlifts."

I watch the ground, following the way my boot shuffles the dirt around, hoping that it will hide the beginning of a smile.

"Alright, Dwayne Johnson. Let's see what you got."

WREN

Even though you can see one of the pumpkin fields from the entrance to the farm, the walk towards it is further than you think. Mix that in with the fact that I have to try and keep up with a man twice my height whilst I'm in heeled boots and I've essentially run a marathon from the office to the field.

I'm out of breath and I chastise myself internally because I know it's not just because of the walk. There was ... something there when Gus and I were outside of the office—something alien and frightening. It's almost as if there was no space for arguments or disagreements, not when what was there in its place was so ... raw?

It felt like something I should have felt during all of that time with Adam, something every person should get to experience at least once in their lives. And of all the people to experience it with, mine just so happened to be with the one man I can never seem to see eye to eye with.

The pumpkin field when up close is gorgeous. From afar it looks like a picture for a postcard, but up close you can see the true size of both the field and the pumpkins within it. Cinderella wouldn't have needed a spell if she'd just bought her pumpkin from Goldleaf Farm.

Suddenly, it's as if that vision I had of my children playing and working as a team to lift just one of these seems idiotic and naive.

Each row sits surprisingly neatly, each pumpkin seeming to know its place and grow accordingly, making it easy for someone to walk up and down the rows.

Gus continues to walk towards the leftmost row, carefully observing each pumpkin as he does.

"So, do you need to check every single one before harvesting it?" I ask, genuinely curious.

He nods confidently, his attention not straying from his task. "Usually, I would do so as we harvest, leave the ones that can't be harvested in the plot for afterwards, but to save time I set myself the task of doing so today. It helps to get a gist of how well we'll do this year in terms of inventory."

My eyes catch on one pumpkin that sits nestled between two large ones. My guess is that the poor little thing hasn't had the space to grow because of its neighbors, forced to grow in the shade. The quality of it still looks superb—bright green and white outer layer with an almost fairytale-like curl to its vines, but it's no bigger than a box of tissues.

"What do you do with ones like these? Do people ask for small ones like this?"

He stops his checks to walk back over and stoop down beside me, surrounding me with the smell of pine. His head tilts to the side as he looks at the tiny pumpkin I'm pointing at.

"Sometimes. Over Halloween, some businesses like the café use the small ones for decorations, but lately they've taken to using fake ones because the pumpkins don't like the warm environment for too long."

"Can you still use them to cook?"

He frowns, but not in a way that shows annoyance, more like concentration.

"I wouldn't," he answers as he leans in closer. "It'll taste quite bitter. The more orange the skin the better it'll taste. I might just have to throw this one away which will be a shame."

He glances in my direction, his eyes dipping down to my lips once before standing up and continuing on.

"Surely there's other things that can be done with them?"

"Like what?"

I take a second to think. "Maybe you could take those ones and do a mini pumpkin patch for children? That way they can harvest their own pumpkins without getting hurt. Or you could offer them to festivals? There's a Halloween festival in Beckford where they do those haunted hayrides and stuff. I'm sure if they happen to have a pumpkin that starts to slowly rot it can only help the whole 'haunted' thing?"

"You sound like you've given this a fair bit of thought."

"These are just ideas I'm having off the top of my head."

He turns to me. "These are just spur of the moment ideas?"

I nod but don't respond. Adam used to hear my impulsive ideas and shut them down as soon as I had them. I don't think I was willing to admit how much it bummed me out back then, but now I can admit (at least to myself) that I would hate it if that started happening again.

The sun tears its way through each strand of Gus's hair making it look about three shades lighter. It brightens up his face and adds to the appeal of those chiseled good looks.

Or, maybe that's just due to the lack of a frown.

"Those are good ideas," he says with a shrug before continuing his observations.

My eyes widen. "You really think so?"

"They're well thought out for such impulsive ideas. You're

thinking about reducing waste, safety and ways of getting the name out there without breaking the bank."

Pride swells within me, almost breaking my rib cage, and I nearly let it.

"Well, thanks." I beam, a goofy smile taking over my entire face.

For the next ten minutes, I follow Gus down the first row of pumpkins, intently watching him as he assesses each one. Without me even asking, he explains to me what it is he's checking for and what it means, and it's the first time I see it— passion. For once I can clearly see that this is something that Gus is genuinely interested in and enjoys talking about. I can see it in the way his eyes light up even when the sun isn't hitting them; the way his hands move animatedly as he points to various parts of the pumpkins and explains how you can tell if it is in good condition or not.

It pulls a smile from me, one that Gus doesn't see, even though I don't bother to hide it.

Chapter Fourteen

WREN

"So, how exactly does the harvesting process work?" I ask once we're more than halfway through the first patch. My feet are aching in these heels and I'm starting to shiver as the cold penetrates both my turtleneck and my jacket, but I keep that to myself, especially since Gus is walking around in nothing more than his usual t-shirt, plaid shirt, jeans and work boots combo. He's decided to give his arm a short break from the sling, letting his shoulder relax in its natural position.

He was right when he said I was making baseless assumptions when it comes to his ability to carry out selfless deeds. He's found a way for the barn to be finished on time after all, and even though he hasn't said so, I'm pretty sure he did that for me. I've been so wrapped up in my frustrations towards him that I unfairly struggle to think of him doing something for someone else.

It's beyond admirable that Gus would have gone to such

lengths to save someone or something so innocent, so young. I can't imagine how scared that puppy must have felt: lost, alone and in danger. Thank God Gus was there to help it.

Gus clips his arm back into its sling, wincing as he does so. "It's a slow process," he says. "You literally have to go down the rows one at a time and cut the vines off of the pumpkins before placing them onto the sled. My hope is that the time will be shortened at least a little since I've done this check the day before."

"And you have three fields to do?"

He grunts in confirmation.

"How long does it take you to do all three fields?"

"We'll usually find ourselves harvesting throughout the whole month."

I blow out a breath. "Wow."

"It used to be a lot less time. Once upon a time we had at least twenty farmhands here to help out. Now it's just Bash and myself. Sam helps when he can."

"What happened to all the workmen?"

Gus's expression darkens, his usual frown slipping back into place. "Money dries up and you have to make sacrifices. It's the shitty side of running a business."

"You couldn't keep any of them?"

His jaw starts to work, moving from side to side. "For a while we managed to keep five of them."

"Then what happened?" I know it's probably none of my business, but seeing the way the topic affects him makes me ache to know more and I struggle to stop the questions from flying out of my mouth.

He lifts his head and when I see his face, I'm taken aback.

Unshed tears swim across his eyes, his previous passionate twinkle now replaced by the shimmer of water meeting light. The tension in his jaw makes me worry for his teeth and the way he's clenching his hand cannot be beneficial for healing bones.

His eyes glue themselves to mine as he says in a low voice, "Then my dad stole all the money we had and I let everyone go."

I've been refraining from asking anything else. It's one thing to wonder what's happened to the progression of a business, but it's another thing entirely to ask about personal obstacles.

But you can see the effect it's having on him. It's clear that the mere mention of his father is pushing an arrow into his heart. It's a heartbreaking thing to see, to know that there is a pain within someone that they can't escape because they're surrounded by it every day.

I've been trying everything I can to distract him: talk to him about the barn, ask him about the coffee I bring him every morning, but all I'm met with is one-word answers and low grunts of approval. I had to leave him briefly to answer a call from Teddy, a guy I know who handles all of my lighting needs for events, and even the time alone did nothing to ease him.

In a last-ditch effort, I ask, "So when you've harvested part of a row, where do you put it? Do you have to carry them all the way to the entrance?"

Gus, who is currently checking the last row, turns to me as

if I've finally asked a question worth his time. "No, we have Mori pull a cart that we switch out for an empty one after each row."

"Mori?"

He sniffs, the cold finally reaching him, and motions for me to follow him. The sun is beginning to make its descent as we wander over to the main building, but instead of going inside, Gus veers us around it towards a second, much smaller barn that looks to be in much better condition.

As we make our way closer to the building, the animal sounds I always hear when I jump out the car become louder. How did it take me a week to ask about the animals when I hear them every morning?

Gus pushes the door to the green barn and saunters in. The most I do is peek around the corner. I can't see the entire interior, just one side which contains two pens, each containing its own horse.

Hay lies all over the floor and in the corner is a large container full of what I'm assuming is feed. It's bright and warm and both horses snicker happily.

A tiny yap by my feet makes me jump, but when I look down I'm met with one of the cutest sights.

"Oh, well hi there, cutie!"

I bend down and the little bundle of joy affectionately licks my hand before playfully nipping at my fingers. I scratch behind the puppy's ear and it lets out a playful bark.

"Aren't you just the cutest little thing, oh my God."

The golden retriever leaps up until its front paws rest on my knee. As if it needs to make my heart melt any more than it already has.

I can feel eyes on me, a heated gaze. Gus is back at the door, watching me interact with the puppy whilst he shoves his hand into his pocket. His eyes only dip down towards the cutie currently licking my hand once, the rest of the time he seems to focus on the smile on my face. If it isn't for the way his tongue darts out to lick his bottom lip, I'd think he's daydreaming.

There's no mistaking this for daydreaming now, though. Not when there is such intensity and heat in the way that he tracks every time I worry my lip, or open my mouth to say something before the words become lodged in my throat. The side of my mouth tilts upwards and it seems to wake him up from whatever trance he's in. He blinks constantly whilst he shakes his head, eventually having to move his hair from in front of his glasses.

"You going to introduce me, or you just going to stare at my lips until they turn blue from the cold?" I jest.

He doesn't laugh, but I wasn't expecting him to. "This is Cliffhanger, but I call him Cliff for short."

"Cliffhanger? As in …"

He nods towards the pup. "This is the little shit responsible for this happening." He lifts his broken arm as best he can.

"Oh, well now it all makes sense," I chuckle as I pick up the little troublemaker. "I'd risk everything for someone as adorable as you, too." As I bring him closer to my face, his little legs—which are now suspended in mid-air—start to kick in an effort to get closer. The moment I cuddle him against my neck he lifts his head and nuzzles into my hair, tickling my neck with the occasional excited lick.

I imagine this little cutie in danger, and the idea of Gus

doing something so unbelievably reckless makes more sense than it did before.

"He was probably looking for his family."

"Most likely," Gus agrees. "I think he was the runt and the mom left him behind in order to keep the others alive."

I cover the puppy with the collar of my jacket. "That's horrible."

Gus shrugs. "That's nature. Animals do what comes naturally to them. It's not up to us to judge it."

———

Gus tries to lead me into the animal barn, but I halt my steps.

"What?" he asks.

"Is *he* in there?" I glare at the doors, hoping that the little rascal can feel it.

Gus looks understandably confused. "Is who in there?"

"Your little biter."

"Emilio?" Gus's tiny smirk doesn't escape my notice. "Maybe."

"He still hasn't apologized, so I'm not going into an enclosed space where he can sneak up behind me again."

"Oh? Is that how he did it last time? He snuck up behind you and just decided that your ass looked delicious."

My hand moves protectively to my behind. "It is delicious, I'll have you know."

Gus tilts his head in amusement, eyes glinting mischievously in the moonlight.

"Okay, screw you. That's not what I meant."

He says nothing as he turns and heads into the barn,

knowing that I'm not going to stay outside in the cold with a new puppy dozing off in the crook of my neck. With an exasperated sigh, I reluctantly follow.

The inside of the barn is far warmer than outside. With only a skylight in the roof, only the sunlight that passes over during the day would be making its way in, trapping in the warmth. On the other side of the barn are some pens with various animals. It shocks me to see different animals all sharing three pens, but they all seem perfectly content with each other, some even sitting together and falling asleep side by side.

There are a few chickens, some sheep, one pig and two goats, one of whose teeth I recognize. He looks over at me and tilts his head before bleating loudly.

"He remembers you," Gus jokes, his tone surprisingly light.

"Yeah, he'll be happy to know that the bruise on my behind means that I can't currently forget him either."

"He's in his pen, Wren. You're fine."

"Hmm."

"Oh, come on." Gus's hand lands on my lower back as he tries to lightly push me over towards the horses. Even through my coat, I can feel the warmth that emanates from him. It's hard to focus on much of anything when the tingles start.

"This is Mori." Gus pats the neck of a black and white cob horse. "She's the one who helps us pull the sled from one end of the row to the other and bring the harvest to the main building."

Mori nuzzles the side of Gus's head with so much affection that you can tell Gus takes good care of her. Even when she brings her head back and lets Gus absentmindedly stroke between her eyes, her gaze remains on him.

"She really loves you," I observe.

Gus looks at her and a genuine smile stretches his lips. "The only woman in my life." Mori touches her snout to Gus's cheek. He looks back to me. "You want to say hi?"

I've never really been around horses and so I've never had any reason to fear them, but the closer I get to Mori and the other horse, the more my heart races. It's because it's now very noticeable how much bigger she is than me, how rock solid those hooves look and how sturdy she is. She could crush me in a second without even trying.

Gus must see my trepidation because he holds out his hand and says, "There's nothing to be afraid of. Trust me."

Do I trust him? Surprisingly ... yes.

I slowly place my hand in his and the warmth of it sends a zip up my arm. For someone who has just spent hours outdoors, only the tips of his fingers show any evidence of being in the cold.

When his hand closes itself around mine and softly guides me towards Mori, my apprehension slowly starts to melt away. I can't seem to look away from him, and he the same. Today I've seen a new side of August that really has confused me more than it's helped to explain anything, because why is it that this side of him seems to fit him so much better? Why is it that trusting him feels right, and joking with him feels ... warm.

I don't even notice how close I am to Mori until she starts to sniff my hair.

"She's sussing you out. Trying to see if she likes you or not. To help her you can give her this." He slips a carrot into my hand. "Hold it so that she can eat as she goes and when it gets too short just hold it on your palm and keep your hand flat."

I do as he says, holding the end of the carrot and extending the other end towards Mori who snickers before chomping on it happily.

My breath hitches when I feel a firm chest against my back. I have to remind myself that I'm still also holding Cliff, otherwise my arms would be turning to lead with the way the small shocks seem to try and deaden each nerve with an overload of pleasure. Gus leans down and the moment I feel his warm breath on my neck, I almost lose control of my legs. He breathes thoughts into my mind that I've not had about another man since long before Adam.

"Now, let it fall into your palm," he whispers, and when my hand doesn't move straightaway, he gently takes it in his and helps me rearrange the carrot in my hand. "Hand flat."

My breath is shaky as Mori finishes the last of the carrot. She looks up at me and leans forward, giving me permission to stroke her mane.

"Here." Gus moves my hand towards the thick line of hair that falls against Mori's neck. I lay my hand against it and slowly stroke her, to which she snickers happily.

"She likes you," Gus mumbles, and the way his voice reaches my ear tells me that he's looking down at me as he talks, not needing to see Mori to know where to show her affection.

Would he be this much of an expert with me as well?

I huff out a pathetic attempt at a laugh. "Good," I breathe. "I like her, too."

Mori continues to act as a buffer for several minutes, and to me it starts to feel as if Gus almost uses her as a reason to keep his hand on mine, even after I get the hang of petting her.

Eventually, Cliff wakes up and starts to squirm in my grasp and so I have no choice but to remove my hand so I can set him down on the floor. I stand back up and turn around, only to find that Gus hasn't moved an inch. His eyes remain trained on my beauty spot, the one thing about me that seems to hold his attention. I swallow hard and his gaze shifts to the motion.

"Do I make you nervous, sweetheart?"

His lips press against each other, as if taking a second to see if he likes the taste the new nickname leaves on his tongue.

My own form a gap when I let out yet another short breath, my lungs desperately searching for any kind of oxygen in the room.

"Do I?" he repeats.

"I..." I gulp. "I'm not sure."

The edge of his lips twitch, but he keeps his smile in check.

"Good enough for me."

Chapter Fifteen

GUS

My attempts at avoiding Wren have so far been successful. I've managed to go an entire week without having to talk to her once. When she comes to drop off my coffee, I make sure to disappear for an hour, coming back to a cold coffee that I drink regardless of temperature. It really does help that she respects the coffee deadline I gave her. I work with Finn on the barn, but only when Wren has left, and as for going into town ... well that's never really been something I do much of anyways, so doing it even less hasn't been a problem.

The harvesting period has been off to a slower start than I anticipated. Even Finn noticed and offered to help for a few hours when my shoulder was giving trouble. It's been stiffer than usual on account of me putting more pressure on it than I should. Whilst my forearm is what's broken, it's my shoulder that consists of two muscle strains from all my efforts to reach

Cliff when he was about to fall. The painkillers that Doctor Shakari prescribed help with the break, but the muscular pain is still there. A warm compress here and a bit of recommended exercises there and it's just a matter of time before it heals.

Except this doesn't seem to want to heal.

Might that be down to me not doing the exercises she recommended? Possibly. It's not something I've necessarily had the time to do. Not when I have to check on the silos, harvest as much as I can, work on the barn and avoid a certain brown-haired girl who I'm pretty certain I wanted to kiss last week.

I'm booked solid.

Which is why, when I begin my pathetic attempt at lifting Nigel's order off of the back of my truck, I'm frozen mid-lift by an annoyingly high-pitched, "August Finch!", causing me to pause, an ache deep in my shoulder along with my temple.

I close my eyes and pray that this isn't the person that I think it is.

"August Finch, I know that's you."

Fuck.

Large pumpkin on my shoulder, I turn around and come face to face with Sandra, the clerk in the library down the street. She's a sour woman—always finding something to complain about, always gossiping, and always telling me that I'm doing something fucking wrong.

"Sandra," I greet.

"Nigel ordered that pumpkin from you a week ago. Why has he had to wait so long?"

"Is this Nigel asking, or you? Because if it's Nigel then he can ask me himself in about thirty seconds."

I try and walk away, but she steps up onto the sidewalk before I can. She's unusually limber for a sixty-year-old with a walking cane.

"I'm asking for him. You know what he's like. Nigel is too nice, too lenient. If you're going to own a business then you should run it properly."

"Thanks for the tip."

I finally manage to maneuver myself around her and step into Flora and Flowers, where Simone and Nigel stand behind the counter, wrapped in each other's arms as they give one another affectionate pecks on the lips.

I think most people would expect me to gag but I find it quite sweet. I'm not a romantic by any means, never really had enough experience to get the hang of the idea, but I do acknowledge the appeal of being with one person for so long. The idea of being able to have the most stressful day imaginable and coming home to that one person who can make the noise just stop.

Have I ever imagined myself finding that person? No. Because whilst I'm not opposed to the idea of love and relationships, I'm still realistic enough to know that the chances of finding what Nigel and Simone have is about as likely as someone who has never been in the sea getting eaten by a shark.

Bash found his person, he was just stupid enough to let her go. Sam thinks everyone is an idiot who doesn't know about he and Jamie, and me? I'm too much of an asshole to convince anyone to love me. Especially not the only woman who seems to be in my life right now.

As I watch Simone and Nigel smile at one another like the

sun shines out of each of their asses, I feel a weight on my chest that I've never had before. To offer myself a reprieve, I clear my throat and step further into the store, thankful that it doesn't sound as if Sandra has followed me in.

Nigel looks over and smiles. "Ah, Gus, what a pleasure."

Simone makes her way over to me, a small limp visible when she walks. She holds her hands out to me, gently takes my shoulders and reaches up to kiss each of my cheeks. She's the only person I allow to do that.

"How are you, Gus?"

"I'm fine," I reply. It's my go-to response.

Her smile turns serious. "Sandra giving you trouble at the town hall meeting like that was out of order."

"It is what it is."

"Well, if you ever need help you come straight to us, you hear me?"

I don't smile back, but I do at least allow my face to soften. "Yes, ma'am."

The light returns to her eyes. "You always were such a beautiful boy."

"Simmy, my love, let the poor boy put the pumpkin down. You see he has a bad arm." Nigel chuckles.

She gasps as if she's just noticed and takes a step back so I can place the pumpkin on the counter. I nod to Nigel in gratitude because that genuinely was fucking up my shoulder.

"I apologize for delivering it whilst Simone is here," I tell him. "I know it was supposed to be a surprise."

He chuckles again. "The only person that is owed an apology is my wife. I shouldn't have assumed that after so long, I could pull a fast one on her like that."

"Forty years later and he still has so much to learn."

The weight on my chest returns, especially when they look at each other with that glint in their eyes. The one that shows me I've vanished from the room right now.

Growing up, Nigel was friends with my father despite the age gap. They were close enough that I used to see him several days a week for lunch or dinner.

I never minded. Nigel was always kind, and when I received my official diagnosis when I was eleven, he was the only one who didn't seem to act as if the world was ending. He simply clapped my dad on the shoulder, smiled and said, "Doesn't change him, just helps you to understand him. Most parents don't have that privilege." He was always on my mom's side, even after she died.

He and Simone never treated me any different to Sam and Bash, but they still made sure to try their hardest to understand. Hell, they used to buy books on Autism just so they could try and grasp the complexity of the disorder. It feels as if they're the only people in Eaglewood who can at least understand that I have a neurological disorder ... not a mental one. Two extremely different things.

"Want me to take it to the kitchen at the house?" I ask as I awkwardly try and look anywhere else.

"Thank you, Gus," Simone smiles.

After nodding to their goodbyes, I drive the pumpkin over to their house which is only around the corner, and I let myself in through the back door that they always leave open. They're too trusting.

I place the pumpkin on the outdated counter and wince.

I'm not even holding the pumpkin on my bad shoulder and yet the effect seems to jump between my shoulder blades.

A few deep breaths, a second to close my eyes and acknowledge the pain and even though it doesn't make it any better, it does make it easier to bear.

I don't think Doctor Shakari will be too pleased at my next appointment.

I mentally tick the delivery off in my head and hope that I remember to physically tick it off when I get back to the farm. Some days I think it's a good thing I don't have any staff anymore because my head appears to be all over the place. I'm forgetting one thing after another.

I start to leave and pause just before heading out the back door. I picture Nigel with the bad back he thinks no one notices trying to cut this pumpkin into smaller pieces for that pie he wants to make. He won't be able to handle that. Neither will Simone with that hip. But why do I care so much? I've spent years sitting comfortably in my mindset that I would prefer to avoid everyone in this town, even the ones that either feign niceness, or actually are nice.

It's easier this way. It's easier to think to myself that if I avoid people then there isn't a reason for me to anticipate disappointment or cruelty from others. So why am I hesitating? Why do I almost feel compelled to help when I usually feel so content leaving people to their troubles the same way they leave me to mine?

I know the answer before I accept it. It's because of a pair of hazel eyes that looked almost green as the surprise flashed across them when she found out how I broke my arm. The way she found it so hard to even for a second believe me capable of being good enough to try and save an innocent animal has rubbed me the wrong way more than I thought it would.

Why am I so concerned about her opinion? The woman gets on my nerves more than anyone ever has before, and that's a difficult title to earn. She acts as if I'm the Devil's spokesperson and yet I care what she thinks? The logic is so backward.

Maybe we had a moment, and maybe it is making me have certain thoughts about Wren that really shouldn't be passing through my head…

… Okay maybe I was having those thoughts before that moment…

… And the moment we shared before that…

… Whatever.

Mathematically, logic isn't necessarily on my side either. If my calculations are correct there would be around a fifteen percent chance of me feeling this way towards Wren after the initial meeting we had. That's only when you take into account that the way in which our meeting panned out could have been avoided if we had settled our differences straight after.

My current problem is that when you add in the fact that we are about to have consistent interactions with one another, it introduces a probability of something more that I'm not ready to acknowledge.

And of course, because my mind has been spending the past ten minutes overthinking everything simply due to my hesitation at the door, I only now realize that I've cut the pumpkin into smaller pieces for Nigel and put them in the fridge.

And of course, because my mind has been on a certain

woman for nine of those ten minutes, I end up leaving Nigel's house with a tiny smile on my face and a blossom of pride in my chest.

Just as I finally begin to settle down and work my way through pile seven of the paperwork on my desk, my phone rings beside me. Typical.

I pull it out of my back pocket and freeze, wondering if, despite my glasses being on my face, I'm somehow reading the name wrong.

I press decline and toss my phone onto the table. Immediately, it starts ringing again.

"For fuck's sake."

I reluctantly accept the call.

"What the fuck do you want?"

"I need a reason to call?"

"Everyone calls for a reason, asshole."

My father sighs. "Always nice talking to you, August."

"Don't try and act like I'm the problem, Winston."

"Show some respect, boy," he snaps.

"Earn some."

He sighs again, as if this phone call is somehow inconveniencing *him*. I refuse to let this silence make me squirm. If he's the one that's called me then he can get the guts to tell me why.

I lean back in my seat, putting my phone on speaker and placing it on my desk.

When he realizes that I'm not budging, he clears his throat and speaks up. "I wanted to know how the farm is getting on."

"You mean if it's still running ever since you stole all of our money?"

"August, if you're going to be difficult about this."

Does this asshole seriously have the audacity to be annoyed at me?

"I'm angry. Rightfully angry. If you have a problem with that then you should never have dialed my number."

"It's still my farm, too."

"Then you shouldn't have left it."

"August." He sounds desperate, eager for me to see his side without explaining himself.

A headache starts to hit my temples and I angrily slam my glasses against the table. Ripping them off of my face and throwing them doesn't make me feel any better, though. I want to do a lot more than flick away a pair of silver-rimmed glasses. I want to scream as I punch him in his face that unfortunately looks so much like mine, hurt him physically so it reflects the way he hurt my family mentally.

It doesn't bug me. Not in the slightest. But it bugs my brothers and my grandfather, and that means that he'll never be forgiven. Not by me.

"Why are you calling me?" I ask, wanting to just get straight to the point.

He pauses, and I can hear some kind of movement happening around him.

"I want you boys to sell the farm and come live here with us."

I want to vomit. I want to bend over and throw up all over this scratchy rug under my feet until there's nothing left. My dad has to be out of his goddamn mind if he thinks I would ever let my brothers move from one side of the US to the other. When my brothers made it clear that they didn't want to take over when Dad decided to retire, I made a promise to my mother that I would always look out for them and make decisions that are in their best interest. Any and all decisions I make about the farm are for them, so that they can be supported. If I lost the farm completely, they wouldn't have anything to fall back on. Bash, who works here with me, would have to quit.

"No," I snap, anger seeping into my tone. "Was that everything? Are we done?"

"No, it's not. I want all of my family here together."

"You turned your back on your family. You don't get to want us with you when you so easily left."

"August, it makes sense." He pushes. "You all move here and we can use the money for more important stuff."

There it is. It's subtle, but it's there. I learned my dad's tell long ago. When he wants to say something, but knows it won't go down well, he goes quiet, speaks the words he knows will cause a fuss in a way that he hopes no one will hear. This time, he doesn't want me to hear the desperation, but his mistake is that it's been there since the beginning of this useless phone call.

"Money. That's what this is all about," I tell him, refusing to give him a chance to lie and say it isn't.

He's silent for a while.

"It's not just about the money."

"Un-fucking-believable," I murmur. Hell, even my shoulder seems to hurt the more I listen to this idiot.

"I genuinely want you boys to come. Especially now."

"What's happened now that didn't happen last year?"

He hesitates and this time my chest does tighten. "Melina and I are expecting and I lost everything gambling."

If the phone was in my hand, I would have dropped it. I can feel the overstimulation—the tingling under my skin and the constricting walls that make up my office. I can hear him calling my name again, but it's nothing but a noise in the distance, like a fly buzzing around the room.

I hang up on him mid-sentence and ignore the tear of frustration that streaks down my face.

I will never understand it.

I will never understand the contradiction that arises when everyone thinks I feel nothing at all, even though it's those around me that are heartless.

Chapter Sixteen

GUS

"Purple? Are you fucking kidding me?"

As I look over all of the paint swatches on the outside of the barn, my skin starts to heat and itch. The imaginary ants under my skin take their imaginary legs and let them bite into every inch of my flesh. I clench my fists to stop myself from ripping off my own skin to flick off every one of the tiny assholes. I bet every one of them has Wren's teasing face on them.

I loosen my hand just enough to scratch at my palm with my middle finger. The ants die down a little when I feel my nail nick my skin. Sometimes pain distracts from discomfort.

"What's wrong with purple? It's a bright color. Eye-catching." Wren asks.

"It's purple." When I look down at her, I only have a clear view of the top of her head and the way it quizzically tilts to the side. "It was red and blue before."

"So what? It has to stay the same color?"

"If I say it does, then yeah."

She looks up and folds her arms. "Because your ego has its own sovereign nation?"

"Because I'm the owner of the fucking thing, Wren. We're working together on this, but the final decisions still land with me."

"The purple was a *suggestion*, Gus. Not a decision. You see how it's surrounded by other paint swatches?" She dramatically gestures towards the other swatches on the wall.

"I know it wasn't a decision," I argue back. "The decision was me telling you that it's not even an option."

"God, you are stubborn," she huffs under her breath. She tries to move past me, but I block her path with my body.

"*I'm* stubborn?"

Bash stops working when he hears my voice rise. Wren's chin is now stubbornly in place, chest heaving and hazel eyes bright with fire.

"This coming from the woman who couldn't leave me alone for more than twenty-four hours so I could make an informed decision about *my* business!"

"Because I knew that nothing about your decision would be 'informed'," she yells, forming air quotes with the last word of her sentence. "You couldn't even bring yourself to believe that a goat bit me on the ass!"

I did admit to myself that Emilio may have actually done that the moment he nibbled my finger a few days later, but I never admitted that to Wren. Any chance for me to be wrong and she would have jumped at it and never let me forget it.

"If I could just interject here—" Bash begins nervously, but we both hold up a hand to stop him. "No one is telling you that this barn isn't yours and no one is trying to take over, Gus. Get your head out of your ass for two seconds so you can see that not everything is about you and your needs. Have you even considered that this is your brothers' farm just as much as it's yours? Have you asked them about *their* preferences?"

There is a tone that floats its way into people's voices when they can see I'm not going to agree with them. Back when I was stupid enough to share my thoughts and feelings with others, their voices would take on a distinctly patronizing intonation. Their heads would tilt just like Wren's, their eyebrows would lift just like hers and their lips would purse in the same manner. It's the look that used to tell me that they thought they were talking to someone with the same mental capabilities as a fucking child. People use my neurodivergence as a way to make themselves feel superior, because, to them, what would an autistic know about simple matters such as sharing?

I take a step back from her and Bash, the latter of whom has his eyes closed mid-wince.

The fact that I'm already overstimulated is enough to have my head spinning, but then comes the debilitating mix of shame and anger that coats my chest. It burns, and yet I refuse to reach up and rub at the area as if it will make the slightest bit of a difference.

A bitter scoff forces its way out of my chest and I couldn't have stopped it even if I wanted to. I don't want to, though.

"I was an idiot," I mumble. When she shoots me a confused look, it breaks the last thread of restraint I have. "Do you think it's easy? Having to run a company knowing full well everyone expects you to fail, not because they believe you to be bad at the job, but merely because they can't be assed to take the time to find the difference between being autistic and being a fucking idiot?"

Those hazel eyes widen. She steps toward me, but I maintain the space between us. "August, that's not why I was asking you, I pro—"

"You think I don't recognize the tone that everyone uses, or the way they all phrase it like they're talking to a goddamn child? I'm more than aware that I struggle with certain things, but none of that means that I'm so fucking stupid or oblivious to what is going on around me. It doesn't mean that every single thing I say or every decision I make is down to my disorder. Sometimes when I make a decision about my company, it's coming from the owner of said company. So, back off."

I leave the barn. I leave the smell of paint and the weight of judgment that suffocates me and walk off to God knows where. I need space and I need to be alone. I feel a breakdown coming and you can bet your ass that that's the last thing I need anyone seeing.

WREN

I stare at the open door for what feels like forever. I stand and hope that he'll come back and I can explain that I never meant it the way he thinks, but at the same time I'm glad that he never walks back in because I know in my heart that it's exactly how I had meant it at the time.

Gus and I have had our differences since day one, but I know better than to think that his most basic abilities are flawed just because of a neurological difference that is so much less understood than we like to think.

I want to defend my actions, and yet there is nothing to defend. I'm in the wrong and that's that. And if that doesn't make my blood run cold.

"He'll be back." I jump because I'd forgotten that Bash was even in the room.

I wipe away a stray tear before I turn towards him, my eyes reluctantly ripping away from the door. "I shouldn't have spoken to him like that."

"You shouldn't have," Bash replies calmly with a shrug of his shoulders. "Especially since he is the sole registered owner of Goldleaf Farm. But when he comes back you're going to apologize because it's who you are. You acknowledge when you're wrong."

"When will he come back?"

It's Bash's turn to stare at the open barn door. "He'll be back eventually, when he thinks that everyone has gone. He was overstimulated before you even asked him the question, I could see it."

"I should have noticed."

"Wren." Bash grabs my shoulders lightly and turns me towards him. "I've grown up with my brother. I've barely had a day away from him and so I know the man better than I know myself. I know when he's struggling and when he's thriving. I know the difference between overstimulation and just plain old anger. You've been here for two weeks. You can't know everything. People make mistakes. He didn't want it to be noticed by you because he has this need to be perfectly normal in your eyes."

My eyebrows flinched. "Why me?"

Bash smiled warmly. "With any guys you dated, did you never get that feeling? That intense need to hide all the things that made you insecure so that he'd see only the best in you?"

"No? I was just myself."

He looked at the ground as he softly chuckled to himself. His hands slipped from my shoulders. "Then you've never been in love."

Chapter Seventeen

GUS

I walk back into my office four hours later when the overdue storm begins to pound against my head. The sun has set and the only sounds around me are the soft bleats of contentment that come from Emilio in the barn, the snorts that sound from Mori and Hector, and Bash's laughter as it floats from my office.

Wait, what the fuck?

As I step into the cramped space, there's Wren and Bash sat on chairs, both facing a laptop that I assume belongs to Wren. They have some show on and his light laughs float around the room. She's snuggled underneath the throw I keep in my bottom drawer for those nights I end up staying well into the night. Mahogany curls cover her shoulders and glint in the soft light of my office as her deep breaths tell me she's sound asleep.

I seriously need to change the light bulb.

Her boots sit beside the chair she is in, and she looks completely at ease in the small space, as if she belongs in it.

Bash, who is sat next to her, is playing head rest and I find myself forcing an ugly, green creature off of my chest.

"Why isn't she home?" I ask as I move past them to sit at my desk.

"She insisted on waiting for you." Bash says quietly, eyes still glued to the screen.

"Why?"

"Why do you think, asshole?"

"I wouldn't ask why if I already knew the answer, asshole."

He throws me a look that I think is meant to say, "Don't pretend to be stupid". He doesn't see me flip him the finger. Or he sees it in his peripheral and decides to ignore it.

"Does she not know that there's a storm starting?"

"I think you know by now that she has enough stubbornness set into her that she wasn't caring about that."

I watch her chest as it slowly rises and falls with each even breath. "She should have gone home."

"She was worried about you, Auggie."

"I don't need anyone worrying about me."

There's a pause, but I don't bother to look up at my brother. I know the expression I'll see on his face—annoyance mixed with concern.

Worry.

"Everyone needs someone to worry about them, Auggie."

"Well, it's a good thing that I have you then, isn't it. Now you can wake her up and tell her to go home."

Like some twisted trick of fate, the main building shakes

with a vengeance as thunder and lightning wreak havoc on Eaglewood.

"For fuck's sake," I say with a sigh. I lower my head until it meets my good hand. I let my fingers grab and pull at the strands of my hair. There is no way she's getting back in this storm.

"You were saying?" Bash asks and I can feel the smug smile he is most likely shooting in my direction.

I refuse to reply as I pretend to look over the various paperwork that is scattered across my desk. As if of their own accord, my eyes keep flicking over to Wren's sleeping form on the chair. Her features are even more pleasant to observe when they're relaxed by sleep. There is no frustration that drags down her eyebrows, no downward tilt to her lips. Her nose twitches occasionally when she breathes out and even when she is asleep, she still bites her lip as she dreams of God knows what.

Even in the dim light, there is a glow to her brown skin that absorbs the light instead of reflecting it. She shines in a way that I've never seen another woman do before.

It pisses me off.

How dare she be so gorgeous whilst also being the biggest pain in my ass? It has my head ticking from one thought to another like it's a goddamn metronome. The moment I left the barn earlier, I had been weighed down by the well-known feeling of rejection. I thought I had been used to feeling that way and yet when Wren had spoken to me the way she had, I found myself with a foreign arrow in my chest.

And despite that, by the time I had made it to the edge of our land, I had forgiven her. I had forgiven her ignorance because somehow, I knew deep down that it had been just that: a lack of knowledge.

I abruptly shoot up from my seat, my gaze still stuck on Wren's sleeping form. There's no way I'm getting her to the house by myself with my arm in this stupid-ass sling. I release my arm from it and my elbow twinges in protest.

"Woah, woah, what are you doing?" Bash jumps up, his features filled with worry as he looks at the orange cast on my forearm.

"She can't drive in this weather. I'm taking her to the house."

I move towards her, but Bash blocks my way. "And how do you expect to do that with a broken arm?"

"The bones have been slotted back into place and there's a stupid splint. Now move."

"Auggie, think logically. I get that you want her to be safe, but neither of you will be safe if you end up injuring your arm even more whilst you're carrying her."

"It's pouring with rain out there. I can't just take her out there without something shielding her."

Bash sighs. "Honestly, when she's safe in the house, we really need to have a nice long chat about how to know when you like someone."

"Shut the fuck up and move." I try to maneuver around him.

"No!" Bash shouts, causing Wren to shift in her sleep, the start of a frown pulling at her eyebrows.

I shoot Bash a warning look. "If you wake her, I swear to God I will shove my foot so far up your ass, you'll be smelling leather for weeks."

Wide-eyed, he holds his hands up in surrender.

I let out a resigned sigh because as much as I hate to admit it, he's right. Doctor Shakari told me to keep my arm in the sling for at least the first four weeks, and it's only been three weeks and two days. Plus, if I accidentally drop Wren, then I would never forgive myself.

Never.

Feeling useless, I clip my forearm back into the sling. "Fine. What do you suppose we do?"

"I'll carry her, Auggie, it's fine. You grab her car keys and we can take her up in her car. God knows it has to be cleaner than the truck."

She's on her side now, her face nestled against her loose fist. She looks at peace for the first time since I've met her. She can try and fool everyone, but I see the wave of fear that passes over those honey-colored eyes each time she's here. She doesn't believe in herself. Or maybe she doesn't believe in me. Either way, she's scared of the unknown and what will happen if anything were to go wrong with this party.

The party isn't even for her and yet, she's treating it as if it were her own, and when it comes to how she handles her business, you can tell that she really cares. She works with precision, with passion. She listens to what the customer wants and does everything she can to deliver as close to their vision as possible.

How all of this is clear in a glint of fear, I'm not sure. Ever since I met Wren, I've found her easier to read than anyone I've ever met before. Sometimes it feels like I understand her more than I do Bash and Sam.

"Fine," I relent. "But if you drop her..."

"I won't drop her, Auggie." Bash rolls his eyes. "This isn't the first woman I'm carrying and I can promise you that she won't be the last." He sends me a wink.

Unfortunately for the world, Bash is statistically considered to be someone desirable. His charming smile and pale green eyes make it hard for women to realize that what he has in looks, he lacks in decorum. And yet, somehow, when it comes to me it is incredibly easy to see that what I make up for in muscle I lack in social skills.

Bash squats down so that he can pick up Wren's boots before slipping his hands under her knees and at the top of her back. As he picks her up, she lets out a little moan that has me itching to adjust my pants. Who knew that when coming from someone you find attractive, a seemingly innocent sound could have such a devilish reaction?

Even though she remains asleep, she instinctually wraps her arm around Bash's neck and nuzzles into it, making my cheeks heat up in envy. Bash awkwardly looks over at me, but says nothing. When he starts to head towards the door, I stop him.

"Wait."

I pick up the blanket that was over her moments before and gently cover her with it again, making sure to cover her face in a way that won't suffocate her. The rain outside is pouring.

Bash bites his lip to hide a smile.

"Don't you dare," I whisper.

He chuckles quietly before once again moving towards the door.

Chapter Eighteen

WREN

L ight streams in through the open window, showering my closed eyelids in a golden glow. The smell of freshly brewed coffee reaches my nose, and I inhale it happily. Soft, warm sheets envelop me in a hug, and I snuggle in further. Soft, warm, yellow sheets.

Wait.

I don't have yellow sheets.

I fly up into a sitting position and watch the space around me cautiously. The unrecognizable bedroom is a naturally dark, yet cozy room. The large bed I find myself on is against a wall opposite the door, another door to the right stands ajar leading to the adjoining bathroom. A white dressing table sits by the door, photos that I'm too far away to see, on top. The window to my left lets in a lot of light, but the dark blue and the dark green that decorates the room almost absorbs it.

On one bedside table sits a book and a pair of glasses. Glasses that I recognize instantly.

When I stand and cautiously make my way over to the dresser, it confirms what I already know.

Somehow, I've woken up in August Finch's bedroom.

My mind flashes back to last night, the memories flooding in like a tank filling with water. We were looking at paint colors for the barn, Gus stormed off and I waited for him. I waited and waited and waited, but I must have fallen asleep.

I look down and sigh in relief when I see that my clothes from yesterday are still on. He must have left my boots off when he brought me here. Do I even want to know how he did that? The man has a broken arm. Knowing him, he was probably feeling spiteful enough to dump me into a worm-infested barrel and wheel me into his truck. And yet, my clothes are clean, my hair—despite being the usual rats' nest that it is in the morning—is clean and there's no smell resembling worms or anything that is creepy-crawly related.

And if I have woken up in what is clearly his bed, judging by the glasses and the photos on the dresser, and the plaid shirt peeking out of his laundry hamper, then where did he sleep?

Quietly, I open the door which leads out into a long hallway. The sound of sizzling comes from one of the open doors and I follow it along with the smell of the coffee.

All the air in the room evades my lungs when I'm met with the incredibly unfair picture in front of me. August Finch stands with his back to me, a kitchen cloth hanging over his shoulder as he cooks bacon over the fire.

His bare shoulder.

Which leads to his bare back.

Which means that even though I can't see it, there is most definitely a bare chest that completes the set.

His usual distressed jeans hang low on his waist as he moves barefoot around his space. He's humming to himself, some tune I can't recognize, and he surprisingly has a beautiful voice. A pumpkin farmer who sings: who would have thought?

I mentally prepare myself for the even more gorgeous sight I'm about to see.

"So does this count as kidnapping, or are you planning on telling the court that I went with you voluntarily?"

It all happens so quickly—one second he's calmly singing and cooking bacon and the next he's jumping in surprise, causing him to knock over the frying pan which proceeds to fall and spill hot oil onto his bare feet.

"FUCK!" he screams, hopping from one foot to the other, trying to avoid the bacon grease that slowly streams across the light wood floors.

Wide-eyed, I scramble for the kitchen cloth that is still draped over his shoulder and run to the large farmhouse sink to run it under the cold water.

"Sit down," I instruct him. He doesn't listen because he's too busy listing off every curse word he knows. "Sit down, August!"

He glares at me, but sits down at the small oak dining table. I grab some ice from the freezer and wrap it in the cloth. I gingerly place it onto his feet which have turned a nasty shade of red. He hisses and curses again, sending me a signature glare before closing his eyes.

"What were you thinking?" I ask.

"What was *I* thinking?" he seethes. "What the fuck were *you* thinking? Sneaking up on someone like that. Are none of my goddamn door frames safe from your skulking?"

"Oh, ha ha, you're so funny."

Gus hisses through his teeth as the cold penetrates his burnt skin, working hard to cool down the area so that it doesn't get any worse.

I balance the ice on his foot so that I can get up and find a basin.

"What the hell are you searching for?"

"A basin, or something that can hold your big-ass feet and some cold water."

I hear him groan as I start to search the pantry. "I can't believe people think you're nice."

"Oh, yeah, I'm sure that me trying to make sure you keep the skin on your feet is me being an absolute bitch."

I can't find anything large enough, so I whip another dishcloth off of the side and drench it under the tap. As softly as I can, I slowly lift his leg and move a chair underneath it. He winces a few times whilst I wrap the ice and his foot in the cloth. His tanned skin is beginning to blister.

"We need to get you to the hospital."

"It'll be fine," Gus growls, trying to rip his foot away from me.

"You need to let the doctor look at it," I argue.

"The doctor is going to tell me exactly what I already know. That my foot is burnt."

"By oil, August. Not steam or hot water. Oil is more serious."

"It only splattered onto my foot, it's fine."

"August." His head whips up and he watches me with wide eyes. I know what it is that catches his attention. It's the way I say his name, the desperation that coats each syllable and the way it mixes in with pure frustration.

I'm pleading with him. That's something I haven't done before, not even when I was trying to get him to agree to work with me and that's because I don't beg ... ever. My dad always said that if you need to beg for something from someone, then the answer will always be no in the end.

This time, though, I need him to listen to me. I need us to temporarily break through this constant back and forth we're a part of so that I can get him the help he's pretending he doesn't need.

"Please let me take you to the hospital."

Time slows as he watches me with that analytical gaze of his. Thankfully, he eventually nods, and I sigh in relief.

"Wait here," I tell him before I rush to his bedroom to find him a t-shirt and some socks for when the doctor is done. I toss him the t-shirt and he catches it without any effort, sliding it over the torso I never got a chance to admire properly. I shove the socks into my back pocket and hold a hand out.

He gives me a look. "You *really* think you can help me to the car?"

My expression turns deadpan. The man honestly just cannot be helpful for one second. "I think you need help to the car."

"Yes, from someone who can handle my weight, not from a woman I'll crush as soon as I stand up."

"I'm stronger than I look, August."

"I don't doubt that, but I don't think you're strong enough

to take some of the weight of a two-hundred-and-sixty-pound farmer."

There's a moment of silence.

"Two hundred and sixty? Really?"

"In case you haven't noticed, being physically active isn't something I've been able to do lately."

"That's not what I meant, ass."

He grunts but ignores me as he tries to stand on the foot with the least amount of burns. He buckles slightly and instinctively. I throw my arms out ready to try and catch him. A dirty look is all I get as Gus slowly hobbles over to the front door.

"Wait," I say when I realize a problem. I roll my eyes when he sighs dramatically.

"What now?"

"You can't put shoes on."

"So?" he asks impatiently.

"So, asshole, how are you going to get to the car?"

His back is to me, but it's obvious as he looks down at his feet that he knows I have a point. The ground is more mud than grass. He tilts his head back and sends a sigh to the ceiling, mumbling a string of curse words that I'm pretty sure are being sent in my direction.

I spot a set of car keys by the door. "Stay here," I say as I pick them up. "I'll bring your truck as close as I can."

I thrust the front door open and the cold hits me, sending a shiver down my spine.

"My truck is back at the office."

"Why?"

"I took your car so you could fuck off from my house as soon as you woke up," he growls.

"This coming from the guy making me breakfast?"

"Shut up."

"Okay, clearly the pain is getting to someone, so like I said ... stay here."

Whatever rain presented itself last night has since moved on, leaving a blue sky dotted with gray-tinged clouds and a strong wind that bites into the skin. I spot my keys on the glass side table by the door and run out to the SUV, the almost gale-force winds whipping my hair into my eyes as I go. By the time I've maneuvered the car so that it's as close to the front door as I can get it, there's an impatient Gus stood waiting, two jackets in hand.

I'm about to jump out the car to help him, but he holds up a hand and makes his way by himself. A pang of guilt hits my chest when I see him like this, already missing some of his independence because of his arm, now hobbling over with even more injuries. The harvest isn't finished yet and I know that he's going to fret and panic over it, blaming himself for any setbacks he and Bash experience from here on out.

As he finally makes it into the car and struggles to put his seatbelt on, I pull off and rush to the hospital.

Chapter Nineteen

GUS

My feet fucking kill, but one look at Wren as we wait for Doctor Shakari has me trying to hide the pain. As much as I wanted to blame her when I was deep in my anger, now I know it wasn't her fault. Well, not entirely anyway. I had been lost in the music whilst I was cooking and wasn't paying attention to the shiver that ran down my spine when I felt her watching me, or the subconscious urge to flex the muscles on my back knowing she was looking.

There is this need within me that drives me to try and be some perfect version of myself in front of Wren when she first arrives. Within the first five minutes of being around her, there is an urge to mask and hide anything my mind considers not good enough for someone like Wren. And yet, once we start to argue it almost feels like a safe space—a messed up, extremely weird safe space where I can just not give a shit about masking or being anything other than a pissed off version of myself.

"Gus?" Doctor Shakari enters the room we were led to where I'm currently lying down with my feet up. "What on earth has happened now?"

Before I can explain, Wren jumps up from the seat beside the bed and says, "It's my fault, doctor. I surprised him out of nowhere and it caused him to accidentally knock over the pan and the grease went all over the floor."

Doctor Shakari moves to speak, but Wren isn't finished. "I promise it wasn't on purpose! Well, no, that's not entirely true, I was standing there quietly and waiting to say something. So, I guess if you think about it, yes, it was on purpose, but I never wanted anyone to hurt themselves, especially not with bacon grease because I'm pretty sure an oil burn is like the worst burn you can get! And that's also not to say that I wanted to cause a less serious burn because I didn't, I just—"

"She gets it," I snap, cutting her off.

Her mouth shuts closed, and I must fight down the urge to apologize when I see the hurt swimming behind those hazel eyes of hers.

"Okay," Doctor Shakari says slowly. "Well, why don't we take a look at the injury and see? I'm sure no one burned anyone on purpose."

Wren moves her hurt look to the floor as she slowly sits back down. She starts playing with her finger nervously. We've had good moments, Wren and I, and in each of those moments I realize that maybe she isn't a bad person—not that I ever thought she was. Maybe she's someone who I can get along with. After all, she's funny, smart and a force of nature when she sets her mind to something.

And therein lies the problem. There is room for more with Wren than there has ever been with anyone else. It's not just her good qualities, it's the way she can disarm me with a single eyebrow raise, or that when she's close I have to actively tell myself not to touch her or move closer. There have been times where I've blatantly ignored my own warnings, and it's lead to situations like yesterday in the barn.

If I let my guard down, then I'm giving Wren the power to do what everyone in my life other than my brothers have always done…

Leave.

"Well, the good news is that the skin will be fine," Doc says as she inspects both feet. "Your right foot got more of the splashback than your left but it's still not going to leave a scar or anything thanks to the quick thinking with the cold wrap."

I want to tell her that it was all Wren's idea. That I was being stubborn and knew that if I let her touch me, I'd combust and so I argued, but I roll my lips and don't say a word. Surprisingly, neither does Wren.

"I'm going to wrap them both and give you a prescription for some cream you can put on them along with some more painkillers. The same ones I've given you for your arm and shoulder, don't worry."

"Thanks," I mumble.

"Since you're here, I may as well check the progress with that as well. Any problems with your shoulder? If so, I may have to refer you for some physiotherapy."

"My shoulder feels fine," I lie.

The good doctor who has been treating me since I was five

years old stops trying to take my arm out of the sling to give me a look. "Oh, really?"

I nod once and avoid her scrutinizing gaze.

"August," she pushes.

As I look to the side, my eyes meet with a pair of sad, hazel ones and I almost groan at the way she pleads with me.

For fuck's sake.

I turn back to Doctor Shakari. "It's been stiffer than I assume it should be, and the pain has been spreading to my left shoulder."

Doc's eyebrows dip. "The pain has been spreading? Have you been taking it easy?"

"I can't afford to take it easy. I told you that when you patched me up."

Her eyes flare as she lets out an exasperated sigh. "August, this is never going to heal if you don't take care of yourself. I know there is pressure to get the harvest finished in time, but you can't keep overexerting yourself like this."

"I have no choice."

"I asked you about asking people in the town."

I scoff bitterly. "Ask who? The people who sat in a town hall meeting just to tell me that they think me incapable to run my business?"

Her face turns sympathetic. "You need the help, August."

"I—"

"He's going to have help from tomorrow, Doctor Shakari. It'll all be arranged by the end of the day."

Doc and I both wait patiently for Wren to explain.

She pauses before continuing, and even though she looks

more worried than anything else, I can still see a small flame in her eyes turning them from sandstone to the color of summer leaves. She looks at her phone which she's holding loosely in her hand and I'm wondering what she's just done or is planning to do.

"We're going to pause the work on the barn and everyone currently helping with that is going to work on the harvest with Bash so that Gus can rest. Me included."

Wait, what?

Doc looks relieved and appeased, but I know that my confusion and anger are showing clear on my face. I can feel the tension in my jaw as my teeth grind together.

"That's not what's happening," I argue. "There's a deadline on that barn."

"You getting better is more important, Gus," Wren says softly. She steps closer to me, and I can't move away because I'm still on this goddamn bed. "The barn can wait."

"What about your party?"

She tries to make her shrug look indifferent, but I see the concern in those soft features. "I'll move it to a backup location."

This stare down isn't like our usual ones. There is no anger mixed with unresolved tension coming from her, only me this time. Wren's stare is softer and kinder than I've ever seen it before. She, like me, wants to move away from our toxic habit of arguing in order to settle our differences, even when they're not different at all.

I let in a deep breath just as Shakari starts to move my shoulder. "We agreed you would have it in the barn."

"We also agreed that I would have a backup location just in case."

"And do you?" I ask through gritted teeth.

She looks down and even if she tries to tell me a pathetically put-together lie, I'll know the truth.

A rather sharp move of my uninjured shoulder distracts me and brings forth a wince and a groan that I couldn't have stopped even if I was prepared.

Doc hums as she examines my shoulders. "You're further damaging the muscles and putting pressure on the nerves. You seriously need to rest from here on out, Gus, it's no longer a suggestion."

"You need to ignore what she said," I tell Doc. "She's having her friend's party in my barn and so I don't have people to help with the harvest. I need to work."

Doctor Shakari, who is looking more and more confused by the second, flicks her gaze from Wren to me and back again before shaking her head and smiling.

"What's so funny?" I ask, slightly annoyed.

"Nothing, nothing." She rips off her gloves and throws them away. "I just remember when my husband and I were like this. Always fighting and pretending that what was new love at the time was so much less than that."

Wren chokes on absolutely nothing whilst I close my eyes and sigh. Why the hell does everyone seem to think that I have feelings for this woman?

Am I attracted to her? Fuck, yeah. Who wouldn't be? I'm not so blind to the normalities of the world that I would overlook Wren's beauty, but am I stupid enough to introduce something as stupid as *feelings*?

Hell, no. Wren and I would rip each other apart if we were ever in a relationship.

"We're not together."

"Yes, at the time my husband and I weren't either." Doc laughs. "But you'll be surprised at what a tiny bit of tension and good intentions can do."

Chapter Twenty

WREN

Things became a little complicated after Doctor Shakari examined Gus.

Doctor Shakari gave strict instructions for Gus to remain on bed rest for at least a week to allow for the skin to start to heal. No socks, shoes or hot showers.

I made sure to call Bash and explain the situation, to which he just spent the entire conversation laughing and saying that it serves him right. He also said that he is in Renford with Finn so that he can take a look at Finn's other projects and won't be back until tomorrow morning.

When I asked him if there was anyone else that Gus would accept help from, I could pretty much picture his smug smile as he said, "*Accept* help? No. But imagine getting help from a pretty girl with curly brown hair and a sharp tongue? Oh, I think he'd love it."

Let's just say it was the first time I felt any dislike for Bash.

And that all leads to our current situation, me helping him out of the car and leading him back into his house. He accepted my help, but holds up a hand as I attempt to let him lean on me as he hobbles down the worn path leading up to the house. I stay close to him despite him telling me he can manage, which I can see is annoying him.

I ignore the side eye he sends me every two seconds and grab his keys which I picked up when we left. He tries to hide his limp as he makes his way into his living room which is joined to the kitchen.

The last of today's light pours in through the large windows, illuminating the bright space. Gus's cream sofa makes the softest creak as he plops himself down onto it. He leans all the way back and closes his eyes, not bothering to move the brown waves that sit against his annoyingly long lashes.

I feel for him, I really do. I can't imagine the amount of stress that he must be under. It must feel like the world is against him: to be so overwhelmed and behind with work and then to have all these obstacles in his way any time he tries to push through. The worst part I realize, as I awkwardly stand in the doorway, is that a lot of it is my fault. If I hadn't come in, guns blazing about that stupid barn, I would have been able to see that it's more of a hindrance for the farm's business than anything. I was so caught up in myself and my own troubles that I didn't see the problems I was causing for other people.

Maybe that's why Gus dislikes me so much, because I forced him into this position. A position that anyone else would have found overwhelming let alone someone like Gus who thrives on routine and order. Maybe my ex was right … when I think about this job, I only ever think about myself.

"Gus?"

He grunts to let me know he's listening. I sheepishly take a step forwards.

"I want to apologize."

He opens one eye as he turns his head towards me.

"I've been really selfish with this whole thing. I pushed you to do everything with the barn when it seriously shouldn't have been done at this point in time. Not when you're injured and overwhelmed with the harvest."

I have his full attention when he opens his other eye and lifts his head off the back of the couch.

"I was so blinded by the chance to bring my business back to life and help out my best friend that I didn't even take a second to think about anything else and because of that you're where you are now. If I had just left and searched elsewhere then you wouldn't be this stressed or this … injured."

He looks bored and I have no idea how to take that. Gus's facial expressions really are an entire language in themselves; one I am really struggling to understand. He's looking at me the same way I used to look at my college professor when he spoke about how kids these days needed to have stricter driving tests.

"That's part of the reason I want you to let Finn and the others help with the harvest. I need to make things right. It's what should have been happening from the beginning."

After a minute of silence, a silence so delicate that even the quietest of noises would sound like an explosion, Gus sighs and lowers his head once more, closing his eyes and clasping his hands in his lap.

I shift my weight from leg to leg, unsure of what to do in this silence Gus has created.

Eventually, he opens one eye again, spots me standing exactly where he left me, closes it again and mumbles, "Are you going to stay standing there all day, or are you going to come in and sit down?"

"You want me to stay?" I ask, surprised.

"I want you to sit the fuck down."

I keep my mouth shut, swallowing a snappy retort, and sit down on the other end of the L-shaped sofa.

When, again, no one talks, I speak up.

"Gus?"

He groans and sits up. "What do you want me to say, Wren? You want me to tell you that you're forgiven? There's nothing to forgive except you scaring the fuck out of me and making me burn my foot."

"But the other stuff—"

"There is no other stuff, Southwick. I don't regret agreeing to do the barn. If I did then I would have opted out of the trial period, but I didn't."

"Why didn't you?"

"Because like I said, I don't regret it."

I watch him as intensely as he watches me, brown eyes blazing and screaming so many emotions that I can't make out a single one.

"I don't understand," I say in a whisper, but he can hear it clear as day when surrounded by the noiseless bubble he has me trapped in.

He groans once more, as if what he's saying should be obvious. "There's nothing to understand. I don't regret you breaking into my barn and bugging me to work with you."

"But why not, August? So far, you've gained nothing from it."

"Not true," he argues.

"Oh, really? Tell me one thing so far that has worked in your favor. You're still behind on the harvest and the paperwork *and* you have an incomplete barn. What the hell could you have gained?"

"I gained you, idiot."

Time stands still as my eyes almost bulge out of my head. There are a lot of things that I expect from August Finch—what can be either a vacant or bored expression, a complaint, an insult, but never ... this. What even is this? Is it a compliment? How does he expect me to know when he says it like he says everything else; like it's the most basic fact known to man?

"Me?"

The man who hates eye contact holds me captive with an intense gaze. It makes the room feel smaller and hotter having his attention so fixed on me. Never before have I held the attention of someone else this easily, as if just my breathing is something he finds so interesting. Every part of me stands to attention, waiting for a response, a movement, anything that will end my suffering. The zip of electricity that fires across every nerve is almost pleasurable under his gaze.

Eventually, he speaks again. "Like I said, Wren, I don't regret anything."

I smile but Gus cuts off the reaction with a raised hand.

"But, if you keep looking at me as if I've just asked you to marry me then I will regret letting you in my house."

My smile is immediately replaced by an exaggerated roll of my eyes. This man really can be dramatic at times.

Gus's sofa has a matching foot stool which I roll towards him. Before he can protest, I lift one foot at a time onto the stool. Just for today, Doctor Shakari has wrapped his feet in a bandage specifically meant to protect healing burns. She's instructed him to wear it for the first twenty-four hours.

He glares at me, but after all that he's just said, I'm desensitized to it.

"What?" I ask. "You shouldn't be putting pressure on your feet and you know it."

"Can you just sit down?" Gus sighs.

"Aren't you hungry?"

"What does that have to do with you sitting down?"

"Well, you can't stand up and make yourself food, so someone has to."

"Then I'm not hungry," he says matter-of-factly.

"Has anyone ever told you that you're stubborn?"

"Funny, I was thinking the same about you."

"I prefer to think of myself as sensible."

Gus smirks in a way that sends a tingle down my spine and between my legs. "Am I not sensible, Southwick?"

"Nope, you're stubborn as previously mentioned as well as extremely grumpy."

He's subtly leaned forward, his face now just inches away from mine. So much so that I can see the way his brown eyes darken to inky black as he smirks, and the fact that his beard has hints of blond in it. I can see the long eyelashes that are so effortlessly full.

I can feel his breath fan my lips, and that mixed with the fact that he's only dressed in his sweats and an unbuttoned shirt makes this entire moment feel so abundantly intimate that I can feel each breath shorten. In the heat of the moment, there was no time for me to notice the corner of a tattoo that peaks out from under his shirt.

"I'll give you grumpy. I've never been one to smile much. But stubborn is just not true, sweetheart. I happen to be very open to other ideas so long as they are the *correct* ideas."

My laugh is breathy and quiet, but as my breath touches his face, his eyes close, like he's trying to savor the feeling.

Unable to take any more of this, I pull away and mumble, "I should make you some food."

For a second, I'm able to fool myself into thinking that my disappointed expression is the mirror of his.

In a pathetic attempt to lighten the mood, I add, "Probably best to avoid bacon this time, though."

Chapter Twenty-One

GUS

"Would you turn down that ridiculous music?"

Wren sighs through the phone. "It's the only way I can hear it over your stupid TV show!"

"It doesn't surprise me that you think it's a stupid show. Judging by your taste in music, I don't imagine your list of favorite programs would be much better."

"Excuse me?!"

I make sure that my chuckle is silenced and my smile is gone by the time Wren is finished stomping over to my bedroom from the kitchen. She stands in my doorway—something that seems to be a habit of hers—arms folded, a bitter yet somewhat playful glare sent in my direction. Being stuck in such close quarters with someone so fucking gorgeous, but so obnoxious, really is the world's version of a sick joke. Long, wild curls frame the soft edges of her face, a total contradiction to the full breasts that her arms are pushing up until they're almost spilling out of her tight shirt, and the prominent lines of her figure.

"Is there a problem?" I ask, feigning ignorance.

"My taste in music is *bad*?"

"I believe I implied that it is stupid, not bad. Although bad *is* probably a more fitting word."

My lips twitch as her glare intensifies. God, it's fun to rile her up. It's the only thing other than finally being able to catch up with admin that is keeping me mentally stable. It's been two days since Doctor Shakari put me on bed rest for a week. Five more days until I can rid myself of the stress of knowing that I've left Bash on his own to complete the harvest. Five more days of constantly wanting to both be close to and be so far away from the beautiful woman who has been helping me look after myself. Like a child, I've been throwing my toys out the pram; angry that I can't have what I want, when I want, which is to help my brother get shit done.

I feel useless here, absolutely stir crazy. I have a business on the verge of bankruptcy, a shit-ton of orders, the most beneficial of which will all be delayed because of the quantity of the order. I need to have enough money to run the farm throughout the year. That includes feeding the animals, purchasing the seeds for sowing, paying to fix equipment and now—thanks to a woman who I struggle to get out of my head —pay for the upkeep of a brand-new barn.

The weight of my responsibilities sits heavy on not just my chest, but my head, and even my shoulders, making my already sizeable injuries even worse.

I'm ashamed to say that there are times I find myself wondering if it's just easier to give up. No one in this town believes in me, so why should I? They would all rather have back a man who abandoned his home, his children and his business for a woman he knew for less than a week. That became a preference over a man who is just as dedicated to running this farm as the man who started it.

Wren tries her best to look menacing. "Take it back."

My head tilts. "And if I don't?"

"I'll have to come over there and … do … something."

That piques my interest. "And if I want you to … do … something?"

I enjoy the way she wriggles, fiddling with her fingers as she bites her lower lip. "That's not what I meant, and you know it."

"All I did was repeat what you said."

"You put a twist on it."

"No, sweetheart. I said it exactly how you said it. Verbatim. If there was a hidden meaning in there, that's only because you're the one that put it there. Something you're not telling me, sweetheart?"

Between twenty and thirty percent of the population are born with dimples.

Wren has dimples.

"Yeah, there is something." She takes a step further into the room and my palms grow sweaty in anticipation. "You're difficult."

I attempt a dispassionate shrug. "Only when I know it'll rile you up, sweetheart."

She rolls her eyes, but there's no real malice behind it.

A swell of pride puffs out my chest as I realize that I knew that straightaway. I'm usually so bad with figuring out people's facial expressions and vocal tones. One behavior, one tone can mean a hundred different things and it throws me off. I allocate one emotion to one movement, that's it. Add in any more and I'm lost. And yet with Wren, figuring out her emotions when she's arguing with me is almost as simple as breathing. When we're talking to one another normally, then I'm a bit lost. Wren's different shades of anger and annoyance are black and white to me.

"Any luck with the party planning?"

My question throws her off. She can't seem to comprehend how I've gone from being annoying to conversational at the switch of a button.

"You actually want to know?" she asks warily.

"Why would I ask if I didn't want to know?"

She shrugs as she perches herself at the end of my bed, her eyes darkening as her gaze lands on my bare chest. "My ex used to ask me, but he never really cared. When I would come to him with good news, it somehow seemed to make him angry, as if my success was an inconvenience to him."

"What a fucking asshole," I say, and I mean it. Who the fuck looks down on someone else's success?

She shrugs once more and this time she just looks defeated, her eyes blank as she seems to relive each and every time her pathetic ex-boyfriend would shut her down.

"Tell me," I press, wanting her to be able to open up to someone about the good things.

Her entire face brightens, appreciation swimming behind hazel eyes that I'm starting to have dreams about. Like a kid at Christmas, she hops up, crawling up the bed until she's sat beside me. Her smile is even more dazzling up close, a gift to someone as grumpy as me.

"Okay," she begins, and I make a show of putting down my papers, shifting to face her even more. Her smile softens. "So, I've got Lori from the bakery doing a bunch of cakes and stuff for me thanks to you, and she's doing Oakleigh's birthday cake. I tried one of her strawberry tarts and I almost died, it was *so* good."

"She does make good tarts. Her lemon ones are my favorite."

She nods in agreement. "And apparently a good Samaritan by the name of August Finch asked someone named Colin to spot the drinks and Mickey to do the food."

"Colin loves a party, so the chances of him saying yes are high."

"Is he your friend?"

"No. Friends have never really been my forte. But I went to high school with him. He was in my grade. By the time we made it to senior year, he was the one known to throw these insane parties every weekend."

"Did you ever go?" she asks.

"I went to a couple, but I never really fit in. Eventually the music would get to me, or I would snap if someone merely brushed past me. I learned early that that kind of environment wasn't for me."

She looks deep in thought and I'm wondering what could possibly have her so. Is it something I said?

She says, "Do you think you'd be okay at Oakleigh's party?"

I watch her. "I wasn't aware I would be wanted there."

"August, you're one of the planners. You've put in the work for it as well. It's only right that you're there, too. If you want to be."

I try my best to ignore the disappointment that sets into my chest. I think a part of me expected her to say that she, herself, wanted me there. I also think that I *wanted* her to say that she wanted me there. It would have been nice to have someone proud to be in that kind of environment with me. Alas, Wren is someone with whom my relationship thrives on anger, not pride.

I change the subject, afraid that my despondency will be reflected in my tone. "Did you want me to ask Colin for you?"

"You already did, didn't you?"

"Not yet, no."

Her eyes widen. "And you would do that for me?"

All of this shrugging is starting to really hurt my shoulder. "It's not a big deal."

"It's a big deal to me, August."

Why do I enjoy the sound of her calling me August?

One final shrug has her dropping the question, for which I'm grateful because, to be honest, I'm not entirely sure what the answer would have been.

"Are you hungry?" she asks.

"Is there something below my neck that you like the look of, Southwick? You seem to be looking down a lot. I don't have something on my chest, do I?" I pretend to look for a stain on my bare chest.

Her face falls and she sends me a look of feigned annoyance. "You're shirtless."

"So?"

"It's distracting."

"You sound like every male teacher the moment a girl decides to wear a top that shows her shoulders."

"I do not!" she shouts.

"Yes the fuck you do."

She groans loudly, her eyes searching the ceiling of my bedroom for some patience. "You're impossible."

"Impossibly attractive according to the way you stare at my torso."

"I am not staring!"

"Uh-huh."

She jumps up from the bed. "Bash can get you food. I don't like you anymore."

I laugh, she storms off, and I enjoy the view of her walking away.

Chapter Twenty-Two

WREN

"The planning is going great," I lie as I stare into the brown eyes of my best friend. "Everything's peachy. Just perfect. P-e-r-f-e-c-t. Perfect."

Oakleigh gives me a look of disbelief. "How have we been friends for this long and still not become any better at lying?"

I sigh and let my head fall into my hands. "Honestly, it's embarrassing how bad I am."

Oakleigh sips her coffee whilst she watches me. After finally having a day off after almost a week and a half, my best friend is now visiting me and the farm here in Eaglewood. It's reached the point where I'm considering renting an apartment whilst I'm here because I've barely seen my house in over a week. After bringing the morning coffee to the gang on the farm, I've started sticking around for even longer so that there's someone around to make sure that Gus doesn't try and run around harvesting pumpkins when he should be resting.

Spending this amount of alone time with Gus has been ... different. Gone are the days in which we argue with malicious intent and unkempt rage. Instead, they've been replaced by disagreements which are underlined with a subtle smirk or a quiet chuckle on his part.

It's awkward, that's for sure. Partly because it's new, but mostly because the change came out of nowhere. A watershed moment that presented itself without any warning and therefore refused to allow for us to adapt accordingly.

Gus will usually remain in his bedroom, and I will make myself scarce in the living room, only stopping in to give him food or make sure he hasn't snuck out of the window.

Now that the week is over, Gus is back to being up and about, but he's only allowed to continue with his admin work. He managed to catch up quite quickly whilst on bed rest thanks to the laptop I let him use. But now he's back in his office, grumbling away about how the fact that he can't work is bullshit and sending glares to anyone who checks on him.

In other words, things are back to normal.

"So, what's the problem?" Oakleigh asks.

My gaze strays to Jamie who is reluctantly taking Sandra's order behind the counter. When he catches me watching him, he sends me a "help me" look to which I respond with a "hell no" look of my own.

I turn back to Oakleigh. "I won't lie to you, Lee, I never should have pushed to have it in the barn."

"Why? What's happened?"

"It was just such a bad time for them. Gus has a broken arm and a fractured collarbone which has put them behind on the harvest. You should see him, Lee, the man looks like he's holding the entire world on his shoulders."

"Is there no one helping him?"

I shrug, keeping my voice low in case those around us are listening in. "His brother Bash works on the farm with him but they had to let everyone else go to save money. Now, because of me, Bash feels obliged to split his time between the harvest and the barn and orders are even more delayed than they would've been had I not come along."

Oakleigh smiles gently. "Wrennie, it's not your fault. You were conducting business, same as them. If it was a bad time then this Gus guy should have said no."

"He did say no." I shake my head. "I pushed. I went to the farm every day with a coffee until he said yes."

She blows out a breath and leans back. "Well, shit, okay you had right on your side until you said that one."

I groan into my hands. "The worst part is that I can see how it's affecting him. He gets overstimulated easily, he is a lot touchier about timings and working order. I've made it so that I've affected someone who literally relies on order to stay functional. I've brought my chaos and I don't even know how to make it better. I've never spent time with anyone with Autism the way Gus has it."

"The way he has it?"

I take a second to think about how to phrase my explanation. "Subtle is perhaps the correct word. I never realized that Autism could be so complex in the sense that it can only be seen in some people when you really pay attention."

"That's the evil beauty that is masking, Wren."

"Masking?"

"Yeah, it's when someone tries their best to hide something that makes them different. A lot of people who are neurodivergent, but who don't obviously display as such, sometimes feel as if they have to hide it because others will treat them as less than." Lee sips her coffee. "It's the same way a lot of people judge those with ADHD because some of the symptoms seem to them like a cop-out. People look at people with Autism who are still able to function on their own and can still communicate with others clearly and assume it's a misdiagnosis or it's nothing more than that person being over dramatic. So, people are made to feel as if they have to try and hide it. Appear normal, I suppose."

"But they are normal?"

She nods. "And now you see the problem."

As Oakleigh checks her phone, I take the time to think over this new information.

It would explain why Gus is so adamant that he needs to work and even overworks himself all the time. He feels he needs to overcompensate just to gain the same amount of respect that someone without Autism would receive in his position.

It would explain why he has so many walls up around him. When I replay that town hall meeting in my head, it reads so differently now. The majority of this town clearly sees him as underqualified, not due to his father's stupidity, but because they see being different as a major flaw. But it's not a flaw. To me, his differences are a strength that shouldn't be underestimated. He's strict with himself and others in a way that warrants a smoothly run business.

"Someone looks deep in thought." Oakleigh pulls me from my thoughts. She smiles when I jump. "Is this Gus dude becoming someone important?"

"What? No, we're coworkers." I avoid eye contact.

She chuckles. "Such a shit liar."

I can't even bring myself to laugh alongside her. I just slump in my seat and play with my empty coffee cup.

Feelings for Gus are not a luxury I can afford right now, but I know it's something that presents itself more and more each day. The anxiety that accompanies even the thought of the possibility reminds me that I'm not yet ready for that. I pretend it doesn't, but my breakup with Adam really left me broken. He has me in a constant push and pull with myself. One minute, I'm mad with myself for letting him make me believe that I'm less than I am. That I'm unable to be a strong businesswoman who can also have a family and a life outside of that business. But the next minute I'm wondering if he was right, if my determination to do something that I genuinely love and enjoy doing made me lose sight of what was really important. Maybe it's just not possible for someone to have both, and whilst I really do want to find someone who I can spend my days with and with whom I can build a family, Second Nature Events is something that I've dreamed about doing long before I longed for kids and a husband. Doesn't that mean that if I have to choose, my job would be the correct choice? Wouldn't that be the choice that would leave me feeling the most fulfilled in life?

And yet, lately something has been stirring inside of me and I'm not blind enough to notice that it's stronger when Gus is around. I sometimes find myself excited to make my way to

Goldleaf Farm in the mornings just at the thought of arguing with him. I've spent so much of my life being "nice Wren", "sweet Wren", or "generous Wren". With August, I can just be Wren. All forms of myself including the versions that I hide— "fiery Wren", "stubborn Wren" and "determined Wren". I don't feel that I have to try really hard to please him because he just easily accepts all the parts of myself and I, him.

And recently it seems to be even better despite being awkward. We argue but it's lighter than before. We don't aim to insult, just win. Plus, there's no denying the man is attractive. Over the past few days, he's had a knack for sitting in his room shirtless and I'd be a fool if I lied and said I didn't admire the view.

Beautifully tanned skin stretched over hard muscle. It's clear to anyone that this man is gorgeous.

It may sound vain, but I enjoy the moments when I rile him up enough for him to stand up and leave very little distance between us. The way he towers over me, having to bend down just to allow for his forehead to almost touch mine. There are times when I marvel at how his forearm flexes whilst he types up paperwork, the sleeves of his plaid shirt remaining rolled up to his elbows despite the autumn cold really setting into the bones.

Holy shit, maybe I do like him.

"I'm going to help with the harvest today," I tell Oakleigh, hoping it's enough to distract both of us from Gus.

I'm guessing it hasn't worked judging by the smirk on Oakleigh's face.

"Uh-huh." She chugs the rest of her coffee. "Okay, so

backtrack a bit because you never really said what the problem with the party is."

"Oh, yeah," I mumble sheepishly. "Well, when I took Gus to the hospital, the doctor said that he needs to rest and so I insisted that the guys stop the work on the barn and focus on helping him and Bash with the harvest. Which means…"

"… the barn won't be finished in time," she finishes and I nod solemnly. "And you don't have a backup venue, do you?"

I grimace. "I'm so sorry, Lee-Lee. I've messed everything up."

After a pause which solely consists of me groaning in self-pity, Oakleigh says, "Wren, look at me."

I do as she asks. "Wren, I didn't want you to put so much pressure on yourself to get this done. I asked you because you're my best friend and I trust you more than anyone. I didn't want you to do this thinking that mistakes weren't allowed. It doesn't have to be perfect. Hell, half of the people that I invited I couldn't even give a shit about, it's just to boost numbers." She reaches out for my hand and squeezes. "The only people I really care about are my parents, my sister and you. So, if at the end of the day all we manage to plan is a dinner with those people then it will still be perfect."

I take a deep breath to try and hold back the tears. "I love you so much."

"Right back at you, biatch." We stand up from the table and when Jamie catches my eye, he holds out a thumbs-up to me and gets started on the gang's coffee order, including his own, before he comes with us down to the farm. "Now, let's go see this barn, shall we?"

Chapter Twenty-Three

GUS

Work on the barn has been coming along much smoother than I anticipated. Finn has managed to put up most of the outside wall and placed some covered scaffolding around the structure until a functional roof is back on it which thankfully means that Wren hasn't had a chance to see it.

He's a nice guy, and I can tell that he really wants his sister's dream to become a reality. He talks about her a lot; a doting big brother. And whilst I entertain it when he's around, in my head I really wish he would stop. I already think about his sister enough, I don't need him initiating thoughts when my brain wants to have a moment's peace.

The only problem I have that currently trumps hazel eyes, a pretty face and an annoying attitude is the harvest. It's been a week since I delivered Nigel's pumpkin and, in that time, the usual six completed orders have been whittled down to two.

Two fucking orders. I'm so screwed.

And on top of that, my shoulder has felt more screwed up than usual. I wake up with it sore, I go to sleep with it sore, I do all but breathe and it's sore. I think Bash is starting to notice because he's been giving me that look. The look that tells me that he wants me to slow down but knows that it would be pointless to ask. And it would be pointless, because I have to help. I had to be a leader and let go of all my staff, so what else is there for me to do? I need to make sure that I get shit done no matter what. The shittiest part right now, however, is that all I can do is fucking admin. Well, it's all I can do when people are watching me.

One field is halfway done. I can see that Bash is exhausted as well and I'm not sure what to do to help. I can't give him time off until the fields are done and I can't help any more than I already am, so what is there left for me to do? Finn and Jamie help out as often as they can, but I need them focused on the barn.

Mori nudges me with her nose which snaps me out of my thoughts. Bash is further down the row, a white puff of air leaving his mouth as he blows out a breath. He leans back, stretching his back with a grimace that I know he thinks I can't see. There are a few pumpkins surrounding him on the ground, waiting for me to follow and add to the crates. He's currently shirtless like I am, his jeans and boots caked in mud thanks to the morning dew.

Just as I start to move along the row, I feel the heat on my back from someone's gaze. A jolt of electricity zips up my spine and I instantly know who it is. My work of avoiding her has been award-worthy up until now, but I've grown lazy with it. Maybe I wanted to slack off, because although it annoys me to admit it, I do miss arguing with her.

I turn around and see her standing at the edge of the field with another woman, coffees in hand. I check my watch and see that she's on time today. I've grown dependent on this coffee over the past couple of weeks to the point that on the mornings when I'm avoiding Wren, I come back to a cold cup and still guzzle it down with the same gusto that I would were it hot.

My eyes meet hers and, for a moment, even Mori's nudges can't drag me away from this sight. Not even breaking my other arm could tear my gaze away from the sight of Wren's eyes lighting up with a heat that I can see even from several paces away. She takes in the sight of my torso, the view clear as day for her. I wipe the sweat away from my forehead and she follows the motion as if in a trance.

I let myself take the same liberties—dropping my line of sight to those sinful knee-high boots, to the tights that offer a glimpse of those legs which are barely covered by the turtleneck jumper dress than sticks to her hips and breasts, provoking some rather dirty ideas. Brown curls sit in a messy bun atop her head, but the wind threatens to free it, and for the first time in my life, I find myself jealous of the fucking wind.

Her eyes catch on my chest, and I realize she's staring at my tattoo—a pumpkin seed with the initials "CF" engraved into the middle and vines curling all around it. I see one dark eyebrow curve upward with curiosity. It's not the first time she's seen it. I see that on her face as she makes an active effort to stop herself from asking its meaning.

189

She'll have to work for it if she wants a closer look than what she's had the past week.

Woah, wait, what?

Where the fuck did that come from?

"Oi, Auggie!" Bash yells, making the both of us jump. When I turn, I see that he's made it to the end of the row and his usual puppy-like temperament has completely disappeared. If there's one thing I know it's that if Sam and I are assholes, there's no way that gene missed Bash as well. And it didn't miss Bash, you just have to see him when he's tired…

… or hungry, or overwhelmed, or suffering from blue balls that one time…

He lifts his arms in a "what the fuck is going on?" gesture, and I hold up a hand in return. When I turn back towards Wren, I'm shocked to see she's disappeared and I'm left in the middle of the row with a coffee waiting on my truck bed on one side, an angry brother on the other, and a stiff erection down below.

Yeah … this is going to be fine.

"We're going for a drink," Sam declares as he walks out of the barn just as the sun begins to set.

"Pass," I mumble as I lift the last crate, wincing.

"We all need one," he argues. "Your shoulder is killing you, don't think we've all missed that; Bash is on the verge of starting World War Three and all of us in here are tired as fuck."

It has been a long-ass week. Jamie took the entire week off work just so that he could help. They've made some amazing progress already, more than even Finn thought would be done in this time.

"I'm fine," Bash huffed from behind us, wiping the sweat with his t-shirt. His mood has been sour for a while and people in town are starting to notice. Bernie, who works in the supermarket, came to the farm for his order of pumpkins and during his pathetic attempt at conversing with me, which was hastily declined, he made sure to mention that Bash was shouting at Doctor Shakari in the waiting room of the hospital the other day.

I wasn't even aware he had gone to the hospital, but so far I've kept it to myself since he's extremely unapproachable when he's like this.

Sam looks at our brother with a disbelieving glare. "Sebastian, we're either getting you drunk or laid. Pick one. Look at me, I've had no choice but to turn into you since your attitude is turning you into—"

"You?" Jamie offers from the barn doors. Who decides that purple dungarees and expensive sneakers are appropriate work clothes on a farm, I have no idea, but in all fairness to him, there isn't a single spec of dirt on them.

Sam shoots him a look. "No, you ass." I don't miss the way Jamie's eyes dip down to my brother's behind. I roll my eyes and avert my gaze.

"I'm down," Finn offers. "Can definitely afford to let loose a little since we're ahead of schedule. I've wanted to show Wren, but I haven't seen her today."

"She's been back in Beckford working on the plans for the party with Oakland."

"Oakleigh," Finn corrects to which Sam just shrugs.

A green monster puts its weight onto my chest. "How the fuck do you know that?"

I don't miss the numerous smirks. Even Bash's lips hold a small one.

"Jealous, little brother?" Sam jests.

"No, idiot." I'm lying, obviously. All I can think about right now is how good it would feel to leave my older brother with a black eye.

"Then why so tense?"

"I just didn't know the two of you were close enough for you to know her every move."

Sam's smirk turns to a sinister smile. "Does it matter how close we are?"

"No."

I'm about two minutes away from fucking up my other arm. If I haven't already, that is.

Jamie steps into the space between me and my brother. "Before Sam gets a fist to the face and a knee to the groin, let's get all the animals inside and then go get drunk. Sound good?"

Sam chuckles pathetically as he backs up, heading towards the empty field that currently holds Emilio and some of the other animals that like to munch on the grass. I'm too fucked off to explain why it's an eco-friendly method of reworking the land so it's ready for another round.

Everyone else follows Sam, even Finn who has been helping out with the farm work wherever he can. I appreciate him. The more I get to know him, the more I see similarities between him and Wren. He's kind like she is. Selfless, too. They both make it seem like they were put on this earth to help others and even someone as selfish as me can admit that it's an extremely admirable quality.

It's a blessing and a curse really, knowing someone so similar to Wren. I hate to admit that I like thinking about her— her long mahogany curls; her almond-shaped eyes that could turn any man into an idiot with just one look; the adorable blush she gets when she's flustered … and that beauty spot. I seriously have no idea what it is about that beauty spot that has me thinking about it night and day. I used to think that it's because I'm a sucker for facts and I found the probability of it existing an interesting notion. However, I've realized now that that can't possibly be it.

Maybe it's because of the fact that I now know how much she dislikes it. I know how insecure it makes her, how she wishes it wasn't there. I know that she looks in the mirror and sees it every day and dislikes the way it emphasizes the shape of her top lip, the cupid's bow that sits perfectly in the center. I know how she hates the way it kisses her nose when she scrunches it up in that way that shows she is annoyed or confused.

I know now that I haven't stopped thinking about it because she tries her hardest not to. And what a sin it is to ignore such beauty.

Chapter Twenty-Four

GUS

The Locke and Key is a dingy bar just off of Main Street. It's also the only bar in Eaglewood. If you want anything better than sticky floors, even stickier tables, shitty cocktails and cheap beer, then you'd have to drive to Stanwood which is the town that separates Wren's town from my own. The bars will still be shit, but slightly less shit.

The lights are always dim, I assume so that Roland, the owner, doesn't have to pay too much on the electricity. The moment we walk in, my boots begin to resist me with every step.

I gain myself several curious glances as we walk over to the bar. Coming to the Locke for a drink isn't something out of the ordinary for me, but ever since I broke my arm I haven't been around. I assume that Sandra's stunt with the town hall meeting and my idiocy when demanding Jamie come work on the farm in the middle of the Sweet Cinnamon Café hasn't done me any favors.

The guys all seem to be in lighter spirits the moment that they all find a beer in their hands, each of their troubles being replaced by the taste of hops and malt. Mine, however, seem to stay sat on my chest like an anvil. There's an urge to rub at the area to try and relieve the pressure, but I know it'll be useless.

When it comes to these guys, their troubles are light enough that a couple of drinks at the end of the day is enough to temporarily lift some of the weight, but when it comes to me, there is too much going on for my brain to even think about shutting off. I'm the owner of a failing farm that has been owned by my family for three generations. If I fail, my family fails.

"What's got your face looking like Emilio's ass?"

I only realize the question is being directed at me when my shoulder is nudged. I try my best to hide the wince.

"There's nothing wrong with my face."

"Is that what the girls tell you?" Bash jests.

"They tell me it's a lot better than yours. Actually, they tell me a lot of things are better than yours."

"Hey!"

Out of nowhere, Wren and the same woman from earlier seem to appear, cutting off what I'm sure would have been a pitiful comeback from Bash.

Any hint of a smirk disappears from my face as I turn to the one person I wasn't aware would be here tonight. If I'd known, I definitely would have avoided the Locke … or run a brush through my hair at least.

Our eyes meet and for a second I find myself in that

embarrassingly corny part of a movie where the music slows and everything around me just seems to fade away. Wren with make-up on is a sight to behold, but bare-faced Wren who I'm looking at now is something that only a world more advanced than ours could have thought up. Gone is the usual light make-up that she wears—the black stuff on her eyelashes, that stuff that makes her cheekbones sparkle. The only thing that remains from her usual look is the lip gloss that coats her lips and tempts me like a snake in a garden. I clutch the bottled beer in my hand a little tighter to stop myself reaching for her and finding out what that lip gloss tastes like. Not that I really need to taste when I can always smell it on her. Coconut.

"What are you doing here?" I ask her as my eyes trail down her open jacket which shows a cropped t-shirt and low fitted jeans which show off a sliver of light brown skin. She must have gone home to change. My voice sounds hoarse and dry and I'm aware it's not from the alcohol.

Usually, her eyebrows would dip, the sides of her lips would mimic their action and those hazel eyes would flare with a spark of fire that would travel down and heat her words. But this time there's no dip anywhere, just a blank look that finds my now confused expression.

Something is wrong.

I catch a glimpse of Finn on the other side of the booth we managed to snatch up and I instantly know I'm right. He's frowning at his little sister the same way I am.

"Hey, newbie!" Jamie yells over the live band, completely unaware of her current expression. "Glad you could join us! Make room for her, boys."

She steps forward and before I can even think about it, I'm

up on my feet. She watches me, waiting to see what I'll do, and even I'm now wondering what the fuck my plan here is.

I close the gap between us and lower my head towards hers so she can hear me.

"What's wrong?"

A small spark of surprise widens her eyes. "What do you mean?"

"Don't play dumb, Wren. What's the matter?"

She shakes her head. "Nothing."

"You're lying."

This time when she looks at me, her gaze is steady and bold, and for a second I feel vindicated enough in the knowledge that the Wren I know and dislike is back.

"I said I'm fine, August."

"And I said that's bullshit, Wren."

We match each other's intensity in a staring competition, my stubbornness fueling her, and hers fueling me. When I see the way she shuts off her eyes, letting them become dull and blank, I take a step back. I'm not going to get anywhere like this. I sit my ass back down and resume showing all of my attention to the bottle I've put back in my hand.

"Okayyyy," Sam says awkwardly, and only now do I realize that everyone on the table and even some people standing around us were watching the interaction between Wren and myself. "Moving swiftly on from whatever *that* was ... who's ready to get another round?"

Something tells me I'm going to need to get a little drunker than I planned.

WREN

The fact that he seemed to just immediately figure me out scares me. When I helped to look after him, he told me that he struggles with reading people and situations. Struggles to understand what one look can mean, especially when it has multiple possibilities. And yet, both then and now it's like he can read me as if I'm made in only his language. And that kind of feeling isn't going to help me right now.

The atmosphere here in the Locke and Key bar is exactly what I need to take my mind off of my current problems. The smell of malt needs to be a taste in my mouth right now, and thankfully since Sam is currently getting drinks, that will soon be a possibility for me.

"So any exciting new plans for Oakleigh's thirtieth?" Finn asks, concern hidden behind feigned interest.

I throw on one of my fake smiles and Oakleigh lets me answer since she hates to reply to Finn. "Oakleigh knows that we've had to halt work on the barn and so we're talking about plan B and what that entails."

The fact that I've avoided the question hasn't escaped my brother's notice.

Finn nods slowly and takes a sip of his beer. "It's a shame we've had to put a pause on it, but you insisted we help with the harvest."

"How is that? The harvest, I mean. I promise I'm going to start helping from tomorrow."

Surprisingly, it's the man who hasn't spoken since he called me a liar ten minutes ago who answers my question. "Shitter than we expected."

"It's the first year you guys have had to do it with only two of you. Cut yourself some slack, Gus."

"If I cut myself some slack, I lose half of the pumpkins in the third field. And since people won't let me work on it, it looks like we're losing it anyway."

"You mean won't let you do the work you've been secretly doing anyway since your bed rest ended?" I ask. Gus ignores me, choosing to instead sip his beer.

"We can always start on the third field," Finn suggests. "Split the responsibilities?"

"By the time you guys finish in the barn it's too dark for us to work on the fields."

"We stopped working on the barn … *remember*?" Bash growls the last word and I watch the boys suspiciously as they exchange sheepish looks.

"Oh … yeah," Gus grumbles.

"My point is that you don't have to do it alone."

"And my point is that if I don't do it alone then it doesn't get done." Gus moves to lift his beer to his mouth and a pained sound leaves his mouth. He flinches so hard that the beer bottle drops from his hand, hitting the edge of the table and shattering all over the table and Gus's shirt.

"Damn it!" he yells, banging his hand on the table and narrowly missing a piece of the broken bottle.

"Gus, stop." I cover his hand with mine and he tenses beneath me. "It's okay."

He looks around him at the broken bottle shards scattered around the table, and I see his frustration slowly dissipate. His shoulders start to relax as he lets out a heavy sigh.

"I'm sorry," he mumbles. "I'm sorry."

Bash claps him on the back. "It's okay, man."

There might be something going on with me, but I know for sure I'm not currently the only one struggling. I am not the only one bowing under the debilitating weight of stress and high expectations.

"Is now a bad time to say hi and let you know that my name is Oakleigh and I'm part of the reason you are pretending to have stopped working on the barn?"

Finn sends Lee a warning look and I send Gus a glare. That lying little shit.

Sam lifts a hand. "I'm Sam, and no it's not the wrong time. Your intro would have been awkward regardless since it had to follow their unresolved sexual tension."

The others introduce themselves, minus Gus who ignores Oakleigh's existence completely, and just like that, my best friend becomes a part of this crazy group I've grown to love.

Chapter Twenty-Five

GUS

By the time midnight rolls around, my hourly number of beers has pretty much doubled. Now, there's two stages overlapping one another against one wall and things seem to move slower than they did before. The live band finished about an hour ago and a DJ has since taken their place. And when I say DJ, I mean Sarah from the library who is one of the rare people who knows how to plug a phone into a sound system.

Sam and Jamie have conveniently disappeared at the same time, and even an oblivious and drunk idiot like myself can decipher why. Bash and Finn are now starting their third round of pool. Finn is getting easily distracted by Wren's friend, Oakleigh, who is busy flirting with Jonathan Brine who works at the hospital. Which leaves me on a table beside them, watching them as best I can with no glasses and a shit load of beer in my system, trying to ignore the somewhat distracted, but also drunk, woman beside me.

She's been keeping up with me, I think. Whenever I go to buy another I see that hers is also done, and vice versa.

That doesn't mean that the drinks aren't affecting her, though. Whenever she comments on our brothers' pool game, she does so in a way that makes her even louder than the music. Her words have been slurred for a few hours and when she gets up to pee, Finn pauses the game to help her make it to the bathroom.

All in all, it's an okay night. It will be a hell of a lot better once I'm able to stop thinking about the woman beside me, though.

Am I wrong for blaming her for the way I am now? Maybe, but that's not going to stop me from doing it. As much as I look at her and want to have what would probably be the best sex of my life, I'm aware that it would also be the best *hate* sex of my life.

"Suck it, bitch!" Bash yells as he pots another two striped balls.

"Says the one currently losing two out of three."

A hazy chuckle leaves Wren. "I hate to admit it, Bash, but you're not doing too good," she slurs.

Bash feigns hurt. "Why break my heart, Wren? You're supposed to be on my side."

"I'm always on your side, sweetie." She blows my brother a kiss and I find my green monster growing.

Wren and Bash have become very close over the last few weeks. If he wasn't in love with some other woman, I would think he has a crush on my woman.

Hold up ... my what?

I attempt to shake my head free of idiotic thoughts and take a long slug of beer. The endless flow of it has my mouth dry and I'd kill for a glass of water.

The more I drink, the more aware I become of Wren's presence beside me. I feel it every time she turns her drunken gaze towards me, even when I'm not looking. That lick of heat that crawls its way up my spine deliciously each time I hold off on turning around. It feels like a game I'm playing with her and she doesn't even know I'm a participant.

I lean back in my seat and let the ethanol guide me. One of her hands remains hidden under the table and when I think about the way she reacted to me in the barn, I can't stop my hand from moving closer.

Bash and Finn's cries of competitiveness blur into the background as I shift closer and move my hand closer to hers. The moment my fingers brush against her warm hands, she jumps. I keep a cool exterior and repeat the action again, earning myself the same shocked inhale.

"What are you doing?" Wren asks me under her breath, only loud enough for me to hear her over the music.

I run my finger softly in a circle on the back of her hand before grabbing it and lacing our fingers together.

"I honestly don't know."

An hour later, and I'm about ready to bounce, the need for alcohol now replaced by the need for a woman who I've been enjoying torturing for an hour.

It started with a brush of my fingers against hers, back when I was trying my best to ignore my own feral urges. But soon I grew bolder, worried that my actions were becoming too subtle. I'm not great with social cues, but when it comes to others who don't share my struggles, how subtle is too subtle?

Light touches turned to a possessive hand on her lower back. That turned into the dire need to lean over and smell her hair, let the scent of vanilla wash over me and sober me up.

Okay, so maybe I have been torturing myself more than her, but whilst I'm oblivious in social situations, there has been nothing subtle about her reactions.

It's been all too easy to know what the way her eyes close when I touch her means, or the way she lets out the quietest moans that I can hear over the music, a sound so sweet that even molasses could take a lesson.

The erection I've had to hide from everyone this entire time has become painful and any alcohol I did have in my system has completely left my body. That's the effect she seems to have on me. I've known that since the moment I met her. I knew she would create these kinds of problems for me and if I'm being honest that's a big part of why I was so angry around her. I was angry that after such a long time of not finding any woman attractive, after spending years deciding that I was better off alone, she had to come along when I'm at my lowest and make me want her.

The problem with that is she doesn't just make me want her body. I want all of her. Her mind, her body, hell, her goddamn soul. I've never been so attracted to someone that it could resemble exactly what Bash told me about. The way he loved that girl so intensely. He didn't think about each part of her as separate entities; he just wanted her. I just want Wren.

Fuck, I need to stop drinking.

"I should really get going." Oakleigh yawns before picking up her bag. "I have a sixteen-hour shift tomorrow and if I want to be able to find a vein or intubate someone I should really get some sleep."

I'm assuming she works in medicine.

"I'll drop you home," Finn tells her.

"Wow, how unusually nice of you, Finley."

He glares at her and it's the first time I've seen Finn look anything close to angry. "Not really, I just don't want to have to console my sister when she finds out her best friend went missing between here and Beckford."

Oakleigh glares at him. "Asshole."

"Right back at you, Michaels. Let's go."

They say goodbye and Oakleigh and Wren share a long hug during which she whispers something into Wren's ear. Wren nods occasionally and gives her a kiss on the cheek. They clearly share a close bond.

After they leave, Bash claps me on the back and I try my best to hide my wince. "I should get going, too, dude. We have an early start tomorrow." He turns to Wren. "You joining tomorrow?"

"You're damn right I am," she replies. "I'm ready to be put to work."

I'm more than willing to put you to work, sweetheart.

Seriously need to stop drinking.

Bash gives her a sideways hug. He gives me one, trying to be gentle to avoid hurting my shoulders.

"Make sure she gets home safe," he says in my ear. I nod once. "And make sure you stop being an idiot. Tell the woman how you feel."

"Don't know what you're talking about."

"Uh-huh. Don't think I haven't seen you've developed a case of wandering hand syndrome."

I lightly shove him away. "Mind your business."

"Mmhmm." He smiles at me and then leaves the bar, leaving me alone with the most beautiful distraction.

"I should go," she says quietly, nervously staring down at her hands. Hands that I will never forget the softness of.

"Why?"

She looks up at me and my hands itch to reach for her. Especially after she says, "Because I don't know what I'll do if I stay."

I reach up and gently move a strand of soft brown hair behind her ear, letting my fingers trail down her jawline until I can grasp her chin.

"And if I want you to stay?" I ask.

Those almond eyes look up at me so innocently and yet they still manage to look so seductive. The moment my dark brown eyes meet hazel, I'm lost.

"Then I'll stay." She takes a step forward. "But I thought you hated me?"

"I hate the way you make me feel, but I could never hate *you*. Like I said last week, I don't regret anything because it gave me you, sweetheart."

She chuckles dryly. "You wouldn't be saying any of this if you hadn't drunk so much."

"True. Doesn't mean I'm lying, though." After a brief silence, I ask, "What was wrong earlier?"

She shakes her head, but answers my question regardless. "I'm just stressed, and mad that I put you in this position. I've made things harder for you and for myself when all I wanted to do was help us both. I suppose it's all just got me a bit down."

She tries to look back down but my fingers on her chin keep her head up.

"Wren."

"Hmm?"

"Come home with me."

Surprise lights up her face. "Repeat that?"

"If I do, will you do it?"

"Yes."

A smirk stretches my lips as I lean down towards her, letting my nose kiss hers. "Sweetheart?"

"Yes?" she whispers.

I move my lips to her ear, "I need you to come home with me."

Chapter Twenty-Six

GUS

The tension within the cab is thick enough to suffocate me. The silence is enough to bring me back from the dead and suffocate me again.

The only good thing is it gives me time to think about what to do once we reach my house.

I don't want to just jump straight in and try to fuck her. I'm not someone who can do that. Don't get me wrong, I've had one-night stands. Even tried the whole friends-with-benefits thing, but only with women who approach me for such a thing first. My mother taught me that when you're interested in a woman, you always treat them with respect. You buy them flowers, you take them on a date, you open the door for them, that kind of stuff.

So far, I've done none of that with Wren.

When it came to a woman I wanted more with than the

basic sexual urges, my mom had even written me a step-by-step guide.

- **Step one:** Introduce yourself.
- **Step two:** Strike up a conversation to see if you have a connection.
- **Step three:** Ask her out on a date.
- **Step four:** Bring her flowers.
- **Step five:** Make her smile.
- **Step six:** Ask her to be your girlfriend if you're interested.

Six steps and I'm currently zero for six. So even though I know for a fact that if she doesn't come home with me tonight, I may lose my mind, what is it that she's coming with me to do?

Sex is secret step seven. Surely, you can't skip straight to seven? Especially not with a woman like Wren. For women like her ... well, that's just it, there are no women like her. So, do the steps even still apply?

God, I wish my mom were still here.

As we pull up to my house, my hands start to shake, and my palms feel clammy. I can't control the bouncing of my leg and as I hand the driver a twenty, I'm ashamed to say I drop it before it reaches his hand.

I flick the lights on once we're inside my house and I take off my shoes and leave them in their correct spot.

Wren slips off her shoes and sloppily leaves them by the front door.

"Your shoes go on the end of the row," I tell her.

I keep all of my shoes in a neat row on the shoe shelf underneath the ottoman by the door. Each pair is placed in height order. Since she has knee-high boots on, they go on the end. She pauses and sees the shoe rack, taking a second to compute what I've said before picking up her boots and placing them in the correct place.

I breathe a quiet sigh of relief.

"Come on."

I lead the way into the kitchen, deciding to get us another drink to buy myself some time. I keep a four-pack of beer in the fridge for whenever Bash or Sam come by. I grab two, screw off the cap before passing her one.

"Does this mean I'm in store for more truths?" Wren asks with a mischievous grin.

"You never know, sweetheart. You could be in store for more than that."

When I see the way her eyes widen, I internally panic. Was that too forward?

I take a step back, nervously scratching at the back of my neck. My shirt feels too tight, my kitchen too small. I'm not usually timid around women so why am I suddenly feeling as if I'm meeting the fucking Queen of England?

An adorable flush of pink winds its way up her neck to her cheeks and across her nose.

"I apologize if that made you uncomfortable."

She shakes her head. "No, no, you didn't. I'm just surprised is all. I'm not used to men being so forward with me."

"I didn't mean it like that. I merely meant that we might end up sharing more than truths."

She looks up at me with a shy smile.

"Okay, yeah that still sounds bad."

Her laugh is light and raspy and I'm finding myself wanting to hear it all the goddamn time. "I'm not used to hearing you sound so nervous."

I move over to the couch, dropping myself down onto it with a sigh. My hand roughly moves itself up my face and into my hair. "I'm sorry, I'm just not used to talking to you in a way that isn't an argument."

Timidly, she makes her way over to me, choosing to sit right next to me. A small hand rests on mine. "That night when you introduced me to Mori and the others, you seemed to speak to me just fine, if I remember correctly."

Shit, I'd completely forgotten about the confidence I felt that night. I simply just went with what felt natural. There was no awkwardness, no hesitation. I didn't follow the steps then, I just said what I wanted to say to her in the moment. I wanted to see that heart-stopping smile of hers, be close enough to her to breathe in the smell of her. I just did what felt natural.

"August."

I move my gaze to her.

"If it feels natural for you to argue with me, then argue."

My expression turns quizzical. "Argue about what?"

"How about the fact that you lied to me about stopping work on the barn?"

I down half my beer. "No idea what you're talking about."

A perfectly manicured eyebrow raises. "Why did you lie?"

"I didn't lie. Technically, I didn't say anything at all, I just didn't mention that we weren't stopping work."

"August," she sighs.

"When did we move from Gus to August?"

She leans forward and I instantly smell her. It takes everything in me not to take a deep breath. "When did we move from Wren to sweetheart?"

"You're asking the wrong question."

"Oh?" she asks, her smile widening with each verbal exchange. I find my lips trying to match hers. "What question should I be asking you then?"

I twist my body until I'm completely facing her and I let myself lean even further, so close that our breaths mix together as we exhale in tandem.

"The question isn't why I started calling you sweetheart. It's when did the intonation of sweetheart move from condescending to flirtatious."

"Okay, well then that's my question."

"Well, the answer is that I don't know. It just ... happened."

WREN

Silence swirls around us but I can still hear the pounding in my chest.

How did we even get here? Two weeks ago, we're arguing maliciously, constantly annoyed by each other's presence. Now, when we argue it's heated and filled with a tension that makes me weak in the knees.

There are so many things I want to do, but I have no clue where we stand. I have no idea if this tension between us is as far as things go, if we're forever to remain halted in this moment of both ecstasy and torment.

"Wait here."

I watch Gus as he saunters towards the front door, leaving me alone in the living room that's dimly lit by the lamp on the side table.

When he returns, he looks sheepish as he sits down, holding out a couple of wildflowers.

I gasp when I see him beside me, waiting for me to take them. "What's this?"

He shrugs. "I didn't buy any, but I always thought the wildflowers that grow outside look quite nice."

I slowly take them, admiring the yellow and purple flowers.

"For me?"

He nods and sniffles awkwardly. "They're cool because they grow even in colder months. Giving them to you is step four," is all he says.

Step four?

"And how many steps are there?"

"Six."

"So what's the next one? And does that mean I've passed the first three?"

His eyes dip down to my lips for a split second. "The next one I'm not sure I know how to do."

He lifts my head with two fingers on my chin and the look he gives me when my eyes meet his has my breath halting in its tracks.

"Step five is to make you smile."

Well he's now accomplished step five because that's just goddamn adorable.

"And step six?"

He looks uncomfortable as he answers. "Step six is ... a complicated one."

"Interesting." I chuckle lightly. "What are these steps leading to? What do they do?"

I become nervous as he leans forward, and seeing his eyes darken in such a dangerous way sends my smile running.

His gaze flicks down to my lips again, but this time they stay there as he licks his own as if he's imagining the taste and thoroughly enjoying it.

He looks mesmerized as he mumbles, "They make you mine."

And then his lips find mine, and I'm lost to him completely.

Chapter Twenty-Seven

WREN

The way he kisses moves past possessive. Gus isn't just kissing me, he's *claiming* me, owning every part of me with the movement of his lips against mine.

A low moan leaves his mouth and it snaps me out of my surprise and spurs me on. My arms loop themselves around his neck, my hand running through what I now know to be incredibly soft waves.

I feel his hand grip my waist tightly as his thumb skates across and even under layers of clothes; it has its intended reaction. Electricity vibrates through me, undeniable and unavoidable. For so long I've been trying to ignore the tension between Gus and I, always trying to convince myself that it's nothing when this kiss shows that it's obviously been somewhat more than "something". Anger and attraction have always come hand in hand when I think of August Finch, and now the two have blended together until it's become a bundle of want and desire that is fueled by annoyance and frustration.

No one has ever kissed me with so much fervor, so much passion. When his tongue skates across my lip, I happily grant him access, excited to see what else he seems to be effortlessly amazing at. He tastes of beer and carnal desire and I allow myself to get lost in the taste of him, the feel of him against me and the sound of him as he growls possessively.

"August." I breathe out his name like a secret shared between us.

"You make me actually like the sound of my name, sweetheart. Be careful, otherwise I might feel obliged to see how it sounds during other activities."

I lean in for another kiss. "You mean like whilst I'm begging you to shut up?"

He chuckles lowly. "Among other things."

"Are 'other things' not what you had in mind when you asked me to come back with you?"

"Begged is more like it, but again, my answer is that I don't know." His hand temporarily leaves my waist to push a curl away from my face before returning. "I never seem to be sure of anything where you're concerned. I think one thing and then it ends up being something completely different."

I smile softly. "I could say the same for you."

He smiles back so softly, a softness that you wouldn't expect to be on someone who comes across so hard and prickly, and yet it suits him perfectly, almost as if for the first time I'm looking at the real August Finch.

I find myself tracing the harsh lines of his face, the jaggedness of his jawline and the sharpness of his cheekbones.

I watch those dark brown eyes as they shine with a hundred different emotions, none of which I'm able to decipher. I like it that way, though. I admire that August Finch will forever remain an enigma to me and everyone around him.

"Stay with me tonight," he says, his thumb rubbing circles on my hip. When he sees my hesitation, he adds, "There will be no pressure on you to do anything, Wren. I just want to spend the night with you beside me."

I huff out a laugh. "This is so surreal."

He rubs his eyes as he chuckles. "You're telling me."

He stands to his full height, holding out a hand for me to take. I do and he leads me down the hallway to the room which I woke up in just the other week.

Which reminds me...

"What was I doing in your bedroom the other week? So much happened that day I forgot to ask."

He glances back at me over his shoulder. "You mean when you made me burn myself?"

"No idea what you're talking about, but yeah."

"Is that a joke?" he asks, genuinely confused.

"Yes, it's a joke."

"Right," he mumbles. We enter his bedroom and I watch him as he slumps down onto the bed. "The storm was too strong for you to drive home. It was the only option."

"And where did you sleep that night?"

He shrugs. "The spare room."

"Why not put me in there?" I ask, moving closer to him.

He shrugs again, looking somewhat uncomfortable.

I think I know why. I think I know the reason without him vocalizing it. I'm pretty sure that he wanted me to be comfortable, and Gus in his own caring way thought that in order to do so, I needed to be placed where he himself felt comfortable. In my own house, my spare room consists of a dust-covered mattress and some boxes of stuff that Adam forgot to take with him. When Oakleigh stays over—usually after several glasses of wine—she sleeps in my bed with me.

I take a seat beside him but he doesn't look over. He looks down at his hand and watches it as it plays with a loose piece of thread on his jeans.

"Do you have a shirt I can borrow?" I ask.

He nods once, moving over to the dresser and pulling one out.

"Do you want me to give you some privacy?" he asks as he hands it over.

"Do you want to give me some privacy?" I ask with a smirk.

"That's a complicated question, sweetheart."

I stand and turn around, quickly pulling my top up over my head before I have the chance to chicken out. I unbutton my jeans and shuffle them down past my hips and I smile to myself when I hear Gus's breath hitch. I challenge myself, deciding to take it one step further and unclip the clasp of my bra, letting it fall to the ground.

"Are you trying to kill me, sweetheart?"

"What is it that'll kill you, exactly—the lack of clothes, or the fact that my clothes are on the floor?"

"Both," he snarls.

My laugh floats around the room as I slowly reach for the shirt, giving Gus as much time as possible to ogle and stare at my bare back, letting him imagine what else I must be hiding from him.

I'm so focused on my actions that I haven't even realized he's moved closer, so close that I can feel his warm breath on the back of my neck. I freeze, waiting to see what it is that he'll do.

"What happened?" he asks, lightly tracing a finger down the scar behind my right shoulder.

"My own fault," I breathe. "I slipped in the shower and the edge of it dug in and cut me pretty bad. It was years ago."

His fingers slide down, taking his sweet time and sending endless shivers up and down my spine. My breathing shortens, moving in and out in rapid spurts. His hands are rough and they cause a delicious amount of friction as they travel down my spine.

"You have another one," he murmurs, almost as if he's talking to himself.

I twist round. "Another one?"

"Beauty spot."

I pull the shirt over my head, letting it fall over my body and shield me from his intensity.

I turn myself around completely. "What is it that has you so obsessed with them?"

He stares at the one above my lip. "You don't like them. At least, I think you don't."

"So?"

"So you *should* like it. There's a less than one percent chance of you having it. I know what it's like to have something *that* rare and hate it at times. Did you know that there is only a one point seven percent chance of someone being born with Autism? Sometimes when people decide to use the word 'disorder', I end up agreeing with them because I despise being different. I still hate that I get overstimulated by the tiniest things, or that sometimes I feel like such a walking, talking contradiction. I feel like a freak. I don't want you feeling like that."

My heart hurts for him. I can't imagine feeling so uneasy in your own skin to the point that you're hyper-fixated on your differences. Living in a town where you feel excluded purely because the way you function is different to those around you.

"That can't be easy."

He shrugs, trying to appear like it doesn't bug him nearly as much as I think.

I hop into Gus's bed and watch him expectantly, waiting for him to join me. He smiles shyly before unbuckling his belt, freeing it from the loops of his jeans with one swift pull.

If he wants nothing to happen tonight, he seriously needs to stop it with the hot guy moves.

When he pulls off his shirt, I can see the tattoos that I caught a glimpse of not too long ago. I tilt my head as I admire the view—the smooth, tanned skin stretched over broad, muscular shoulders and defined abs. I can see the effect that his broken arm has had on his physique. It's softened the muscles a little since I saw him shirtless last, lessened the definition in a way that makes me want him even more. It reminds me that August Finch is human.

I realize now that if we were to take part in any ... carnal activities, I'm not sure how Gus would manage with his broken arm. Various positions would be out of the equation, but I suppose it would give me a chance to do something that

I've always wanted to do. Adam was never one for allowing a woman to take the lead, always afraid that it said more about his masculinity than his personality did. If Gus and I were to take that final step, were we to let that thin thread snap, would he allow me to take control of the situation, or would he be like Adam—old-fashioned and controversial?

I must have truly been in my own world, because all of a sudden, the bed shifts as Gus climbs in, wearing nothing more than a pair of boxer briefs. My tongue runs across my bottom lip as I imagine what he could possibly be hiding underneath his underwear.

I lie down, snuggling under the covers as I face Gus who does the same.

I've never felt such a contradicting mixture of ease and consternation before. I have this overwhelming urge to make sure that I am exactly what Gus needs in this moment and each moment after that I find myself in his presence. Yet, at the same time, I've also never found myself so comfortable just being myself—being both kind Wren and fiery Wren—without feeling insecure.

With any guys you dated, did you never get that feeling? That intense need to hide all the things that made you insecure so that he'd see only the best in you?

Is this what Bash was talking about?

"You look deep in thought," Gus announces.

"Can I ask you something?"

"Of course you can."

I take a deep breath to try and ready my nerves.

"Have you ever been in love?"

225

Chapter Twenty-Eight

GUS

The question has me tensing.

Feelings aren't necessarily a topic of conversation that I strive to have.

"I thought I was once," I begin cautiously. "I soon realized that it wasn't love. It was more like lust mixed with a general liking for the person."

"That isn't love in your opinion?"

I shake my head as best I can whilst lying down. "Not the way my mom used to describe it. She used to say that it was something a lot deeper than that." I smile as I remember the kind eyes and the soft smiles of my mother.

"She said that I'll know when I love someone if I'm struggling."

She looks at me, confused, and I chuckle softly.

"I know, but she knew me better than anyone. She used to say that love isn't about statistics and facts, so I'll know when

I'm in love because I'll struggle with how much I need to feel it and let it happen."

Wren snuggles in further as she listens intently.

"One day, this girl came to town. Her name was Erica." Wren's eyes widen as if she's heard the name before, and it doesn't surprise me. This town loves to stick its nose where it doesn't belong. "We met at the Locke and we got along easily enough. Unfortunately, this was back when I used to be naive enough to think that everyone was as kind as my mother was. We hooked up for a while, I even took her on a date or two and we generally just got along really well."

"So, what happened?" she asks, squirming as if she's preparing herself for the answer.

"Her mom met my dad and they decided to start dating instead."

Wren's eyes widen. "You're kidding."

"I wish I was." My chest tightens as I picture the day my dick dad told me that he and Melina were running off to get married. "They dated for all of two days before my dad told me that they were running off to Vegas to get married. Erica and I obviously couldn't continue with what we were doing and to be honest, I was okay with that. I don't think I would have made a good partner at the time anyway. Especially not when my dad merely sent out a mass text to let us know that he wouldn't be returning, and would instead be moving to California. Apparently, his new wife decided that she wasn't actually a fan of small towns and my father was all too happy to drop everything and leave his family behind at a moment's notice."

Wren looks devastated. Her hand comes up to my arm, but

she's careful to not put too much pressure on it. "I can't imagine what that felt like."

I avoid her sympathetic gaze. "My father and I never got along anyway, so it never bothered me in the way that it probably should have. I wasn't mad that he left me, I was mad that he left everyone else. My whole family, the memories that my mother left behind, all of it. He just dropped it like it never held any meaning to him. That's what had me wanting to fly to California and kick his ass until he was begging me to stop. Bash retreated into himself and Sam became more bitter and resentful than usual, and I joined him. The whole town realized that I was the only one available to take over the farm since Bash wasn't living here at the time and Sam already had a job, and they all instantly decided that I would forever be an inconvenience to their way of life. At least when my father was here, there was someone to 'keep me on track'."

"Keep you on track?"

"The Autism," I say simply. "It doesn't suit their way of life. I need things done in a certain way, and now that my father isn't around, there's no one here to make sure it's done their way instead of mine. Everyone assumes that I laid everyone off because I wanted to do it all myself as if I have some kind of hero complex. Not that I've necessarily bothered to tell them that it's for financial reasons. This whole town hears the word 'disorder' and assumes it means the same as 'stupid' or 'useless'."

"And what does the word mean to you?"

I think on it for a minute. No one has ever asked me this question before. I'm not entirely sure how to go about it.

After a minute, I go with, "To me, 'disorder' is the same as

229

'different'. Even if I see myself as a bit of a freak sometimes, it doesn't mean I'm an idiot or that I'm less than everyone else. No one with Autism is."

Soft fingers lightly trace their way down my arm, leaving a tingling sensation wherever they pass. When they meet my hand, they intertwine with my own until Wren's hand is safely encased in mine.

"I want to know what it's like for you," she declares, her expression set by determination. "Autism is different for everyone, isn't it? I want to know what specific traits you have, what difficulties you experience, what needs you have."

"Why are you so desperate to know?" No one except Bash and Sam have ever really taken an interest like this before. It's hard to imagine someone wanting to take the time to better understand how I differ from them.

"Because I want to understand you. I want to see the world through your eyes."

I'm not sure how to take that. It has been a long time since anyone made the effort to try and envision the way I see the world, to see why I'm so misunderstood, by understanding the misconception.

"What do you want to know? Vague questions throw me off at times, so be specific."

She thinks on it for a minute and I spend that time watching her bottom lip curl in until it's trapped between her teeth. She shuffles closer and the smell of vanilla wafts over to me. I lose all sense and take a deep breath in.

"Do you ever feel like you get overlooked because your Autism isn't like what people stereotypically think it is?"

I chuckle. "Moving past the easy questions already, huh?

No 'Gus, is it true that Autistics hate bright lights and loud sounds?' or 'Is it true you have to do everything by a certain time?'"

She hides behind her hand whilst she giggles and I smile down at the happiness that I caused. "Sorry, I did start off a bit hot and heavy. I just thought that the basic questions are ones that you would have been asked all the time."

"You'd think so, wouldn't you? But I've never particularly been this town's favorite. They don't care enough to ask any questions."

She pushes herself up until she's leaning on her elbow. Brown curls flow around her as her eyes glint with uncontrollable curiosity and now I'm thinking that she's gorgeous for an entirely different reason. She's become the most beautiful person I know for the fact that she genuinely cares about others. She's learning about me with a genuine interest that I've only ever seen on my mother's and brothers' faces.

When my mom realized that I hated something, or that something made me uncomfortable or overstimulated, she would sit me down and ask me to explain it to her, never saying a word until I was finished, even if my explanation took hours. There was never a need to change who I was, never a need to act like I was less than. Before she passed, I never knew that the word "disorder" had such a negative connotation attached to it. She used to use the word with such integrity and respect that until I found myself with only the father who saw his son as a freak, I didn't know that the word meant something completely different to closed-minded people.

I haven't answered her question.

"I do." When I see her confused expression, I elaborate. "Feel overlooked. I think because I'm able to be independent and hold a conversation that people think it was a misdiagnosis. They forget that it's a spectrum that can range from self-sufficient to fully dependent on another."

"Are you dependent on anyone else for anything?"

"No," I answer. "My mother used to help me with a lot of stuff. Holding my hand when I had to go somewhere that would overstimulate me and stuff like that, but when she died, I made sure to do it all myself. For her."

For my mom, I would have done anything. For the woman who had so much unconditional love to give to everyone around her, I would have done anything she asked of me.

Wren loves unconditionally.

As I look at her, as I watch the kindness and anxiety swimming around in her eyes, I know that no matter how many times I argue with this woman and no matter how much we want to act as if we hate each other, one thing I know for sure is that I will always love to hate her more than I actually detest Wren Southwick.

Chapter Twenty-Nine

WREN

"**T**each me how to harvest. I want to help."

Bash jumps, spinning around so quickly that he almost drops the pumpkin in his hands.

After dropping off the usual coffees for the day, for which Sam tried multiple times to slip a fifty into my pocket, I decided to see how Bash was getting on with the harvest. I've spent so much time focusing on how Gus is, that I never took the time to check up on his big brother. Bash is under a ton of stress, too, especially now that it's up to him to harvest the rest of the pumpkins. I can see that it has Gus feeling down, feeling useless because he can't help to do the physical jobs that this season has to offer. When he was on bed rest, I caught him twice trying to slip out the house to go and harvest whilst Bash was on a lunch break. I thought it was both sweet and slightly pathetic, mostly because he's a grown man who was trying to sneak out his own house.

I've learned that Bash isn't one to complain. He gets on with what he has to do and doesn't say anything about it. I think there's a lot more to Sebastian than meets the eye, but I also think that he's just as stubborn as his brother and so he won't show any of it unless he deems it absolutely necessary.

After carefully placing the harvested pumpkin into the crate, he turns to me with a strained smile. "You scared the crap out of me, Wren."

"Sorry," I apologize. "I didn't know I was so light-footed."

"You weigh all of eighty pounds, of course you're light on your feet."

"Not accurate, but I appreciate you purposefully guessing under to save your skin." I laugh.

He gives the field a once-over. "You mentioned something about teaching you to harvest?"

"Yeah, I really want to help you. Gus can't assist at the moment and even though I wouldn't be nearly as fast as you guys, it's got to help at least a little, right?"

He looks apprehensive as he scratches the back of his neck. "I don't know, Wren. It's a lot of heavy lifting. If anything happened to you, not only would I never forgive myself, but I also wouldn't need to because Gus would murder me."

"I promise I'll take it easy, Bash. I'll only pick up the ones that I can handle. Like I said to your brother, I'm stronger than I look."

He still looks hesitant, green eyes bouncing around, looking everywhere but at me.

"Please?" I push.

He groans quietly, and I hear the multiple expletives he

mumbles under his breath before he grinds out a reluctant, "Fine."

I squeal as I throw myself at him, arms wrapping around lean shoulders. "Thank you, thank you, thank you!"

"It's me who should be thanking you," he laughs out.

"I just want to be as helpful as I can. You guys are literally saving my ass with the barn."

He gestures for me to follow him, leading us to the end of the row he's currently on. He stops just before the last pumpkin, stooping down in front of a medium-sized bright orange one. He motions towards the pumpkin.

"Try and lift it."

I take a deep breath, realizing that maybe doing this in knee-high Timberland boots may not have been the best idea. I seriously need to invest in some normal-length boots.

I squat down and position my hands underneath the pumpkin, dirt lodging itself underneath my nails. Making sure to use my legs, not my back, I stand up and bring the squash closer to my torso. It's heavy, but nothing I can't handle, especially if there's a crate next to me.

Bash assesses me, checking to see if my face gives away my struggle to hold onto the pumpkin. Satisfied that I'm not lifting more than I can handle, he motions for me to put it back down.

"Okay, fine, but if you come across any bigger than that, you leave them alone. Got it?"

I salute him. "Sir, yes, sir."

He shakes his head with a smile.

"I'll get in on this."

We both turn to see Finn making his way towards us.

"You want to help, too?" I ask.

"Of course. The barn can handle one man less now that the exterior is complete. Put me to work, boss."

Bash tries his best to hide the relief on his face, but I see it. It can't be easy the pressure that both he and his brother are under. They are under the scrutiny of the entire town, and I know that he can feel it almost as much as Gus does.

He spends the next hour teaching both of us where to cut when harvesting the pumpkin and where to take it once we're done. Finn immediately gets to work, and thanks to his rigid workout routine and his job in construction, it seems to be an easy task for him. He's barely breaking a sweat by the time he's finished his first batch, and by the time he's done that, I've only completed a quarter of mine.

Okay, so I may not be all that much help.

A nudge on the back of my neck has me jumping, but I instantly calm down when I see Mori behind me.

"Hey, girl." I rub up and down her snout, more comfortable with her now than I was the first time I met her. Heat licks my spine when I remember the way that Gus showed me exactly how to do this, his firm body flush against mine even when it didn't need to be. I remember the way his smile almost broke me, so mischievous, but so comforting to look at. The way he asked me if he made me nervous, and the way the word "yes" sat on my tongue, tasting like the spice that hits you when you eat a pepper.

Mori snickers beside me and I realize I must have zoned out. Shaking my head, I reach down for the next pumpkin that is within my weight limit. Unfortunately, there haven't been many that I can help to harvest because the size of these pumpkins is ridiculous. I now understand why Bash and Gus are so physically fit, how could you not be when you need to lift double your body weight?

Mori's head moves to the side as if she's heard something close by, and when I look in the same direction, I see him.

The shock on his face is evident, his body frozen in place by the sight of me working the fields with his brother and mine. It's crazy when you think about how our families have blended together so seamlessly. My brother now hangs out with Sam and Bash without me even knowing and I love it. I love that my brother has found his people.

But it scares me knowing that I feel like I've found mine, too. But not people … just one particular person.

It's scary to admit that the man I'm looking at right now is someone I could actually grow to like … is someone I *have* grown to like. A crush on August Finch is not something that I could have ever anticipated. And yet, as he looks at me across the field as if I'm the only one around for miles, and as if he wants nothing more than to have me all to himself like a man at a buffet, I know for a fact that I'm hopelessly attracted to him.

When we kissed, I lost all my breath. When he touched my waist, I felt like my entire body was on fire. And when I woke up beside him, I felt fear—fear for the way my heart raced as I felt his arm wrapped around me and for the way I found myself never wanting to leave.

As he stands there watching me, I find myself hoping that he'll wrap his arm around me and tell me that he missed me. This morning, his coffee ended up being placed on a slightly clearer desk than usual that stood in the middle of an empty office, and I wondered if he was avoiding me almost as much as I'm avoiding him.

I want him. I do, truly. But the thought of letting myself become vulnerable with another man after Adam causes a wave of anxiety so intense that I struggle to even think about coming back to Goldleaf Farm. I'm overcome with the urge to run and never look back, because it's one thing knowing that if I were to give my heart to Gus, he could break it just like Adam did, but it's another thing knowing that if he were to do so, it would hurt a million times more.

The feelings I have for Gus usurp anything I thought I ever felt for Adam. My ex offered me a false sense of security, making me feel I was loved enough to continue my life with him by my side. But in reality, he made me feel just safe and loved enough to make me feel as if I needed him instead of wanted him.

When Gus walks over to Bash and starts a heated conversation that is clearly about me, based off of the occasional glance thrown my way, I wonder if Gus would ever do that; if he would ever purposefully make a woman feel as if their life would be meaningless without him in it, making her feel obliged to do anything and everything for him.

Judging by the way Gus's free arm gesticulates, I'm going to guess that he's not all too pleased to see me working the field, and from the way Bash doesn't hesitate to push back, I'm going to assume he's sticking up for my decision. He whispers something to his younger brother, and Gus looks around as if for the first time he's noticed that Finn is helping out as well. After an intense stare in my direction, I can see him visibly back down, shoulders slumping forward as he nods.

Disappointment feels prickly as it slides down my throat when I watch him turn away back to the office, despite me not wanting to speak to him just yet. I have no idea what I would say to him.

Hey, August. I know we never really spoke about the other night, but I'm here to tell you that I would really love to repeat it, and maybe even add in a couple hours of bumping uglies!

Yeah, that would go down beautifully. He'd probably spend five minutes asking me to explain the meaning behind the phrase "bumping uglies".

He doesn't look back as he stalks towards his office. Defeat sits heavy on my chest, because as selfish as it sounds, even though I want space from Gus, I was really hoping he wouldn't want it from me.

Chapter Thirty

GUS

My frustration doubles when I check my watch for the seventh time this morning.

All it takes is one fleeting thought of hazel eyes and a warm smile and I find myself checking the clock with a look of contempt. Trying to work is futile, a clear head is nothing more than a dream. I'm on the verge of having a bald spot with the way I'm dragging my fingers through my hair.

"Should I be worried that the stack of papers in front of you hasn't gone down in the last four hours?"

I don't waste my time acknowledging my brother's presence, even though it surprises me. Sam avoids this office like the plague since it serves as a constant memory of the man who sat in it before I did.

I feel feverish when I ask, "Have you seen Wren today?"

Where I expect a smirk, I instead find a frown. "You didn't hear?"

"Hear what?"

I sit up straight once I see him squirm, his eyes avoiding me.

"Sam," I say lowly. "Did I hear what?"

His face scrunches up as he exhales. "It's not a big deal, I just know that you're going to turn it into one. She called and said she's sick, that's all. There was some kind of incident today in town and she had to go home. She said it's to do with her being unwell."

Everything around me slows and Sam's voice sounds further and further away as the worry sets in. Millions of questions flood my mind as I jump from my seat, grabbing my jacket and car keys before pushing past my brother.

I knew it. I knew something was wrong the moment it passed nine this morning and Wren's mischievous smile wasn't brightening up my office.

At first I had spent the majority of time wondering if maybe it was what we did three nights ago. If perhaps the idea of becoming a little bit more than business partners and enemies had shaken her ... or worse, disgusted her.

I had been pretty vulnerable, almost pathetically so. The alcohol still had some effect on me even though I had no longer felt its curling smoke around my blood. A part of me wanted to think it was the puppet strings that were controlling my words, letting them easily dance out of my mouth. I had assumed when I didn't hear from her after she went home that she just maybe needed time. What the actual fuck happened?

My foot is almost floored as I drive recklessly over to the Sweet Cinnamon Café. I sloppily park outside, storming through the doors and easily ignoring everyone who stares at me as if I've lost my mind—which I have.

When Jamie sees me storming over, he begins backing up, hands up in surrender.

"No, man, come on. Last time you dragged me out of here, you ruined my sweater and the one I'm wearing now is—"

"What the fuck happened?"

"With what?"

"Jamie, don't act stupid. You know everything in this town. Tell me what happened to her."

"Dude, nothing happened to her!"

"Then why is Sam telling me there's something wrong with her stomach?"

Jamie sighs in relief, but still keeps his guard up. "Gus, she's on her period. She's fine. She just suffers from really bad cramps."

Oh.

I let Jamie go, pacing across the length of the café with no concern for those who are watching me right now. I don't even know what I thought had happened. Ideas have been bouncing around my head like a ping pong ball since this morning, and each makes sense less than the one before.

Period pains are the least of my problems, and yet my body refuses to relax, the idea of Wren in any kind of distress not sitting right with me. I wish she had told me. I could have been there for her. I could have helped her by…

Hold on.

"How the hell do you help a woman when they're going through that?"

"Do I look as if I'd have been with enough women to know?" Jamie asks.

"You look like you know enough women to know," I retort.

"Touché."

"I just need to know how to help her."

Usually, when there's a problem involving somebody else, I struggle. I can never think of a way to console someone when they're hurt or angry or sad. How are you supposed to know what one person needs when it all depends on who they are as a person? Does a kind person need that same kindness in return? What does that kindness look like—space? A hug? A pep talk? I've always been especially shit at those.

I want to be the kind of person that Wren needs, however that might look to her. If she needs space, it'll probably kill me but I'll move to the next goddamn town if that's what it takes. If she needs a hug, I'll never let go unless I need to use the bathroom. If she needs a pep talk, I'll ask someone to teach me how. Whatever she needs, I will be.

We can pretend to hate one another as much as we want, but for me, it's more like some twisted sort of foreplay that gets both of us riled up enough to temporarily forget that hot-blooded attraction that's been there since the moment I watched her chastise my goat.

It's not just those gorgeous hazel eyes, the softness of her face, or the way her smile makes something in my chest jump every time she directs it at me. It's not just how she is the most stubborn woman I've ever met. It's not just that she is the first person in a while to treat me like I deserve the same amount of special treatment as some regular old Joe on the block. No, it's the fact that she is so effortlessly herself, even when she's trying not to be. It's the fact that she is a whirling tornado of both chaos and order. She's Wren, and it's the fact I care about her enough to want that to be all she'll ever be.

The fact that I like her enough to want that to be all she'll ever be.

I grab him by the back of the jumper, ignoring his protests, and dump him into one of the chairs. The entire café's eyes are on us, and for once, I'm glad. Let them stare. Let them see what I become when someone I care about is hurt.

"Tell me everything. Now."

WREN

I ignore the knock at my door, instead curling up further into my duvet. The tears dried up a couple of hours ago, but that sensitivity to both questions and thoughts about today still remains.

The knock sounds again and I once again ignore it.

"Wren!"

I bolt upright when Gus's voice reaches my ears, quiet yet desperate.

"Wren, are you in there?"

Reluctantly, I wrap my blanket tighter as I waddle my way from the living room over to the front door.

He's holding a cup from the café, the edges buckling slightly from his tight grip. A cowboy hat sits atop wild brown hair and gone is his plaid shirt, replaced by an aging brown leather jacket. He uses the edge of the cup to push his glasses back up his nose. If he wasn't currently standing in front of me looking as if he just lost Cliff, I would take a second to truly appreciate the sight in front of me.

"Hi," I mumble.

"Hi," he replies, completely avoiding my eyeline.

"What are you doing here?"

He looks so uncomfortable, shifting from one foot to another and adjusting his grip on the coffee cup. He motions for me to take the cup from him. Hesitantly, I take it. I'm surprised that the cup is really cold, but also full, so cold you'd think he'd been standing outside with it for hours, not merely driven it over from two towns away.

I try and keep my expression neutral so as not to offend. "Thank you."

He rubs at the back of his neck just as a blush makes its way up from under his jacket. "I, um … I didn't know your order, and when Lola started to make my usual I just didn't say anything."

I hide my smile in my blanket. "That's sweet. How come you've decided to treat me?"

He shrugs. "Every time you come to the farm you bring coffee. This time I was coming to you, so I brought coffee."

"Huh," I whisper wistfully. "Thank you. Although, I should chastise you for bringing it after nine a.m."

He nods once and next thing I know, we find ourselves cloaked in an awkward silence. It's a strange instance that seems to happen when we can't find a reason to argue with one another. It's become such a norm for us to either yell, or stare at one another in a way that shows we have no idea whether we will yell or kiss … again.

I sheepishly move out of the way and motion for him to come in.

He steps inside, immediately taking off his boots and neatly placing them by the door. I've spent this entire time coming to see him in Eaglewood that it's strange to see him here, in my house in Beckford. He looks so out of place—a farmer in a lawyer's town.

"How are you?" he asks.

"I'm okay," I answer, heading back to the couch.

"Why didn't you tell me that you weren't coming today?" he pushes.

"I didn't know I needed to tell you everything," I snap.

A frown mars his forehead as he looks at me, confused. "Are you mad at me?"

"No."

"Well, you sound mad."

"I said I'm not, August."

"Can you tell that to your tone because it seems to be a little confused."

"I'm not—" I stop myself when I hear my raised voice. I swallow a sigh and bury myself deeper into my blanket.

I've been avoiding everybody ever since the incident this morning, the embarrassment causing too much restriction in my chest for me to handle people's pitiful or judgmental stares. Since Gus is the first person I've seen since, I suppose my mind is using him as a substitute for the person I really want to yell at. Myself.

I take a deep breath and soften my voice. "I'm sorry, Gus. I really am not mad at you. I suppose I just needed to get rid of all my pent-up energy."

There's a pause, during which time he looks at me with a kind of understanding that I've never seen on his face before.

"Is that what you need from me?"

"What?" I ask.

He takes a seat beside me, a warm hand landing on my thigh. "Is that what you need from me? To be an outlet for you to get out your frustration?"

"God, no." I turn towards him. "August, no one should ever need that from you. It was wrong of me to do that and I hope no one else ever does."

He shrugs even though he looks almost determined to do it, to be my own personal punching bag until I feel all of my negative energy has depleted.

"Tell me what you need and I'll do it."

Never would I have thought that this is where August Finch and I would end up after just a few short weeks. I never thought that I would be here feeling relief that Gus decided to come and check on me, that he is here offering to help me in the way that I need the help. It's hard to believe that we've gone from arguing non-stop to me harboring genuine feelings for the man. Feelings that I can't act on for reasons that his presence today has cemented.

It's not safe. Dating isn't safe, being vulnerable isn't safe … loving isn't safe. It's at a point where even six months later, I'm paying the price for loving a man who only ever cared about himself.

I'm tired.

Defeated, I look up at Gus, a thick wave of brown hair falling into his eyes, nose scrunched up in such an adorable way that it hurts my heart to know that I must make him off-limits.

Maybe he can be off-limits starting from tomorrow.

"Can you stay?" I ask so softly that it's almost a whisper, but it's enough to break the suffocating silence that threatened to end me if I didn't shatter it completely.

His hand moves from his thigh to grab my hand and he laces his fingers with mine. The warmth from his hand instantly brings me a sliver of calm that's been missing from my life for a long time. Even as his thumb begins to trace small circles against the back of my hand, I find my anger and embarrassment from today begin to drain.

"I'm not going anywhere," he says when his gaze meets mine.

My body instantly relaxes knowing that I'll have him by my side for another night since it's been craving the feel of being wrapped in his arms since the last time. The nights that I've had to sleep alone have been strangely empty—full of tossing, turning and incomplete conversations that were left drifting around the stale air of my bedroom.

I stand from the couch, allowing the blanket to fall from my shoulders. The way he watches me when it hits the ground would make you think I've just stripped myself of every layer of clothing, which isn't much in the first place considering I'm only in pajama shorts and a crop top. I never let my house get cold.

The dark, hard gaze of a man on the edge of losing control is what welcomes me as I hold out my hand to him. His hand slides against mine and I slowly lead him towards my bedroom, the air around us shifting with every step.

His hat is gone, which is a good thing, because if it stayed on for much longer, I would have to ask him to do some very unsavory things to me with the hat on.

The soft greens of my bedroom are comforting, but not whilst the rest of the room is the chaotic mess that greets us as we enter—clothes tossed all over the floor from this morning, my make-up taking up half of the bed, and my multitude of empty glasses that never seemed to tag along for the journey from my bedroom to the kitchen.

"Let me clean this up," I offer as I hurriedly begin packing my make-up back into its bag.

"Wren."

I hastily pick up the clothes from the floor, not even bothering to check if they're clean or not before dumping them into the laundry hamper.

"Wren."

I need to clean up the bedside table on his side, too. What if he wants to put his phone down or something?

"Sweetheart, stop."

Large hands hold me in place before I can move towards the table. I try and move anyway, but when I hear Gus groan, I freeze.

Hang on, there's two hands on me. Two.

"Where's your sling?" I ask.

The wince is still clear on his face. "I left it at the office."

"But your shoulder and your arm aren't healed yet, Gus." I fret as I try to move Gus's hand so he can lower his arm, but he is—as usual—as stubborn as an ox and refuses.

"Sweetheart," he repeats and I huff like a child before looking up at him. One hand moves until it's gently cupping my chin. "I know I'm anal about everything being in its place, but I can deal with a little mess for a few hours, you know. I'm not going to freak out … yet."

He truly is a one-of-a-kind man—always honest no matter what. He's trying to be gentle whilst being honest. A gentle giant.

"Would you like to talk about what happened?"

My head shakes before he even finishes his sentence. "I don't want to."

"Then I won't force you."

Without another word, he brushes past, stripping out of his clothes as if he's just come from a long day at work.

"Wait."

He pauses in the middle of lifting his shirt.

"I don't want to go to bed just yet."

He lowers his shirt. "Then what would you like to do instead?"

"I don't know." Frustrated, I begin pacing the length of my room, my energy so frantic that even Gus moves out of the way to take a seat on the bed. "I just have all of this pent-up energy. I can't sleep whilst I'm like this."

He's watching me again, analyzing every move I make and assessing its meaning. Before, it used to intimidate me, but now I actually find it quite calming. It's comforting to know that someone cares the way Gus does. He's intense, sure, but that's only because his level of care is so high that he will do anything and everything to ensure that those he loves are safe.

Not that he loves me.

Slapping a hand onto his thigh, he stands, towering over me. "Then get into the truck."

"I'm sorry?"

He takes a step closer and the smell of pumpkins surrounds me, making me feel strangely at home. Funny how being in my own house doesn't make me feel this way.

"We're going for a drive. You can tell me what happened, and then…"

"And then what?" I ask.

He leans down, and the mischief in his eyes along with the devilry in his smirk sends my heart racing.

"Then the fun begins."

Chapter Thirty-One

WREN

Earlier Today

The longer I've been coming to Eaglewood and Goldleaf Farm, the longer I stay during the day. Yesterday, after helping Bash with the harvest, I met up with Jamie and Oakleigh and we spent some time in the barn imagining the potential for her party. Three of us laid on the newly laid barn floor, staring up and picturing hay bales, cocktails and black lace. Oh ... and pumpkins, of course.

The thought of them is now permanently linked to brown eyes, matching hair and a headstrong personality. Gus takes over more and more of my thoughts each day and it scares me that a part of me actually wants to let him into my life in a way that supersedes business partners.

Now, as I make my down the street to the Sweet Cinnamon Café by myself, I take a deep breath and let the feeling of contentment fill my chest and zip through my blood. This town feels more and more like home and I chastise myself for spending so much time in a house that's felt empty to me since the day I bought it purely because I once thought I loved a man enough to live within it with him.

Here, the trees along the sidewalk shelter me from my fear, the short buildings that line the street emphasize my relief, and the smell of fresh air that reminds me of my freedom. If I'm being honest, I don't think there is anything that could ruin my day today.

"Have you no decorum, girl?"

I turn to find Sandra behind me, her cane clicking against the paved walkway as she storms over to me. She looks extremely pissed off.

"Excuse me?" I ask, backing up even though she continues to come closer.

"Have you no sense of good personal hygiene?"

"I have no idea what you're talking about."

"I knew you were bad news. I can always tell when there's something to dislike about new people."

"Okay, let's just clam down—"

"Wren!" Lori runs up to me, concern written all over her face, eyes twinkling behind her round glasses. As she reaches me, she rips off her cardigan and wraps it around my waist despite my protests. "Wren, you've leaked."

My blood runs cold.

This cannot be happening to me. This has to be some kind of infernal nightmare, some hideous trick of fate that has decided to give me a reason to fear coming to this town. Neither of us speak, not when I can see the sympathy clear as day in Lori's eyes, not when Sandra's disgust is right there in the set of her shoulders.

"I had no idea, oh my God. I must have forgotten to take my pill the past few days."

"Probably because you're too busy spending an unhealthy amount of time with August Finch of all people," Sandra scoffs, as if the thought of anyone wanting to spend time with Gus to be absolutely preposterous.

"Where is your heart?" Lori asks Sandra. "I would have thought that as a woman, you would have more empathy towards other women when they experience this kind of problem. You're chastising her as if this is her fault. That's not nice, Sandra. Not at all."

A hand on my shoulder jolts me out of my daze, and Simone stands behind me, a comforting smile that extends everywhere from her cheeks to her neck.

"Come on, dear, I have some clothes that may fit you in the back of my shop."

Half of the town is on the street, watching the scene unfold. I have no idea how long they've all been standing there. The street was almost empty when I started walking. Sam stands a little ways off ahead of me, brown hair such a similar shade of brown to his brother's that my heart aches.

The shame floods in soon after, icing the fire that Gus had caused within me. The tears flow from my face one by one, falling onto my green scarf and immediately getting absorbed by the fibers.

Thankfully, Simone and Lori support me, hold me up just as women should do for each other in times such as these. They bring me to Flora and Flowers, where Simone hands me a pair of jeans that fit me perfectly, and Lori pulls a pad out of her bag.

If I hadn't known it then, I would have known now, because almost as soon as I put the pad on, the pain hits me like a truck going seventy miles an hour. The tightening of my stomach and the sharp pain that I feel further down is a mixture that I, and so many other women, know all too well, and yet my advanced knowledge of it can never seem to prepare me for when it hits. It never helps me to build up an immunity towards the aches and pains of womanhood.

I don't allow Simone and Lori to coddle me for too long before I thank them and rush to my car without a second glance towards the two people whose support I'm so thankful for.

As I walk away, heart heavy and mind blank, I think about how I can't stand that all I want right now is a tall farmer to wrap me up and hold me tight without so much as a second thought.

Chapter Thirty-Two

GUS

I'm not even sure what there is for me to say. How do you even begin to find the words to console someone when you know the shame they feel will erase anything you say?

Even as I indicate left and head back towards Eaglewood with Wren beside me, there's a pressure to get it right the first time round, to find the exact words that will make her feel better. When I glance over every now and again and see that very hurt reflected in those big brown eyes, it makes me want to find Sandra and see how it looks in hers.

Wren has been quiet ever since her explanation ended. She's staring out the window in contemplation, probably wondering what it is she did to deserve such treatment. The answer is nothing.

Should I tell her that, though, or is it something she already knows regardless of whether or not she questions herself?

"Penny for your thoughts?" I ask.

She coughs out a laugh. "You struggle to understand the point of 'eager beaver', but 'penny for your thoughts' is fine?"

"That's because the phrase makes sense when you look at its history. Your phrase rhymes. You know, it's actually quite interesting, the phrase 'penny for your thoughts' is seen being used by Sir Thomas More in his works from fifteen thirty-fi—" If I wasn't driving, I would look over to give her an annoyed glare. "Okay, I see what you did there."

I don't look over to see her smile, but I can feel it ... somehow. It's as if air in the car is lighter, easier to breathe. That's the effect one smile from Wren Southwick has on not just me, but the world. All the more reason to want to beat that prick to a pulp for hurting her.

"When I'm in a better mood, you'll have to tell me more about the phrase. It really did sound interesting."

"I will," I promise, making a mental note in my head to do so when the timing is better.

"You still haven't said where we're going," she reminds me.

"You'll see."

"That's all I get?"

"That's all you get," I confirm.

She hums in acknowledgment, and I continue driving towards the farm. There's something there she should see. Besides, even if that wasn't where I was taking her, I really should at the very least run back and grab my sling. My shoulder feels as if it's hanging on by a thread, the pain becoming a bit harder to ignore.

When Sam told me about Wren, the adrenaline in my veins burned like fire. It zipped its way around my body faster than a soundwave and I leaped into action without thinking. There was no pain, no discomfort, just a dying need to know what happened to Wren and to make sure that she was okay.

Now, however, the adrenaline has dissipated, leaving behind an ache in my joints and a lingering pain down the entire arm. It's a good thing I don't drive a stick because there is no way I was using my other arm for this.

We finally make it to Eaglewood and I can swear I've just heard Wren breathe out a sigh of relief, as if she's finally returned home. She may have had a stressful day here, but maybe deep down she believes that this tiny town feels more like home than Beckford does.

I pull into the farm, the silence surrounding my land filling me with both comfort and anxiety. This is my home, it always has been, but at the same time I can't help but notice how this silence resembles the level of noise that occurs during business hours. The only real visitors we get are Nigel and Simone when they want to come and check on the poor kid who had no choice but to run a farm all by himself with no training whatsoever. They're kind people—maybe some of the only kind people in this place—but their close eye on me could really be taken two ways. And I really don't need people checking up on me.

I pull up in front of the main building and hop out of the truck. I see Wren make a move to open her door so I press the lock button on the car keys, enjoying the confused expression that is painted across soft skin and full lips. When I reach her side, I unlock the truck and open the door for her, holding out a hand to help her down.

Amusement swims behind dark eyes and a smile threatens to pull at the corners of her mouth.

"Did you seriously just do that?"

"If there's one thing I've learned about you, sweetheart, it's that you're too stubborn to wait in the damn car."

I stretch my fingers so she knows to take my hand before hopping down. She's a whole foot shorter than me, so the distance from the truck to the floor for her is not really one that I want to see her make alone.

I can see the caution in her eyes as she takes my hand, letting me support her as she clambers down.

She looks up at me. "Happy now?"

"Very," I answer back just as sarcastically.

I keep her hand in mine, marveling at the way they fit together perfectly. I lead her slowly towards the second field which currently holds what I think will really help Wren the way it usually helps me. The fields at night are gorgeous, but kinda spooky. The darkness hugs them like old friends, bathing them in nothing but black with the slightest hint of orange when the pumpkins are ready to be harvested.

This field is now empty thanks to not just Bash, but Finn and Sam, and even Wren. When I saw her helping Bash harvest the field, I wanted nothing more than to pull her into my arms and thank her. Thank her for seeing something worth saving, for seeing some*one* worth saving.

When Wren first came along, I was stuck in this ever-shrinking bubble made out of both external and self-appointed pressure. I was made by both myself and others to believe that I am undeserving of this farm which I love so much, and I could never be enough for it to prosper.

When I then had to let go of the staff, it felt like the end, like that was it for not just the farm, but my self-confidence.

I knew when I tried to help Cliff that I couldn't afford for anything to happen to me, and yet I did it anyway; pushed into it by my need to help those just as alone as I am.

I hold a finger up before jogging into the office to pick up my sling. When I run back out to her, my arm is back to being wrapped up and the loss of weight on my shoulder has me sighing in relief.

"Gus, where are we going?" Wren asks, just as we reach the second field.

"Right here," I reply with a smirk.

She tries her best to look around her. "Your eyes will adjust in a minute. When the harvest is over it can be a bit hard to see."

"How come we're here?"

I mark out a safe path for her by walking first towards the middle of the field, careful to avoid the leftover roots and vines. I tell her where to take a big step, where to hop, and there's a swell of pride in my chest as she does everything I say, when I say it. It shows a trust that definitely would not have been there in the beginning.

In the center of the field lies a pile of discarded pumpkins that were considered too damaged or moldy to be sold. We allow it to turn into compost and mix it in with the soil when we sow the new seeds.

"Usually, when the harvest is finished, I come out here late at night to work off some steam."

Wren listens carefully, eyes on the mountain of pumpkins as if imagining a younger Gus running amuck in an empty field.

"I would come when I felt alone in the world, alienated for

something I can't control. I used to come out here, grab a mallet or an axe and just let loose."

"You were out here smashing pumpkins?" Wren laughs.

"Better to say that I was out here smashing demons. Why let them continue to plague my mind when an empty field is just as dark?"

She hums in agreement and I take this moment in which she's unaware to appreciate the sight of her—eyes large, bottom lip stuck between her teeth in quiet contemplation. She wants to ask questions, I can see it; wants to know a million things about me all at once and can't think of which question should take precedence. She's very inquisitive, Wren is, seemingly trapped by the urge to know everything but having to think before she speaks.

I don't do that. It's not an autistic trait—unfortunately, I can't blame every one of my difficult qualities on that, as easy as it would be. That seems to be a problem I have with others —they assume to those who are not "conventionally autistic", their struggles or their quirks are merely cop-outs to get away with murder. A necessity is seen as a choice, a need seen as a preference.

"It must be hard," Wren says, pulling me from my thoughts.

"What must be?" I ask.

"Being different somewhere where no one really wants you to be."

I shrug lightly knowing she can't see me when she's looking in front of her. "I wouldn't say no one. My brothers want me to be myself. And I suppose there's the occasional person here and there in town that I don't think is terrible."

I turn towards her. "And I guess there's also this girl I met a few weeks ago who doesn't really mind it either ... I think."

The smile on her face when she looks at me could be a beacon for the lost with how bright it shines. It makes her cheeks glow, her eyes sparkle. I think it might be my favorite thing about her.

"You're annoying," she says, her words completely void of malice. "You're stubborn, you're difficult and a know-it-all ... but none of that is down to you being neurodivergent, Gus." She surprises me by stepping towards me and reaching up to plant the softest kiss on my lips. "It's just because you're an ass."

The laugh flows from me smoothly, no longer being restrained by my stubborn personality. It still feels strange, it's something I used to do so easily and often but now it's a rarity, only offered when I'm trying to be polite to customers. Laughing with Wren is easy. I haven't had easy in a while.

I grab a mallet from the ground beside the pile and hold it out to her. "Have at it."

A perfectly manicured eyebrow raises. "Don't trust me with the axe, huh?"

"I'm not an idiot, Southwick. It's going to take more than a gorgeous pair of hazel eyes to trust you with something sharp."

Chapter Thirty-Three

WREN

Gus's way of helping me feel better is the very thing I needed without even knowing it. The ability to remove one's frustrations by smashing something that doesn't know pain is truly a cathartic experience. The moment my shoulders couldn't take any more, the pain in them was nothing compared to the lightness of my chest.

I felt like a new woman. It's not just that the embarrassment that I felt over my incident the other day has dissipated, but also the pain and betrayal I once felt towards Adam is now replaced with a determination to become a better version of myself—a version that respects me and values my heart. I deserve love, I do, and even though I'm not sure if I'm ready for that yet, I think I deserve to at least know that I can be open to it despite being burned in the past.

I'm pretty sure that's all clear on my face as I pull up to Goldleaf Farm. This time, there's no coffee. This time, my excitement following Finn's phone call has taken over and made me keep my foot on the gas as I drove past the Sweet Cinnamon Café.

The barn is finished. Seven weeks of work whittled down to four weeks thanks to a group of guys who are all too kind to put into words. I will forever be grateful to them. Grateful to my brother for pushing pause on other jobs just so he could do this one favor for his little sister. Grateful to Bash for still helping whenever he could despite having to do the harvest by himself for God knows how long. Grateful to Jamie for taking time away from his job to help, and Sam for coming as soon as he was called. And oh so grateful to Gus, who gave me the chance in the first place. None of this would have happened without him, without him having a determination that matched mine. Whether it was to rid himself of my presence or not, it fueled him to get it done and done it is.

The exterior gleams in the autumn sun, red walls and blue roof. Freshly sealed windows reflect the light and a large door stands open, letting the ghosts and demons escape from the interior. I chuckle to myself as I think back to my first moments in this barn—scared out of my mind, furious with a goat and a sexy pumpkin farmer who is now someone I can't imagine not seeing each morning.

Speaking of sexy farmers…

"Morning," Gus smiles. He strides over, his gait and posture seeming so much more relaxed than usual. When we're standing no more than a single step apart, he surprises me by slipping his arm around my waist and planting the gentlest kiss on the side of my head, as if both actions are the most natural thing in the world. "Feeling okay?"

"Funny, I was just about to ask you the same thing," I chuckle, following him as he leads me over to the barn, arm still wrapped around me.

He shrugs lazily. "I'm great. The harvest is over, the barn is finished. Two of my biggest stresses are done."

"Was the harvest enough to get you through the year?" I look over when I realize what I've asked. "Not that it's any of my business how you do financially."

"It's okay for you to ask, sweetheart." His arm leaves my waist as he slips his hand into mine.

This is a very new Gus I'm looking at. I don't know whether to be scared or to be impressed.

I tug on his hand until he stops moving. "Was it?"

He tries to pacify me with a smile, but even his glasses do nothing to hide the concern swimming behind them. "We'll be okay, Wren. Don't forget, the new barn is going to do good things for us. We have a whole year to test-run it, starting with your party."

Another kiss lands on my forehead and he moves us on once more. "Who knows … maybe I might even be okay with Second Nature Events conducting business with Goldleaf Farm on a more regular basis."

I stare at the back of his head like his brain has come bursting out of it. "Who are you and what have you done with August Finch?"

His shoulders move as a warm chuckle leaves his mouth and melts down my spine.

The inside of the barn is warm thanks to all the trapped sunlight. Finn has rebuilt the upper level and has even placed four windows in the roof to allow for even more natural light.

It's empty now, awaiting the moment that I think of exactly what needs to go where and decorate accordingly. There's only one problem...

I don't know.

Looking at this empty space, it all seems so real. Before, the idea of throwing Oakleigh her party was nothing more than a dream in my mind, with not even my best friend literally asking me to do so making the idea feel real. Now, here I am, standing in the middle of the venue that will be used to hold such an event in a week's time and I'm lost for ideas. There's too much space, too many possibilities that my mind has gone blank, like when someone asks you for your favorite movie and all of a sudden every movie you have ever watched leaves your head.

Panic creeps into my chest like blood seeping into an open wound.

"You okay, sweetheart?"

My eyes stay glued to the open space. "Yeah, yeah," I mumble.

The walls feel closer than they did a minute ago, the room brighter, the silence louder. All of it is just ... *more*.

"Okay." All of a sudden, a wall of muscle blocks my view of the rest of the room and before I know it, I'm being lifted up with one arm by a pumpkin farmer.

"August!"

"God, I love it when you say my name."

"August, put me down! Your shoulder—"

"—is fine, Wren."

"Gus, put me down, right now!"

I hear him sigh before mumbling a whiny, "You're no fun,"

before he drops me. Of course, because I have the balance of a newborn giraffe, I end up falling on my ass, glaring up at a very amused Gus Finch. "Oops."

"What the hell was that?" I snap.

"I may not be the best when it comes to reading expressions and reactions, but I know enough to see that you were overstimulated. Pretty sure I spend ninety percent of the time overwhelmed by the world around me, I know what it looks like behind the eyes."

My heart stops. "That's what that feels like? That's what you feel?"

He nods once and I see the way his shoulders drop, as if the feeling of someone understanding even a fraction of his struggles is enough to ease that pressure inside of him.

I can't imagine feeling that more often than the one time I just experienced it. It feels as if the entire world is closing in—nowhere to run to, nowhere to feel like there's enough room to breathe again. Hopeless. That's the word I'd use. The feeling of being so overwhelmed that your brain cannot even begin to comprehend half of the things your senses are experiencing in that moment.

"How often do you feel like that?" I ask him.

He shrugs again. "How many hours are there in the day?"

"Gus," I breathe.

His smile is soft, calming, his fingers coarse as he brushes my cheek. "I'm overexaggerating. It's not as bad as that. By now I'm more than aware of what and where to avoid. Most of the time it's down to stress."

I open my mouth to respond but he winces and asks, "You're not going to say you're sorry, are you? Everyone tells me they're sorry when they hear I struggle with something they don't."

"I wasn't going to apologize," I assure him. "I was going to tell you that I think you're kinda cool."

Seeing Gus Finch blush has to be one of my new favorite things. The way that flush of pink bleeds into his tanned skin like a flush of color that kisses the horizon at sunset. The way he goes from sexy to nerdy and shy in an instant as he lowers his head and pushes up his silver-rimmed glasses.

Thankfully, by the time Bash and the others make it to the barn, I've long since calmed down and Gus is back to his quiet, grumpy self, only offering one-word answers when it suits him.

We're all sitting inside the barn, lounging on the floor as the boys offer ideas for the interior. On the way here, I called Oakleigh and she said the moment she finishes her shift she'll be down.

When she steps in, she gasps, green eyes wide as she takes in everything.

"Holy shit," she breathes. "This is amazing! Way better than what it used to look like. Now would be a great time to update those photos on your website."

When I glance over at my big brother, he seems put off by Oakleigh's presence, pulling his knees closer to his chest and staring straight ahead. I really hope that they get on eventually. Sometimes it seems to be a form of hatred that's been spurred on by unresolved sexual tension. Not that I particularly want my best friend and brother knocking boots, but it's not my place to say what they should and shouldn't do. They're adults, after all.

Oakleigh comes and sits beside me, bringing me into her side in a tight hug. "I'm so proud of you, boo."

"I didn't really do anything, Lee. All I did was ask to redo it. The guys are the ones who put in all of the hard work."

She sighs dramatically. "Yeah, but I can't bring myself to say thank you to your brother."

"Your maturity knows no bounds," my brother sneers, and, because annoying him just doesn't seem to be enough, Oakleigh blows him a kiss.

I look around me whilst they begin their usual argument and breathe out a sigh of contentment. This all just feels so … right. For the first time in my life, I feel as if I'm where I'm meant to be. I'm surrounded by the right people, doing what I've always wanted to do with my life.

I haven't even realized until now that Gus is nowhere to be seen. He's slipped out at some point, probably whilst I've been so lost in my own head. I look around, but nowhere is there a tall, grumpy farmer wearing his usual plaid shirt.

"Missing a certain someone?" Oakleigh whispers in my ear.

She doesn't need an answer from me, not when I can feel my ears burning like there's a lighter held beneath them.

"It's okay to want that, you know," she says, eyes boring into mine. "To want something with someone. Something real."

I stare at the open doors. "I'm scared, Lee. I know that they're not all like Adam, but it's scary knowing that you have to trust them to find out which ones are and which ones aren't."

When I set my sights on my best friend once more, she's

watching me with a look of sympathy. "Gus doesn't strike me as the type to hurt someone on purpose, Wren."

"He isn't," I confirm with a surety that I never had with Adam. "He's not like Adam at all."

"Well, then maybe he's worth the risk."

As if to prove her point, Gus walks in with a small bunch of wildflowers in hand. He perches himself next to me, closer than someone who is just a friend would, and holds the flowers out to me.

My heart feels like it's floating on air as I take the bunch of freshly picked flowers. "How sweet."

He shrugs like it's no big deal. "They were outside."

When we all stand up to leave, eager to get on with the day and sort what needs to be sorted, Bash floats at the back of the group until he's shoulder to shoulder with me.

"Those flowers really must have made you smile last time," he says with a low voice so only I can hear.

"Why do you say that?" I ask, staring at the flowers with a soft smile.

"Those wildflowers only grow by his house. They're nowhere near the barn." And with that little nugget of information, he walks off with a smirk, leaving me speechless and wondering if my feelings are reciprocated by Gus Finch.

Chapter Thirty-Four

GUS

"Gus! What a pleasant surprise."

I walk into Flora and Flowers like a fish out of water. I'm not used to stepping foot in this store unless I have an order of pumpkins to deliver. I'm not really the flower-buying type. I used to always just try and find the nicest flowers I could for my mom when I was little; run around the acres of land that we own to find the perfect bunch.

Poppies grow wild near the cliff-face at the edge of our land. They were always my mother's favorites. She said that despite their somber meaning and dark uses, she liked to believe that their beauty and distinct spark of color meant that they were just as alive as the rest of the world, even though they symbolized death.

I distinctly remember the first time I picked one for her, the smile that lit up her face like fireworks on the fourth of July.

From then on, once a week, on the same day I gave her the first poppy, I would run and find the most perfect poppy I could.

When Wren smiled the first time I handed her wildflowers, I'd had this urge to give her a fresh set every day I saw her, but I refrained. But, when I saw her in the barn, a smile on her face and hope in her eyes, I wanted to try and make sure it stayed the best day for her.

Since then, when she brings my coffee—something she could have stopped doing the moment the barn and the harvest were over—she finds herself leaving with a new, rather rumpled set of yellow, purple and red wildflowers. The joy in her eyes as she walks back to her car with them makes me want to put a smile on her face every day and make sure it never dims. I would buy her a set of flowers whilst I'm here, but to me it lacks a personal touch.

"Morning, sir," I say as I make it to the counter.

"Sir?" Nigel smiles. "How formal."

"Despite what everyone says, I haven't forgotten my manners."

"Well, we've known each other long enough, lad. No need for such formalities."

I look around the store, trying to see if there are any flowers which might be useful for Wren.

"Looking for something for a special party planner, perhaps?"

I scoff nervously. "No offense, Nigel, but there's nothing beautiful enough for her here."

"No offense taken, son. I feel the same way about my Simone. Everything in the world seems dim compared to her."

"And yet nothing has seemed so bright, right?"

If he's surprised by my rather chipper mood, he doesn't show it, he only lets his usual smile widen further until I'm worried it's going to stretch his aging skin. "Spoken like a man in love."

I wouldn't go that far. Would I?

I shrug it off, continuing to look around the store.

"What can I help you with if not flowers for a beloved?" Nigel asks eventually.

"I'm trying to see if you can help her out with the party she's holding next week. It's some kind of scary theme I think."

"*Nightmare Before Fall*", Nigel elaborates. "Wren told me about it last time she was here."

"Yeah, that's the one."

"There are several options I can order in if you'd like— black-sprayed roses, maybe some delphinium and baby's breath to even it out?"

Wren did say that she was going to keep it black and red, throwing in some orange with the pumpkins.

"Can you throw in some red roses, too?" I ask.

"Of course I can," Nigel beams. "Anything for that girl."

I like that she's made friends here, people who can see the goodness in her as clearly as I can.

Yes, I miss arguing with her, and yes, I still do find it easier than talking to her, but that doesn't mean I've always been blind to the light that clings onto her like it clings onto the moon at night.

When it comes to emotions, I feel a lot more than people expect. However, when it comes to people, I've always either formed a logical connection or an emotional one. Logical connections are just that—logical. I connected with my father because I needed him to survive, so when I realized that he hated that I was different, it never bothered me as it might somebody else.

Emotional connections, however, can be quite … intense. I don't just connect with them, I cling to them, I rely on them. I reach for them during any emotion and sometimes it feels like I struggle to live without them.

My mother was an emotional connection. When I woke in the morning, I looked for my mother, when I did all but sneeze, I looked for my mother. When she died, I didn't talk for three months, lost in a void that I thought I would never leave because it was always her who pulled me out of it. I would reach for my mother's hand and would come up empty. I would call my mother's number and no one would pick up. I would scream for her at night and no one would come … except my brothers.

Bash stepped into that role as easily as if he actually were a parent. He looked out for me, he supported me, he learned what I needed and what I struggled with. He knew what foods to avoid because of the texture, he knew what paths to take to school and to work because there was always a right one and a wrong one.

It's been a while since I formed that kind of connection with anyone. What's more, I've never made that kind of connection with someone that included a romantic aspect, and that's what scares me. The more I realize that I have feelings for Wren, the more I feel this call to her. She's the siren calling to me whilst I'm lost at sea, but the problem is I have no idea where the rocks are. How the hell do I navigate a relationship when I've never felt this need to rely on her like I do?

I don't want to rely on Wren, I want to *want* her, not need her.

"Will a hundred of each be enough?" Nigel asks, pulling me from my own thoughts.

"Should be fine." I pull out my wallet. "I'll pay for it now."

Nigel holds a hand up. "Oh, no, mister."

"Why not?"

"Because you doing this is enough for me."

"Nigel, you're talking about three hundred flowers. That's not cheap, you can't just give that away for free."

"Are you going to be charging Wren for those pumpkins she ordered from you?" Nigel asks with a smirk.

Okay, he's got me there. I don't think I was ever planning on charging her for those.

He chuckles when he sees my face. "The things we do for the ones we care about sometimes come across as crazy."

"Are you saying you care about me?"

His expression softens and the sympathy swims clear in his eyes. "August, you and your brothers were the closest I ever came to having sons. How could I not care about you?"

Huh. "I had no idea."

He moves from behind the counter, quite spritely for an old man. He places a comforting hand on my shoulder which is thankfully no longer hurting. Though I refuse to tell Doctor Shakari that the bed rest was a good idea.

People touching me makes me uncomfortable and a lot of the time, angry, but when it comes to Nigel and Simone, you can tell that every touch is filled with care and appreciation, so I let it happen.

"August." When he sees my face, he corrects himself. "Gus. I know it's been hard for you. You lost Caroline, your father left, and you've always struggled to get people to understand that despite being independent, you still see the world differently than we do. I understand that doing that has led you to shut yourself off, push people away, but I always knew it was temporary. All you needed to do was actually believe that you were deserving of love, even if there were people around you who refused to give it. It doesn't matter if you struggle with certain things, because the right people will appreciate that it's what makes you who you are. Simone and I will always appreciate you for who you are, that will never change, son."

Nigel's words aren't what make my eyes start to sting with unshed tears. It's the fact that in that one speech alone, Nigel sounds more like a father than mine ever did. I don't think I realized that the town's rejections ever made me feel unworthy of acceptance, but that's exactly how it's always felt. I think because I know that there are some things that make being around me a little difficult, I mistook that for me being difficult and therefore unworthy of anything. But who the fuck isn't difficult sometimes?

So what if I'm a picky eater? So what if loud noises make me want to scream? Because of that, I deserve to be alone my whole life?

"You're right," I say to Nigel, my chest swelling with something I can't yet explain.

"You're damn right I am," he smiles. "Now here." He picks

up a yellow rose and hands it to me. "Go and tell that woman how you feel."

I can't give her the rose.

I've been so nervous about talking to her that I've unknowingly been crushing it in my fist. The now-crumpled flower lays on my passenger seat. How am I fucking this up already?

Leaving the rose where it is, I hop out of my truck, making sure to lock it behind me. I head into the Locke and Key where Sam and Jamie are already sat at the bar, sitting too close for any two people with nothing going on between them. Bash and Oakleigh are arguing over whether or not one of them potted the white ball in a game of pool. And as for Wren ... she sits exactly where we sat last time, and the memories come flooding back from that night; the feel of her hand as my fingers brush against it, the way she shivered as I whispered in her ear that I wanted to bring her home with me.

Ever since that night I've had the most sinful thoughts. It took everything in me not to push her up against the wall and take her right then and there, steps be damned. Even now, I'm stuck between wanting to storm over to her and scream at her that I want her to stay with me in Eaglewood, and wanting to bend her over the table and show her just how to worship a woman.

As if sensing that I'm watching her, she looks up, hazel eyes catching me from across the bar. A tingle dances across my skin as her gaze rakes over my tall frame. She takes in my broad shoulders, my toned legs hidden behind worn-out jeans. She looks at me like a woman starved, a woman on the edge, and that in itself almost tips me over until all I can hear is a ringing in my ears.

I don't take my eyes off of her as I stalk over, and when she licks her lips, I almost lose control entirely.

"You look at me like that for much longer, sweetheart, and Colin might have an early show on tonight."

Her eyes widen at my promise and I eat up her reaction like it's my last meal. There's something else I would ravage with just as much given the chance.

I take a seat beside her, letting my thigh brush against hers.

This is not why I've come here. I came here to tell her that I want her to stay, to tell her that I want her to come to the farm and just never leave. Is that too extreme, though? Is that too fast? Fuck knows, all I know is that if I don't tell her something, then I'll have wasted a chance to be with a one-of-a-kind woman.

Right now, though, with the way one touch from me has her breathing heavy and has her body charged and sensitive, my mind is finding itself being invaded by a different kind of need, a different kind of desire.

I still want her to stay with me, but I want her to stay so that I can bring her flowers, kiss her hair before carrying her onto my dining room table and eating a meal that would make any man jealous.

I need to tell her this.

I open my mouth to tell her this.

"Can you take me home?"

Okay, maybe I don't need to tell her. Not when she's just

asked me to take her back to my place with a desperation that has my cock straining against my jeans.

I shift towards her, allowing myself the chance to tuck a stray curl behind her ear. The blush that creeps across her cheeks when I let my finger glide behind her ear has me biting my bottom lip. I know what it feels like between my teeth. I know what it tastes like when I kiss along her neck. I know what her lips taste like.

And I'm desperate for more.

"Sweetheart, let me tell you right now. Be sure that you want to step foot in my house, because if you do, you'll be coming to my house, and then coming all night. So, decide now. I won't be mad or think less if you change your mind."

She shakes her head so violently that her curls fall back into her eyes. Her eyes are wild and dark with lust.

I almost combust with the look of fierce determination as she says, "Take me home, Finch."

Chapter Thirty-Five

WREN

He doesn't waste any time, doesn't even let me take my shoes off—let alone line them up in size order—before he lifts me up with one arm like I weigh no more than his smallest pumpkin.

There's no space between us. It's his chest against mine, the tip of his nose nuzzling mine intimately. There's no space to breathe, and yet I wouldn't want it any other way. This is what I need. This is what *we* need.

Gus crashes his lips against mine, a desperate act that could bruise. Not that I care. We're a frantic mixture of lips, tongues and teeth. The way he nibbles at my bottom lip has zips of electricity jolting throughout my whole body.

"Gus," I moan as his lips trail along my jawline and down my neck. "Gus, your arm."

"What about it?" he mumbles, refusing to stop.

"I don't want you to hurt yourself."

His face is back in front of mine. "Shut up, Wren."

His lips find mine once more, and any snappy retort I had ready to go dissipates. I gasp as my back finds the wall in his hallway. A firm chest presses against me so tightly that I'm held in place, allowing him a chance to move his hand from my waist to my ass, his grasp firm even though my jeans are thick and stiff.

He touches me in such a way that my whole body feels like it's on fire.

He unclips his sling, tossing it to God knows where, giving me a chance to tug on his shirt until I'm able to toss it to lands unknown. I rip off my own top, the air too hot, and my desire to have his hands on my bare skin is too much to ignore. He pulls back to allow himself the chance to look at me.

His already dark eyes become black as they rake over my braless chest. There's no stopping him as he uses his bad arm to reach for me, cupping my breast in his hand and expertly kneading it, tweaking and stimulating my nipple so easily, you'd think he'd slept with hundreds of women.

The moment his mouth latches on, I'm lost. There's no time to breathe, no time to think. My only option is to revel in this feeling and lose myself to the pleasure he's causing.

"I've had thoughts about this, Wren," he murmurs. "Bad thoughts, terrible thoughts, but they all end so nicely."

I feel myself being carried into the kitchen, my eyes remaining closed as he doesn't take the time to stop his assault on my body. I'm dropped onto something hard—I'm assuming the dining table—and his lips find mine again.

"Couldn't make it to the bedroom, huh?" I laugh breathlessly.

"I brought us right where we need to be." In one swift move, his t-shirt is gone. "I was taught that you always eat at the table."

God help me.

The smirk that stretches his lips is the definition of mischievous. Mix that with the uninterrupted view of strong shoulders, defined chest and lean muscle that covers his stomach, and I'm at his mercy. The visceral reaction that occurs between my thighs may for once be a problem that can be solved exactly how I dreamed it would be.

When he kisses me, he lowers us down until I'm lying on the table before him, a meal ready for him to devour. He grabs my legs, admiring the thin fabric of my knee-high boots.

"Would it be bad if I wanted you to put the boots back on after I take these jeans off of you?"

I lift an eyebrow in response and he mirrors the action. "Or, to make it easier, I can just rip the jeans off?"

"Oh, I bet you'd love that."

"I bet you would too," he retorts.

Slowly—almost painfully so—he undoes the boots, slipping each one off of my feet so seductively, his eyes never once leaving mine.

He trails his hands over my thighs, one finger drifting over that spot between my legs leaving me gasping. He finds my belt buckle, undoing it one-handed, the button on my jeans swiftly following.

Brown hair covering equally brown and wild eyes, Gus has my pants off in a heartbeat and I realize that I'm currently almost completely naked in front of him. Not just naked, but vulnerable, too. I spent so much time being worried about being emotionally vulnerable around August that I never felt the weight that came with being physically exposed. It's something I haven't done in a while. Sex wasn't particularly something I was offering towards the end of my last relationship.

"Hey." I look up at Gus as he speaks. "Stay with me, okay? The moment you want to stop, we stop."

The reassurance calms me enough to relax my arms and legs, letting him fully see me. Goosebumps appear on my arm and I'm not entirely sure if it's down to the cold or the feel of his eyes.

He lingers at the waistband of my underwear, seemingly waiting for permission. I let him take me lifting my hips as his answer, and his smirk tells me he's read it loud and clear. My panties come off in one swift swoop. If this is what Gus can do with one arm, I don't even want to know how sexy he would be with both of them in action.

He's drinking me in, eyes as dark as the night outside.

He bends down until he's up close and personal with me. "Fuck, I'm going to enjoy this."

The moment his mouth lands on me, I'm a bundle of nerves and joy. I can feel my eyes rolling into the back of my head as wave after wave rolls through my entire body, wrapping me up in an overwhelming level of pleasure.

As his tongue flicks up and traces a circle around my clit, the entire world flips upside down. Colors become a fireworks display behind my eyes as he devours me, uses his tongue in such an expert fashion that I'm screaming, begging for him not to stop. I can see the stars in the night sky when he chuckles against me.

"So sweet," he groans against me. "So goddamn sweet."

"August, please."

He's back up, rushing to unbuckle his jeans whilst he leaves a trail of kisses anywhere he can reach.

"Are you ready for me, baby?"

I nod quickly, too overwhelmed to use my words, to trust them. I decide that it's my turn to do the exploring. It's my turn to trace the contours of his body—the hard muscle, the clear-cut lines just above his jeans. This time I get to appreciate the smoothness of his skin, the feel of the ridges as I trace the tattoo inked into his chest.

I let my exploration lead me down, down, down, until I reach the freshly popped button of his pants. Insecurity makes me hesitate, makes me realize that it's been a while since I last did anything like this. It's been too long since I've felt the hard ridges of a man's cock in my mouth. Am I out of practice?

Gus's breathing becomes more and more shallow as he waits for me to make the move. His gaze is fierce but gentle, a reminder that if I want to stop, all I have to do is say. No questions, no double-checking, I know that Gus would just let it go immediately.

I take a deep breath and jump into the deep end, pushing past the waistband to grasp him. His inhale is sharp, and for a second I think maybe I've grasped him too hard, but when I look in his eyes, the glint in the darkness is enough to tell me that it feels good.

I give him an experimental stroke, and another, and then another, and his groans of pleasure spur me on, make me bolder in my attempts.

He grasps my hair, pulling tight on my curls until I'm

arching up into him. I stroke his cock with a vigor that is new to me, enjoying the feel of him in my hand. I become more confident with each movement, enjoying the tightening of his grip, the biting of his bottom lip with his teeth.

"I need to feel you," I breathe.

"Someone's feeling impatient," Gus chuckles.

"Now," I plead, writhing beneath him in an attempt to scratch an itch only made worse by his mouth on my wet pussy.

Not needing to be asked twice, he lowers his pants all the way and positions himself at my entrance.

The one thing that I find truly admirable is the way he keeps checking on me. He doesn't need to ask when his patience says it all.

I close my hand over his and together we guide him in. The feeling of him filling me up is a stretching sensation I won't soon forget. We groan in unison and Gus buries his face into the crook of my neck.

He starts pumping in and out slowly, each thrust measured, calculated. The pressure inside of me builds, like a song reaching its crescendo before drifting into a satisfied silence. My legs are wrapped around Gus's waist, clinging onto him tightly so that even when he pulls out, he's never too far away.

He moves faster, harder. The more I beg, the more he moves until he's pounding into me in a way that has my back rubbing against the table. My climax finds its way closer and closer to the edge, waiting for Gus to push me off that cliff into paradise.

"Fuck, sweetheart, you feel incredible," he murmurs into my neck. "I knew you would."

I let my fingers run through his mahogany waves, each strand even softer than I remember.

"Come with me, sweetheart. Clench my cock."

And just like that, I fall. I fall far. I fall for the song as it finally reaches its most pivotal moment, and I fall for the man who made it so. He falls over the edge with me, filling me up in a whole new way.

Neither one of us moves, stuck in place by the overwhelming feeling of satisfaction, lust and something more that we can't yet voice.

I inhale the scent of him hidden beneath the smell of sweat and sex—something sweeter and woodsy. It's calms me down as I take deeper breaths each time just to smell it.

Light, sweet kisses are peppered up and down my body as Gus slowly pulls out. He moves over to the cupboard under the sink to find a cloth, giving me time to admire the other side of him—the firmness of his ass, the muscular tone to his back.

He smirks when he turns around again to see me watching him, and I'm feeling confident enough to not bother pretending I didn't. I refuse to take my eyes off of him as he stalks back over to me and takes the time to gently clean me up.

I'm pretty much purring at the way his hand kneads the inside of my thighs, the strain of keeping them wide open for so long finally dissipating with each stroke of his fingers.

I'm lifted up, again with only one hand. I gasp at the sudden movement, and the shock at the way he lifts me so easily.

With a dark chuckle, he kisses me once and says, "Something wrong?"

"No," I remark with a smile. "Just wondering where it is that you're taking me now."

"Oh, sweetheart, I really hope you didn't think I was done with you."

"You're not?"

"Fuck, no." He begins carrying me to his bedroom. "I'm a growing boy, Wren. When it comes to you nothing more than three meals minimum will fill me up."

Chapter Thirty-Six

GUS

T he sun shines, turning the backs of my eyelids red.

Something in my arms nestles closer into me, a low hum vibrating against my chest.

I open my eyes, looking down to see the most beautiful sight. Wren sleeps peacefully in my arms, her curls spread out behind her. Her naked body is warm against mine and for someone who hates physical contact, I find myself reveling in the feel of her skin pressed to me.

Her breathing is deep, her face relaxed. It's exactly like when I put her to bed the night of the storm. When I laid her down, it may sound creepy but I stayed and watched her for a second. At the time, it was just nice to see her when she wasn't yelling at me or shooting back some retort laced with an abundance of attitude. Looking at her like that, I was able to take a minute to truly appreciate her—appreciate the way she didn't need the sun to make her skin glow, didn't have to try and pout those full lips.

Now, as her eyes flit with dreams, I'm able to do so again—admire the beauty even though nowadays it's clear as day even when she frowns and even when she shouts.

I have a plan for today, one that I'm hoping she'll be happy to carry out with me, especially now that I've helped her to sort out most of the work for her friend's party.

Maybe, today, if I'm brave enough that is, I'll be able to accomplish step six. If I'm lucky.

She stirs, moving her head from my chest as she slowly blinks herself awake. She looks around, the sun showcasing the green in her eyes.

"Good morning," I smile, kissing her softly. She hums against my lips and a zip runs down my spine.

"Morning," she replies, stretching as she yawns.

"Sleep okay?"

"Considering you knocked me into a coma thanks to all the orgasms, I'd say so, yeah."

A chuckle leaves my chest, coarse from all of the sleep. I plant a kiss on the side of her forehead.

She lightly traces my tattoo causing goosebumps to erupt all over my skin.

"What does 'CF' stand for?" she asks.

"Caroline Finch," I reply lowly, the subject of my mother causing my chest to tighten. "My mom."

She looks sorrowful as she stares at the tattoo, now with the new knowledge behind its meaning.

"You must have loved her very much."

"More than anything," I mumble as I rest my hand over hers. I shake my head, ridding my mind of the memories of my mother's funeral. How the feeling of remorse and grief making me choke on the air around me. "As much as I'd love nothing more than to stay in bed all day, I have an appointment to get to."

Her face deflates and I realize I've said that quite bluntly. I lean forward until I can feel her breath fanning my face.

I firmly grab her chin. "Relax, sweetheart. Don't go running into your own head. You're coming with me."

She looks at me with curiosity burning in her eyes. I love the inquisitiveness that shines through her when I surprise her. She looks for the reasoning behind things and I wonder whether or not that's because she thinks she's undeserving of such attention. It's a criminal thought to have and if that is the case, I plan on eradicating the notion entirely.

"Get ready and meet me in the kitchen. And this time, don't surprise me whilst I'm cooking the bacon."

An hour later, we're in the car on the way to Liliton, our stomachs full and our spirits high.

Wren hasn't stopped smiling the entire journey and it makes me want to do all I can to keep it on her face.

"Okay, can you seriously tell me where we're going?" Wren asks.

"This time, yes, I can." I signal left. "There's a sanctuary in Liliton that houses animals with nowhere else to go. Sometimes, they become over capacity, and when that happens they usually give me a call to see whether I have space for them on the farm."

I can feel her eyes on me, watching me in that way she does whenever I reveal something about myself. I know I don't give her much. If I'm being honest, it's down to shame. I used to be so ashamed of anything that showed me to be soft, more than what I appear. It felt like something that could be used against me. If anyone saw that I have a weakness other than my Autism, I assumed it would be used as further reason for me to be considered useless, pathetic.

Now, however, I'm starting to see that my love for animals isn't something that needs to be hidden like some dirty little secret. And more to the point, I've realized that my Autism isn't a weakness. Wren has helped me see that. I should appreciate that I'm different, not be so hard on myself for needing to live my life a certain way. The world is ... a lot. Too much sometimes. I'm finally learning that that's okay.

"That's why there's so many different animals in the barn."

"Mhmm." I adjust my grip on the steering wheel. "I love animals. They're ... easier to understand."

"Are they?"

"Funnily enough, it's easier to know what someone needs when they don't use words. When all they can go off of is instinct and survival they don't bother to lie or hide their emotions."

When we reach the sanctuary, a wide-eyed Wren takes in the pens, the barns and the open space for animals to run around. I became acquaintances with the owner, Reena, about five years ago when I found Mori.

I drive us up to the main lodge where Reena stands waiting.

"Gus Finch," she greets as I step out of the truck.

"Hi," I reply as I help Wren out of the passenger side. "Thanks for calling about Trixie."

"My pleasure," she says.

I smile down at Wren as she straightens herself, my heart jolting as I see the excitement and happiness clear in her eyes. I just want to spend more time with her, show her a part of myself and my life that means just as much to me as the farm does.

"I see you brought some company this time," Reena says with a suggestive grin.

I let my arm wrap itself around Wren's waist, pulling her close into me. "This is Wren."

The enclosure that Reena leads us to holds a group of animals I've never dealt with before. I don't actually think that anyone has dealt with something like this before.

"This is Trixie."

In the enclosure is a cougar. Not yet fully grown, but definitely not a cub.

"Is that a goddamn cougar?" Wren asks.

"Indeed it is," Reena replies.

"Explain." My fury rising by the second.

"She was raised by a couple in the mountains for four months, so she can no longer survive in the wild. We've kept her around other animals, so we know that she won't hurt them. She's docile now. She needs a home."

I turn to Reena. "You told me you had a cat."

She at least has the decency to look sheepish. "I mean technically I didn't lie. She is a cat. A big cat."

"I own a pumpkin farm, Reena, not a fucking safari. I have nowhere to keep a goddamn cougar."

"I just thought that you'd be able to give her a home, Gus." She shrugs, brushing my concerns off like this is no big deal or just some game to her.

"Besides ... who doesn't love a cougar?" Wren teases, giving my side a squeeze and Reena a conspiratorial grin. The ring of her laughter mixed with Reena's makes my stomach churn. "Can you imagine a cougar running around the farm?"

I wanted to show the woman I like a side of me that I don't share with many people. People in town don't know that it's me who fosters and adopts the animals. But I don't just feel as if I want to her to know. I *need* her to know. I need her to know I'm someone with substance, someone with depth. The fact that she's joking about this feels like an attack on this side of me. Sure, it might not be at all, but my sensitive and bruised ego refuses to allow me to see it as anything else.

I'm going to throw up.

I pull Wren even closer to me, her stiff frame making me feel safer even if her words chisel against my confidence bit by bit.

"I can't take her."

"I don't have space for her, Gus." Reena argues.

"Then you need to call someone with expertise with these kinds of animals."

I gently but firmly steer Wren back towards the truck, pissed off that I've not been able to show Wren exactly what I had planned to. Wren struggles to keep up with me, and even though I'm aware of that in my mind, I still walk quickly, wanting to remove myself from this embarrassing situation.

Reena is calling after me, but there's no way I'm wasting my time with her. They all deserve a permanent home, the animals, especially the ones that are in their last few years, but I also have to stay realistic. The only problem with that is now I seem to have become some kind of joke to Wren.

"Gus, slow down," Wren pleads. I keep my hand on her waist firm. We're almost to the truck.

"Gus! Please, slow down."

I open the passenger side door and wait.

"Get in, Wren."

She's shocked by my tone, and to be honest, so am I. It's unnervingly low and harsh, primed for a fight with someone I'm not even angry at.

"Will you just calm down for a minute, please? You're having a really big reaction to this."

"No, Wren, I'm reacting exactly as I should."

"You're behaving like an ass," she challenges, and it only fuels my frustration more.

I take a step towards her, my frame shadowing over hers easily. Her eyes widen on my approach and her back hits the car door.

"Get. In. The. Car. *Please*. There, now I'm being polite."

"Oh, my God," she groans. "Why are you being so pig-headed all of a sudden?"

"Pig-headed?" I step forward again. "*Pig-headed?* I'm the one who woke up this morning wanting to show the woman I want that there's more to me, only for that to be ruined by shitty communication and frustrating jokes ... and *I'm* the one being pig-headed? Because I'm angry at the situation?"

"If you're angry at the situation then fine, but don't you dare direct that at me."

"I'm not, I'm just..." I'm just what? For fuck's sake, what am I doing?

I'm in way over my head. How the hell did I mess today up so badly? I should have checked. I should have asked for a photo of Trixie before schlepping Wren across three towns. If I'd known the truth, I would have been able to spend the day worshiping her body and staring at her smile instead, making sure that I knocked her into another orgasm-induced coma before I put a vase of wildflowers on the bedside table for her to wake up to. I could have made her come, and scream for me over and over that she's mine and will always be.

Frustrated and overwhelmed, I storm over to my side of the truck, jumping in and slamming the door behind me. I stew in my own anger whilst I wait for Wren to get in, and each minute I sit there staring ahead of me is another minute of me feeling worse and worse.

The door slams as Wren enters the truck. She sits beside me quietly for the entire drive back, arms folded as she looks out the window solemnly. My fingers tighten on the steering wheel as I pull up to the house.

"Wren, I—"

"I need to get home," she interrupts, jumping out the truck before I can respond.

I scurry out after her, catching up to her easily. "Wren, please, wait."

"I need to go, Gus."

I manage to catch her arm and twist her towards me. Just like the first time we met, I find her nestled into my chest, clinging to my shirt with a hint of desperation. Her breathing is heavy, her breath fanning my chest warmly.

"Tell me how to fix it," I plead. "Tell me what I can do to make it all better."

She shakes her head and for a second, I wonder if I've lost her before I even had a chance to have her.

"August, you're frustrated, you're upset. Whilst I understand that, you're directing it at me and that's not okay. So, I need to just go home and cool off, and I think that you should, too."

Dread fills my chest but I still plant a kiss on the top of her head. "I just really wanted to give you a good day; to tell you how much I want this ... want you."

"I know, I had a feeling." She looks up at me, skin glowing as the sun hits it. "But these things happen, and that's okay. Take your time and try again. I'll be here waiting."

Chapter Thirty-Seven

WREN

Today's the day. Today is Oakleigh's party and I am absolutely, positively shitting myself.

I arrived at the farm at seven this morning, wanting to make sure that anything and everything that can go wrong does so early in the day. Thankfully, so far things are running smoothly. Knowing my luck, however, the chances of it staying that way are slim.

Bash has been a massive help, as has Sam but, unfortunately, Gus is nowhere to be found. Hasn't been for a week as a matter of fact. I thought he would only need a day or two to calm down, and yet two days turned to three, three to four and so on until seven days have come and gone and I haven't seen him once, even though I've been on the farm every day since preparing for today.

Even Bash hasn't seen him. The only reason I haven't been concerned is because Bash isn't. He says it's normal for Gus to disappear occasionally, when the weight of the world is too heavy on his shoulders. He leaves so that he can regroup, reassess and return calmer than when he left.

I think about how that would work in a relationship, if that would be something to cause more harm than good, but the more I think about it, the more I know that I would deal with it if it's what he needs. I want to be with Gus as he is, not change him to suit me.

"Not disturbing, am I?"

Nigel stands by the doors to the barn, smiling warmly. I walk over and return his smile, hugging him as gently as I can.

"Nigel, how nice to see you!"

"Right back at you, my dear." He smiles. "I have a flower delivery for you."

Oh, my God. I forgot to order the goddamn flowers.

But wait, if I forgot to order them … then who…

"Someone ordered flowers for the party?"

"Oh, yes," he says with a mischievous look on his face. "A secret admirer, I believe."

Of course Gus would be so thoughtful. It wasn't enough that he sorted the food and drink—even if he was just doing it to try and get rid of me. He had to go one step further and think of the one thing I should have sorted from the beginning. I've been planning parties, both professionally and unprofessionally, for five years now … and I forgot to buy flowers for my best friend's thirtieth?

"Thank you, Nigel," I tell him as he leads me to his truck, where there is a bed full of black and red roses, baby's breath, and delphiniums. My breath is stolen from me when I see the array of bouquets, registering that Gus really did take into account everything I told him. We'd had a conversation, Gus and I, regarding the flowers I wanted. Well, it was more like me speaking and Gus sitting there, so I had no idea that he listened to all of it. But he had. Every single word I said.

"How much is there?" I ask breathlessly.

"A hundred of each," Nigel replies. "I'd be more than happy to help set them up if you would like. As long as there are no ladders that is. I don't think my knees could take the workout."

Nigel assists me with setting up the bottom floor of the barn, the two of us laughing and joking around as we arrange the flowers in a way that looks both beautiful and haunted—beautifully haunted, I suppose. Some of them look to be blooming from the hay bales, others in black vases on the tables. Nigel even managed to direct me on how to arrange them on the railing of the balcony. He even gave me some eucalyptus leaves to add to it so that the metal rail is nearly invisible.

The only thing left are the pumpkins. The pumpkins which I really hoped Gus would deliver. We started this together, it would have been nice to end it in the same way.

"Lost in thought, my dear?" Nigel asks.

I smile wryly at him. "Just nervous. It's been a while since I planned an event and I seem to be all over the place."

"You need to believe in yourself, Wren. You're more than capable of doing whatever you put your mind to, but you need to believe that yourself."

He plants a swift kiss on my cheek before heading back to his shop.

About an hour later, Bash enters the room just as I've

finished setting up all of the treats that Lori made. Working with her has been an absolute dream. She's a kind, interesting woman who really has a passion for her craft.

The pastries she's done for me are amazing—all following the theme of the *Nightmare Before Fall* with their color coordination, and spooky decorations.

I'm still waiting for the excitement to kick in—that rush through my blood as I realize that I have, once again, planned a party. Something that I enjoy doing. I'm waiting for it to flood my veins, replacing the nervous gloop that's clogging them up instead. But it's still not come. The set-up is usually my favorite part, but right now, all I can think about is the fact that there is someone missing.

"Oh, my God!" Oakleigh screams as she enters behind Bash. "My bestie does it again!"

She runs up, throwing herself at me. "I love it! I love it! I love it!"

I can't help but laugh as I hug her back. "It's not done yet! Still gotta set up all the pumpkins."

"Even without them it's amazing!" She turns to Bash. "No offense."

"None taken," he chuckles. "I'm just about to bring them in now, but, um … Wren? I think you should come outside and check them before I do."

"That's not necessary, Bash. I trust you and Gus. I'm sure they're all gorgeous."

"No, no. Trust me. You're going to want to come out."

The smile on his face makes me feel uneasy. I feel like Bash is always knowing something that I don't, always watching me with his sly smile and mischievous green eyes.

Oakleigh and I follow him out together. Thankfully, the weather is on our side today; the sun unobstructed by any gray clouds. The trees around Goldleaf Farm are bronze as the sun hits them, their dying leaves offering a golden glow all around us.

I watch Bash walk ahead of us towards the truck, and my breath stops.

Gus stands beside his truck, plaid shirt replaced with a plain gray button-up. His hat sits atop his head, keeping the sun out of his brown eyes. His sling has disappeared, his cast now a dark gray in color. He must have gone to the hospital during our week apart.

He looks nervous, hands in pockets, feet shuffling on the dirt. On the bed of the truck is a pile of pumpkins with wildflowers stuck in all of the gaps. On some of them, carved into the skin, are pictures from *The Nightmare Before Christmas*. Fake LED candles force a glow from inside of the pumpkins to showcase the scene carved into each one.

"Is it to your liking?" Bash whispers in my ear.

A breath escapes me, sounding relatively like a laugh. "It's perfect."

"Then go and get it."

Following his instruction, I slowly walk towards Gus, each step filling me with that very excitement that I was missing not that long ago. This time, I don't stop in front of him, I don't wait for him to say the first word. I just leap up and wrap my arms around his neck, hugging him tightly. My grip tightens the moment he hugs me back because I was so afraid that he's been mad at me this whole time for needing both of us to take a breather.

"I missed you," he murmurs into my neck.

"I missed you, too, Gus."

He plants a kiss on my lips that steals my breath. "Talk later?"

"You bet."

The way he kisses me is rough, desperate and loving. It's not like at his house, last week—all lips, tongues and teeth. This is hard grips and low moans. I can hear Bash hollering in the background, making me smile against Gus, and he smiles, too. I don't even need to be dating Gus for long to know that he's about to treat me better than Adam ever did.

What's more … he's going to make me treat myself as I deserve.

With respect.

Chapter Thirty-Eight

GUS

The party is in full swing, which means that I'm hiding in the corner, ear plugs lodged firmly in my ears. If Wren wasn't the one that planned this whole thing, then I wouldn't be here. Instead, I would be holed up in my office, avoiding everyone and everything, knowing that overstimulation is just twenty paces away.

Yet, here I am, sitting on a bale of hay, my newly released and now sling-free arm dangling at my side. It's not the same as it was and I still seriously need to take it easy, but thankfully, the break healed well despite my tendency to disregard the need for gentleness whilst it was healing.

The barn seems to be holding the number of guests easily enough, and as the owner of the farm, I make a mental note of it so that for future events, I know the structure's limits.

Wren stands a little way away, chatting with the guests as they enter the new event space. She's animated, energetic, enough to know that this is the kind of environment in which she thrives. She looks so at ease, shoulders relaxed in her dark red dress. She's wearing a pair of heeled knee-high black boots that are so goddamn sexy, I fully intend on showing her the effect that they're having on me later. Her hair is dying to be released from the messy bun on her head, strands of brown curls framing her face and resting on the back of her neck.

I am really proud of her, of everything that she's achieved. She tries to throw some of the credit my way, but I don't need any of it. She's accomplished all of this on her own, all I did was offer the assist here and there. Seeing this party in full swing really does feel a bit surreal. It's the reason Wren was brought into my life, into the life I was wasting away because I was so determined to hide in the shadows. Oakleigh is clearly enjoying herself, her usual laid-back temperament replaced by a chaotic—albeit drunk— version of her that is dancing to the music as if she's the only one in the room. I see the way Wren occasionally glances over at her best friend, joy clear in her eyes as she sees the very thing she worked so hard to achieve currently unfolding. She did this for herself, yes, but knowing Wren, the priority was always making sure that Oakleigh had the party she always wanted.

"You almost look like you're enjoying yourself," Bash jokes as he sits beside me on one of the hay bales.

"I wouldn't go that far."

"Oh, admit it, Gus, you like being here, getting to watch Wren do her thing."

My shrug comes with a minimal amount of pain and that genuinely makes me feel so goddamn happy. "I'm proud of her. I'm enjoying watching her do what she's so talented at, but that doesn't mean I'm enjoying the party itself."

Bash scoffs. "You can never just say you like something, can you?"

I ignore him and continue watching Wren rearrange some of the flowers for the fourteenth time since guests started to arrive.

"So, what happens next?" Bash asks after a few minutes.

"Wren said they're going to cut the cake soon, I think. I'm not entirely sure. Either that or speeches."

"That's not what I meant, Auggie."

"What are you talking about then?" I ask, confused.

"I'm talking about you and Wren. What happens now for the two of you? Have you discussed how you'll go on after Wren stops coming here?"

That pulls me away from watching Wren adjust a pumpkin on one of the tables. "What do you mean when she stops coming here?"

Bash's eyebrows dip as if the notion is seemingly an obvious one. "Auggie, you guys have completed what you set out to do. The harvest is over, Wren's party is underway, and the barn is complete. After today, Wren has no reason to bring us coffee every morning, or come to the farm every day. Eventually, she'll get another job and we don't know what town that will be in. What if the next one is in Liliton? She'll have to go there each day instead."

Fuck. I never even thought of that.

Dread inserts itself into my veins as I replay Bash's words in my head. What if she does get another event in one of the other towns? What then? I own a business where I need to be physically present, I can't afford to come and see her every day like she's been doing for me. What happens to the morning coffees, the tension-filled arguments, the sexual tension? You're telling me it all just … stops?

Besides, Bash says she won't have a reason to come by anymore. So, am I not reason enough?

"Of course you're reason enough, Auggie," Bash answers, making me realize that I've just spoken out loud. "Gus, that girl likes you. A lot. All I'm saying is that it might be easier to talk to her about what happens from here on out. Make a plan so that you know what happens moving forward and can find peace in the knowledge that there's no 'what ifs'?"

But what if there are still "what ifs"? What if after talking, there's still a day unaccounted for, or a last-minute change of plan when one realizes that they still have work to do? Me, I plan my day down to the minute. I know where I'll be at every second of the day, and I always have. Wren, however, is a force of nature. She's a tornado that's swept through my life, with no concern for any structure I already had in my life. Would she even be able to live my way? Would she be able to understand that I need things in order, which could in turn have an impact on her life as well as mine?

"Okay, so then how do I—"

"You got this. I'll be right back."

Bash sprints off towards the side door to the barn, looking like a thief in the night. I stare after him confused. That is, until a familiar voice says, "Hey, Gus."

Holy shit.

Raven Thomas. The woman Bash let slip through his fingers.

She looks exactly the same as the last time I saw her—hair that's the same color as her namesake, startling blue eyes and skin as light as porcelain.

"Hi, Ray. Long time no see."

"Yeah, it's been a hot minute." She looks uncomfortable as she looks to the door Bash fled from. "Have you seen Seb?"

"He ran out of that door," I tell her, pointing towards the side door.

She huffs out a laugh. "You always were honest."

"And he always was stupid. If you'll excuse me."

As much as I would usually revel in fate throwing Bash a grenade when he's constantly been teasing me about Wren, I really don't have the time. Not when my brain is running at a million miles an hour, trying to make sense of his words. Not when I have a million questions sitting on my tongue.

I keep Wren in my sights as I make my way towards her, sticking to the edges of the barn so as to avoid the crowd. Her back is to me by the time I'm all but two steps away. She's in the middle of a conversation with identical twin girls, both of whom look as if they're pleading with her.

"Please, Wren. You have to plan our gala for us. It's the week before Thanksgiving. We need you. Only the best could pull off a party like this in such a short space of time."

I was about to interrupt, but now I'm listening intently whilst hidden in the shadows. I wait impatiently for Wren's response. How convenient for her to be talking about the exact thing I wanted to discuss with her.

"I don't know," Wren mumbles.

"Pleeeeease! You can even name your price! We have quite the high-end guest list, half of which are always looking to host some kind of event. It's the beauty of working in fashion. Plan this party for us and you'll be booked up until the end of next year, easy."

End of next year?

"There's some people even flying in from out of the state. It's the chance you need to take things national."

National?

"Surely, seeing how successful this party has been, you're excited to move on to the next?"

I lean in closer as Wren adjusts her stance. "Of course, I'm excited to plan more events. This is my life. This is my dream. And the chance to take my work out of the state ... it's insane to think about."

"But make sure you do think about it. You can't stay in these tiny towns forever, Wren," says one of the twins. "Who the hell would want to stay stuck in one place forever?"

I've heard enough.

How stupid I've been, thinking that Wren would ever want to stay with me here in this "tiny town". She wants to branch out and I handed over her chance to do so without even knowing it. She told me in the beginning, said that she would get more business from this party, open up more opportunities for her. But she said it would do so *here*. In Eaglewood. In the end, I found no downside to helping her, because I knew in the end, the town would see what she's done and offer me a chance to make her stay and work here.

But how can one little town in the middle of nowhere possibly compete with the chance to travel and work for those who can offer her a life of luxury?

As I storm out of the barn, rejection weighing on my chest,

I wonder how I could have possibly been stupid enough to fall for someone like Wren Southwick.

The night air is exactly what I've needed to cool down some very heated thoughts. The constant thought of being abandoned by the one woman I want to stay more than anything is causing my skin to prick and itch with the harshness of reality.

The reality is that no one is going to stay. Why would they when the idea of leaving me seems to hold so much appeal?

"August?"

Despite my anger, I can still feel the way my entire body stands to attention when she's around. The way every part of me almost sighs in relief at the knowledge that she's close by. I hate feeling like this. I never want to be stupid enough to be so vulnerable ever again.

"Yeah."

"Everything okay? I've been looking around for you everywhere."

"Here I am," I say bluntly.

She pauses, both her movements and her words halting for a split second. "What's the matter? Is the party a bit too much for you, because we can go outside if you'd prefer?"

"No, thanks. I'm fine right here." In my town. On my farm. In my home.

A small hand finds its way onto my shoulder and I tense so not to shrug it off. "August, talk to me."

"What happens from here on out?" I ask, my tone snippy and emotionless.

"I don't understand."

I stand abruptly, taking several steps forward hoping that the distance will quell some of this anger.

"What happens? Where are you going to work after this?"

She watches me cautiously, clearly not sure where this has come from. "Um, I suppose I'll just see where my job takes me."

I scoff at such a vague answer knowing exactly what it means: *If I get to leave, then I'll leave.*

"Right."

"Gus, have I done something wrong? Because you seem … agitated."

"I am agitated." I turn to face her, taking one more step back for good measure. "I'm mad that I was stupid enough to think that there was anything to this."

"To what?" she asks desperately.

"Tell me something, Wren. If you had the chance to move somewhere else—anywhere else—in order to do your job, would you take it?" Her eyes widen, but she doesn't answer me. She simply stands there, rooted to the spot. "If you were given the opportunity to leave this 'tiny town' and everyone in it behind so that you could plan events in some big city somewhere, would you?"

"You heard them," she says. "You heard Cally and Maggie talking about their gala."

"I also heard you. When you told them you would move."

She scoffs in disbelief. "Gus, I never said yes."

"And you never said no either." I pace in front of her, my

fear and anger mixing together and flooding my veins with this unyielding energy. "How can I trust you? How can I trust you to stay when I was stupid enough to trust people when they literally told me they would never leave? My mom died, my dad left, Sam moved. They all leave, all of them! And given the opportunity, you would go and do the exact same thing."

"Gus, I—"

"Well, now is your time to decide, Wren. If you had to choose between your job or the people who love you, which are you choosing?"

She stutters, lost for words as I try and force a decision to be made. If my heart is going to be torn into pieces yet again, I want it done now instead of months down the line when I finally feel safe again. She doesn't move, doesn't even look to breathe, just stands there with her mouth wide open as she tries to find the words.

"Well?" I push, my voice rising.

"Gus, my job is…"

"More important?"

"Important, yes. It's—" She cuts herself off.

"It's what?"

After a minute—a devastatingly long-ass minute—she says the words which I hoped never to hear her say. She even has the audacity to look apologetic as she says them.

"It's the one thing I have which I know will never let me down."

Chapter Thirty-Nine

WREN

G us refuses to see reason.

He refuses to understand that my job is my life. I don't deserve to be forced to choose between my job and my personal relationships before we've even really started a relationship, especially when it's not as if it's a choice he's making, too.

He put me on the spot when there was absolutely no reason to and that is exactly why I gave the answer I did. Not to mention, he did so on the one night that he knew meant the world to me. I did what I had to do to protect my heart, something I should have done with Adam, and never did. I deserve to live my life without the fear of losing someone due to my choices. My job is what I gave to myself and so I should choose it every time.

It's been a week. A whole long, tiring, soul-crushing week, each day feeling more hollow as it passes. I miss him, I will admit, but it's for the best that I stay away from the man who will break my heart even more than it already is.

"So, can I ask you something?" Oakleigh asks, digging her hand into the bowl of popcorn that's sitting between us on my couch. My heart grows heavy when I think about the last time we did this—the very night that Lee asked me to plan that party in the first place and told me about the farm that would change my life forever.

"Sure," I reply.

"I was just wondering how much longer you were planning on being a mopey bitch before you realize that you're both being idiots and decide to run to him and he parts those legs wider than the red sea?"

I stare at my best friend, astounded by her choice of words. Leave it to her to be so unbelievably blunt.

Wait, hang on…

"What the hell do you mean 'both being idiots'? Last time I checked, I wasn't the one who accused me of leaving before I even decided whether I was going to leave."

Oakleigh sighs, sitting up and facing me in an array of sluggish movements, as if turning to face me is a massive inconvenience. "Alright, I've been meaning to have this chat with you for a week now, but I held off because I thought 'hey, maybe she'll eventually see sense and realize she's being a silly bitch' but alas, you've pretended to play dumb, so here we are. I've even had to call for reinforcements, because I'm not dealing with your denial by myself."

She checks her phone before yelling, "It's open!"

My front door opens and in walk Finn and Jamie, each holding a six-pack of beer and a weary smile.

"What on earth is this?" I ask my best friend.

"An intervention," she replies, holding up a hand before I can protest. "And before you even start, yes, Mr. Finch is currently receiving his own one, too."

Finn and Jamie take a seat on the floor and pass us each a can of beer. I open mine eagerly, downing half of it so that I can mentally prepare for what's to come.

"Okay," Oakleigh begins. "Now, we're here to talk some sense into you and make you realize why you're being stupid."

"So you've said," I grumble. "But I'm not being stupid, Lee. I'm simply protecting myself, which is exactly what I should have done last time."

"Protecting yourself how?"

"By saving myself the pain that will come when I'm inevitably let down again. Like I said to Gus, my job is one thing I can rely on to never let me down."

"Your job did let you down, dumbass! Or are you forgetting the part where you had little to no work for almost six months and were struggling to pay the damn bills?"

Okay, I'm not particularly liking my best friend right now. Why choose now to bring up valid points?

"Wren, you can't push people away before they've given you a reason to," Finn steps in. "If you do that, then you'll find yourself alone for a very long time. In life you need to have your heart broken, otherwise how are you going to know when you finally find something that's worth it? Something which we all think you have with Gus."

"Gus is the one who came at me, okay? I never even gave the twins an answer when they told me about working out of state, and all of a sudden he was yelling about me leaving him."

"And you think that—what?—none of that stemmed from some unresolved trauma like your reaction was?"

Okay, another good point.

"Look, I really don't think the three of you can talk. I mean this is all coming from the two people who hate each other more than Gus and I did, but who think we don't know they sleep together once a year. Oh, and let's not forget the guy who thinks he's secretly dating Sam. Thinks being the key word in that sentence."

All three of them look shellshocked, and I feel a hint of vindication. They have absolutely no right to talk to me about my relationship issues when they have their own to deal with.

"Okay, when you come, you come to play," Jamie mumbles. "But for the record, Sam and I are not dating. We're just fucking."

"Oh, even better," I retort.

"It shows you were wrong!"

"Okay!" Finn interjects. "We seem to be veering slightly off topic here. The point is that deflecting isn't going to get you anywhere, Wrennie. You need to understand that it's okay to love someone. The difference between Adam and Gus is that Adam never accepted that you wanted to remain your own person whilst also being a couple. Gus accepts that because he wants the exact same thing. Even when you two were arguing every day, you never once attacked each other maliciously. You both knew exactly who the other one was and carried on anyway. Doesn't that say something about him?"

I will concede that Gus never did any of the crap that

Adam did. He never made me question my ability to run my business, never made me feel like less purely for wanting to do something I love. My job is Gus's worst nightmare come to life, and yet he still helped me, still encouraged me to do it because he knew it's what I love to do.

Gus did the one thing that I wanted someone to do for me —accept me, and I pushed him away for it, all because I'm scared to love again. I'm scared to be vulnerable, knowing I can get my heart broken again.

"I think it's finally landed," Jamie laughs, and the three of them begin a conversation whilst I continue to sit here, wondering what the hell I've done.

GUS

Wren Southwick is someone who would have abandoned me had I given her the chance. I was an idiot to believe that she would have stayed—accepted me for all I am and thought me to be someone worthy of sticking around for.

I understand that this is a small town. Smaller than even her town. But I know for sure that staying in such a town doesn't equal failure. Yes, the people in this town make me want to punch something. Yes, my farm isn't the most successful thing in the world, but it's *mine*. It's not much, but it's a nice life, whether Wren thinks so or not.

If she wants to run off and plan events for the stars in the same place my dad ran off to, then fine. Let her. See if I give a shit.

The wood splits clean in two as I bring my axe down swiftly. My shoulder aches with how much I've been working it, but I don't care. I can finally hold an axe with both hands, and I can finally do more than sit there and do fucking admin, so pain or no pain, I'm chopping wood.

"You're going to wind up back in a sling if you keep this up."

I turn to see Bash and Sam walking towards me from across the field. I roll my eyes, but continue working.

"Ooo, he's feeling sociable," Sam jests.

"What do you want?" I ask, not bothering to stop what I'm doing.

"We're here to lend you a hand."

"I can chop wood by myself, thanks."

"Oh, no, not with that." Bash smirks. "With getting your goddamn life back on track."

That makes me pause. "Excuse me?"

"We're going to help you see reason, little brother, something which you seem to have lost sight of a little bit over the past week."

I scoff bitterly. "Last time I checked, I wasn't the one with the problem."

"Up for debate," Sam mumbles, for which I throw him a death glare.

"Gus, I feel like I put some thoughts into your head the night of the party," Bash says.

"How so?"

He looks guilty as he says, "Well, I'm the one who asked you where you and Wren go from here and stuff. I think it made you paranoid, worried."

"You failed to mention that," Sam whispers to our brother.

Bash shrugs. "I didn't want all you guys yelling at me."

"All you guys? Who is all you guys?"

"Us, Jamie, Finn and Oakleigh. What, did you think we were all just going to let both of you throw away the best thing to happen to either of you?"

"I don't need a relationship babysitter," I snap.

"Then stop acting like you do."

"Gus, you are scared that Wren is going to leave, and that's fine. Dad didn't stay, and he definitely never accepted you. But —and it's wild that I need to tell you this—Gus, Wren isn't Dad."

"She was going to leave just like he did." I angrily chop another plank of wood, this one cutting in a wonky line. I growl in frustration.

"Did she actually say that she was going to leave?"

Okay, so maybe she didn't say those exact words ... but it was heavily implied ... I think.

I let my axe swing instead of answering.

"That's what I thought." Bash chuckles.

"It doesn't matter. She might feel one way now, but she'd change her mind when her business picked up."

"How do you know that?" Sam asks.

"Because who the fuck wouldn't? Not even you guys want to stay in this hick town, so why would she?"

Sam and Bash exchange a glance, one filled with a conversation to which I'm not invited. When they turn back to face me, there's something in their eyes that tells me that I'm misreading something.

"Gus, neither of us would ever leave here," Sam says softly.

"This farm is our home. It may not have meant much to Dad, but it meant the world to Mom. To you. And when it comes to Wren, okay, yeah, maybe she would have traveled a bit for work given the chance. Maybe she would say yes to an event in San Francisco or some shit, but do you know what she would always do that Dad never did?"

"What?" I ask, genuinely curious.

"She would come back."

I hate that my brothers are making so much sense. I hate that now I feel like an asshole for panicking and making Wren validate my abandonment issues.

"It's not just about whether or not she'd stay," I tell them sheepishly, letting the axe fall to the floor.

"What's it about then?"

I take a deep breath, letting my fingers pull my hair away from my face. The weight of my emotions heavy on my mind.

"I've never loved anyone before. Not romantically. But I have connected with people before and it's … messy. I depend on them and I know that if I depend on Wren and she does decide to go then I'll break. I'll fall apart because I do love her and I'm afraid that I'll love her because I need her."

With my admission comes a realization; one that makes the world stop in its tracks as I come to terms with my own idiocy.

I could have just spoken to her, voiced my concerns just like we had agreed to do before the party started, but the more I sat there, watching Wren make friends and form connections, the more I began to panic. I started to think to myself how much Wren shines in a world that, to me, can be so dark, and how with that would come opportunities for her; opportunities that will never find their way to me because I don't shine the way she does.

Yes, I'm terrified of her leaving me—so much so that I added meaning to her answers that I never knew for sure was there. But, deep down, I'm also terrified that I'll mess this up. More than I already have, I suppose.

"Gus, you need to realize that at the end of the day, the right people will stay and the ones who don't deserve you will go, and that it's okay to let them go. If you connect with her then do it. Relationships aren't perfect, but if you talk to one another and actually voice your concerns, then boom: you'll still argue and not like one another some days, but the love won't go."

"Plus, from what we've seen, the two of you have the arguing thing down," Sam laughs.

I let out a wry chuckle because he's right. Arguing is something we seem to have perfected. Now it's time to perfect being vulnerable.

Wren did the one thing that I wanted someone to do for me —accept me, and I pushed her away for it, all because I'm scared to love someone. I'm scared to be someone who is vulnerable with another knowing I can get my heart broken.

My brothers walk away whilst I continue to sit here, wondering what the hell I've done.

Chapter Forty

WREN

Gus stands in the middle of the field, axe in hand. His hat sits atop his head, keeping the sun out of his brown eyes. With his now free arm, he lifts the axe above his head, letting it fall and expertly cut through a block of wood. He looks disheartened, feet shuffling on the dirt before he chops another block.

I sneak over to the barn beside him, making a show of leaning against the side of the building.

"Is it better to scare you when the axe is up, or when it's down like it is now?"

Gus almost drops the axe as he spins around.

He looks tired. Exhausted, actually, as if he hasn't slept in days, and I can bet you that I look the same because neither have I. Dark bags sit under his brown eyes, his usual stubble now a full beard that makes him look older. He still looks gorgeous to me, and seeing his face now makes my heart ache for him all the more. The t-shirt he wears underneath his plaid shirt is gone, allowing for me to ogle at the sight of his bare torso peeking out underneath his unbuttoned shirt.

"Down, got it," I say as I push off the barn. "Oil burns can be fixed, but I don't know how good Doctor Shakari is at sewing on toes."

"Where the hell did you come from?"

"Beckford," I answer simply.

He rolls his eyes, going back to the wood in front of him. He raises his arms, axe in hand, but hesitates. He lowers his head and I see it shake. I see his shoulders lower as the breath leaves him, most likely in the form of a frustrated sigh. He slowly lowers the axe, letting it fall to the floor before turning to me once more.

"I was going to come and see you, but..." he lets the end of his sentence drift off.

"I know."

"I've missed you."

"I know."

"I'm sorry."

I step closer to him. "I know."

"I'm not good at this, Wren." He lets his head fall, looking so defeated that it hurts my heart. "I'm sorry I was gone for so long, sweetheart. Really, I am. At first, I was so afraid because you never really gave those girls a definite answer, and that just reignited the fears that I had tried to ignore, but the longer I went without seeing you, the more I realized that I needed this time. I needed it to think about what I want for myself, what I want for this farm."

"And now?" I'm on edge as I wait for his reply, eager to know whether I have a place in the life of Gus Finch or not.

He lifts my chin, and when I see his soft, warm smile, it feels as if the sun is shining that little bit brighter.

"Now, I know not just what I need, but what I deserve. Sweetheart, I want you. I think I have since the first moment I met you. I want to wake up to you, sleep next to you. I want to kiss you whenever I get the urge, I want to see a smile on your face every day. The reason I needed the time wasn't to realize that, but to think about how to navigate this.

"When I form an emotional connection with someone, it's not a small thing. I rely on that connection in a way that sometimes I think isn't healthy. And I don't want to be unhealthy for you, I want to be exactly what you want and need, too. Even after this short time together, I have this overwhelming desire to tell you not just that I love you, but that I'm devastatingly obsessed with you, and I have no idea if that's a normal amount of time or if that's too fast and if that will scare you off.

"Hell, this is the most I've spoken in one sitting in maybe two years, but if this is the version of me that you prefer, I will talk every minute of every goddamn day. And if that scares you off, or if that is too much then I will have to live with that, because yes, I had to learn how to love you, but I also had to take the time to learn to love myself.

"I want to be with you, but I needed to know that I could also be without you as well. I've been abandoned in more ways than I care to admit. As much as I pretend that my dad leaving didn't affect me, it did. It made me bitter and it made me guarded.

I always assume that people are going to leave because that's what they do sometimes, but it took Bash and Sam knocking some sense into me to make me realize that that's okay. People will leave and people will stay and both are fine because the people who are worth keeping in your life will always come back. And I think you'll come back to me, Wren, no matter how far you go, and if taking your business to another city or another state is what you decide to do, then you'll have my complete support."

I can't breathe. I can't think. How the hell do you follow words that are so raw, so real? How do you understand the weight of his words and get across to him that you want everything he's scared of?

"You want to be with me?" I ask.

Brown eyes flick to my lips quickly. "Desperately."

"Then be with me," I say simply. "Love me. Want me. Do it all. I'm ready for it. I want it, because I love you, too, August."

And I do. God, I do, I just never realized the extent to which I do until I didn't see him for so long.

"Thank God."

He leans forward to kiss me, but I stop him with a hand on his mouth.

"My turn." I take a deep breath, moving my hand to cradle his face instead. "Gus, I owe you an apology as well. I was so set on making sure that my heart never breaks again, that I never took the time to realize that maybe some people are worth getting it broken. When Adam cheated on me, it killed a part of me, the part that believed in myself and trusted my decisions, because how can I trust myself when I choose men like him?

"So, I protected myself. I told you that my job is all I care about because I thought maybe if I say it out loud, it would be true. But, in all honesty, Gus, when the twins asked me to plan their gala, I wanted to say yes, but then they said later on that it would be in California, and I wanted nothing more than to say no. I wanted to tell them that the idea of being so far from my home makes me feel uneasy, even if I'm only gone for a week or two. And when I say my home, Gus, I mean you. I mean Oakleigh, Finn, Jamie and your brothers. I love all of you guys, but you? I will never love anyone the way I love you."

The sigh of relief that leaves him as he brings me into his arms is a feeling that cannot be explained. It feels as if the world is complete, as if the weight on my chest has now crumbled into a million pieces, leaving a light feeling in my heart.

When he kisses me, I smile against his lips, grateful that the one man I want in my life is just as flawed as me, and that those flaws are my favorite part of him.

"I'm so glad you came back, because I'm pretty sure that if I had tried to cut one more block of wood, I would have fucked up my shoulder again. It's killing me."

"Please stop chopping wood," I chuckle.

"Consider it done, sweetheart." He kisses me once more. "Oh, and before I forget. Sam and Bash weren't the only ones who had a chat with me."

"Oh?"

"Yeah, Emilio had some things to say as well. Turns out you were right ... he's still a bit of a biter."

Laughing with him feels so right ... almost as right as

331

arguing, and knowing that I get to both laugh with him and argue with him in the future makes me feel I'm exactly where I'm meant to be.

Epilogue

GUS

"You're doing really well, Gus," Doctor Shakari tells me as she finishes up examining my shoulder. "Really, really well. The physio is working even better than I'd hoped."

"Thanks."

"How does it feel to carry out heavy duty tasks at work?" she asks.

"It's hit and miss. Sowing the new crop was easy enough, but working out sometimes takes it out of me."

I can see that she's shocked I've offered such a detailed explanation, but what can I say, I'm in a good mood.

"And how is the farm doing?"

"Better." I nod. "The barn is doing amazingly for us. The Christmas period was really successful and I've even been able to hire back a farmhand to help out with the animals."

"I'm impressed," she beams.

She finishes up her assessment of my arm. Thankfully, the

break continued to heal correctly even though I really haven't been taking it easy. The need to constantly hold my girlfriend with both arms is too overwhelming.

"Well, Gus, it seems you're doing really well here and I'm happy to officially discharge you. As long as you promise to keep up the exercises that your physio gave you and don't overwork yourself."

"I promise."

Her gaze is analytical, calculating. "You know, Gus, you seem … different."

I shrug lazily. "I'm not really, I'm just done with hiding who I am."

She looks oddly … proud.

We shake hands and I start my journey to Beckford, to what I'm fairly certain is going to be the best part of my day.

When I pull up at Wren's house, the "SOLD" sign outside the front door stands loud and proud. I can see boxes in the living room window, piled up in groups that I organized myself. Yellow tape for kitchen. Blue tape for living room. Red for bedroom. Every day I come by, I take a few boxes at a time. It's been a week and there's still a bunch of boxes to go. Who would have thought that one woman could have so many knee-high boots?

Wren has the door open before I can even knock.

"Hey, you."

"Hey, sweetheart." I plant a kiss on those full lips of hers, basking in the feel of their softness and the taste of her coconut lip gloss. "You all packed and ready?"

"You bet I am. I'm ready to get out of here. Start anew."

"Good." I steal one more peck for good luck. "Bash and Finn will be by later for the rest."

I pack as many boxes as I can fit onto the back of my truck and we head off back to Eaglewood, the place that is about to become Wren's new home. Shortly after Oakleigh's party, Wren decided to sell her house and look for a place in Eaglewood.

It's still early days, having only been four months—four amazing months. But even though it has been the best time of my life, I know that Wren still isn't ready to move in together, and I don't plan on pushing her into it whatsoever. She'll know when it's time.

For now, though, she's moving into her own place not too far from the farm. It's nice, spacious and modern. It's obvious that she's excited, having already seen Eaglewood as her home ever since she first step foot into town.

Me? I'm more comfortable here now than I've been in a while, but still a long way off from being accepted by the town. That's fine, though. I don't need their acceptance. The ones who like me for who I am will stick around, and so far, they have.

We reach her new home, and my hands start to become clammy as I think about the surprise I have waiting for her.

Sometimes, I think I overdo it on the amount of surprises I give her. But I just trust that Wren will tell me if it becomes a bit too much. My problem is that when I do something and see this woman smile even once, I continue to do that one thing until I've rinsed it completely; until I can see the glint of annoyance in her eyes that I know she's too kind to show on her face.

Finn has already put a fresh coat of paint on her new front

door—it's a light pastel orange, the exact color of pumpkins. She said it's to remind her of her favorite place in Eaglewood.

When she opens the door, her surprise comes bounding over, yapping happily at the sight of company.

Wren gasps, hands over her mouth as she takes in the sight of Cliff running towards her, going up onto his back legs so that he can rest his front paws on Wren's thighs. He's much bigger now, and because of that it's time for him to have a home. He's a bit of a diva, refusing to go out when it's raining, and hating bathtime. He needs a proper home, somewhere that he can be in the warm and have constant company.

"What's Cliff doing here?" Wren asks as she bends down to give him a fuss.

"Well, you're moving into your new home. I thought it only right that I give you a housewarming present."

She spins around, eyes wide. "You want Cliff to live here?"

"The best pup deserves the best owner."

She melts into me, and I wrap my arms around her happily, soaking in the feel of her close to me, both in terms of her body against mine, and her new home.

Things are right. Things are good. They're exactly where they need to be and now, more than ever, I'm grateful to Wren. I'm grateful that I've spent the time learning to open myself up to people knowing that, yes, you can get hurt. But when people like Wren come around, you take that risk and jump into the deep end.

What can I say, there's just something about her.

Acknowledgments

First of all, I would like to extend a massive thank you to anyone who has made it to this page. It means you gave the entirety of this book a chance and I will be forever grateful.

I would also like to say thank you to Charlotte and everyone else at One More Chapter who was involved in making this book a reality.

As expressed in my dedication, without Soraya, I wouldn't even have had this opportunity, so thank you to her for seeing my potential and opening the door for me.

On a more personal note, as per usual, I need to thank my rock, Callum. I started this novel whilst four months pregnant and finished it with a newborn, and the entire time I had such a frazzled and fragmented mind that I really didn't think I'd ever finish writing it. My amazing boyfriend, *mi corazon*, helped me to continue pushing through and believed in me even when I stopped doing so. He made sure to give me as much time as possible for me to sit down and just work, all the while being the most amazing new father.

In addition to him, I also have my family to thank – my mom, dad, sister and brother – for all helping me manage to push through both motherhood and a new career at the same time. For looking after my daughter so I could say that I at least managed to write 100 words in a day. Thank you.

Lastly, I would just like to show my admiration for mothers everywhere. Having to forgo any maternity leave whilst looking after a newborn really did put so many things into perspective. The challenges that motherhood has presented me with are wild, to say the least, and whilst my little Aria is the best thing in my life, she's also the hardest. With motherhood comes judgment, pressure and depression. There's this longing for the woman you used to be and an admiration for the woman you are now, and I will forever be proud of both. My eyes have been opened since having a baby of my own, and my respect for mothers everywhere has tripled, quadrupled, and multiplied by infinity. I have gained so many new friends who are both authors and moms like me, and to know I'm not alone in this is truly a weight off of my shoulders. Whilst this novel may be slightly fragmented and not perfect, it is exactly that which makes it reflect real life and the obstacles it brings to us.

So, to all those moms who feel that they are trapped in a universe by themselves … I promise you you're not, and I promise you it will get better.

Thank you x

ONE MORE CHAPTER

YOUR NUMBER ONE STOP

FOR PAGETURNING BOOKS

The author and One More Chapter would like to thank everyone who contributed to the publication of this story...

Analytics
Abigail Fryer

Audio
Fionnuala Barrett
Ciara Briggs

Contracts
Laura Amos
Inigo Vyvyan

Design
Lucy Bennett
Fiona Greenway
Liane Payne
Dean Russell

Digital Sales
Laura Daley
Lydia Grainge
Hannah Lismore

eCommerce
Laura Carpenter
Madeline ODonovan
Charlotte Stevens
Christina Storey
Jo Surman
Rachel Ward

Editorial
Janet Marie Adkins
Sarah Bauer
Kara Daniel
Charlotte Ledger
Laura McCallen
Jennie Rothwell
Sofia Salazar Studer
Helen Williams

Harper360
Emily Gerbner
Ariana Juarez
Jean Marie Kelly
emma sullivan
Sophia Wilhelm

International Sales
Peter Borcsok
Ruth Burrow
Colleen Simpson
Ben Wright

Inventory
Sarah Callaghan
Kirsty Norman

Marketing & Publicity
Chloe Cummings
Grace Edwards

Operations
Melissa Okusanya
Hannah Stamp

Production
Denis Manson
Simon Moore
Francesca Tuzzeo

Rights
Ashton Mucha
Alisah Saghir
Zoe Shine
Aisling Smyth
Lucy Vanderbilt

Trade Marketing
Ben Hurd
Eleanor Slater

The HarperCollins Distribution Team

The HarperCollins Finance & Royalties Team

The HarperCollins Legal Team

The HarperCollins Technology Team

UK Sales
Isabel Coburn
Jay Cochrane
Sabina Lewis
Holly Martin
Harriet Williams
Leah Woods

And every other essential link in the chain from delivery drivers to booksellers to librarians and beyond!

One More Chapter is an award-winning global division of HarperCollins.

Subscribe to our newsletter to get our latest eBook deals and stay up to date with all our new releases!

signup.harpercollins.co.uk/
join/signup-omc

Meet the team at
www.onemorechapter.com

Follow us!

@onemorechapterhc

Do you write unputdownable fiction?
We love to hear from new voices.
Find out how to submit your novel at
www.onemorechapter.com/submissions